The Step Between

Penny Mickelbury

Simon & Schuster

SIMON & SCHUSTER
Rockefeller Center
1230 Avenue of the Americas
New York, NY 10020

Designed by Kyoko Watanabe
Manufactured in the United States of America

10 9 8 7 6 5 4 3 2 1

Library of Congress Cataloging-In-Publication Data

Mickelbury, Penny, 1948–
    The step between/ Penny Mickelbury.
      p.   cm.
    1. African Americans—Fiction. I. Title.
    PS3563.I3517 S74 2000
    813'.54—dc21   99-042199

ISBN 0-7432-4636-5

For information regarding the special discounts for bulk purchases, please contact Simon &
Schuster Special Sales at 1-800-456-6798 or business@simonandschuster.com

Acknowledgments

Writing a book is, of necessity and by definition, a solitary pursuit. But that does not mean that the writer, if she is fortunate, walks alone; and I am lucky in the extreme. Thank you David Forrer, formerly of the Charlotte Sheedy Agency, and Roslyn Siegel, editor extraordinaire at Simon & Schuster, for being there every step of the way.

To Harriet and John Williams,
Marshall and Veronica Thomas,
Felicia Jeter, and Gregory Fraley:
Thank you for demonstrating that indeed one can go home again.

And

To Peggy Blow, my guide on endless, seamless journeys.

The Step Between

1

RUNNING THE RED LIGHT WAS EASY, AS EFFORTLESS as jamming her foot down on the accelerator and engaging all eight of the engine's cylinders, a rare and delightful departure from the routine of bumper-to-bumper city traffic. The turbo Saab made the transition as easily as Carole Ann made the split-second decision to risk the bold dash across Georgia Avenue at the intersection where Military Road changes into Missouri Avenue, despite the fact that traffic was dense in both directions. It was the third light she'd run since leaving the dojo in Bethesda, but that's not what made the illegal scurry easy. The ease was brought about by the fact that the morning's second illegal run had proved correct her suspicion that she was being followed. This third violation was designed to lose the bastard, and the lawyer in Carole Ann didn't experience the slightest qualm or pang of guilt at her outlaw behavior.

It was a white Range Rover. The driver was white and male and enigmatic behind ultradark, reflective aviator lenses. And that's all she'd been able to discern, from the moment she'd first noticed him, when he made the turn behind her onto Connecticut Avenue twenty minutes ago. He'd been the one to run the light that time, and had incurred the horn-blowing wrath of a half-dozen Monday-morning road warriors, which is how and why she'd noticed him. He'd been with her, at three- or four-vehicle intervals, ever since. Every time she changed lanes to position herself for a look at the front license plate of the truck, its driver slowed almost to a halt and shifted lanes. He knew she knew he was there and seemed intent only on preventing her from identifying him—not from being aware of his presence.

Her interest in his presence, though, was beginning to wane, and to change form. She now was annoyed. She wanted to be rid of him. The traffic behind her was dense enough that if she could get across Georgia Avenue ahead of him, there was no way he could follow or catch up.

The third time was not the charm.

"Damn, damn, damn!" She smacked the steering wheel and cussed, relatively inaudibly and completely unintelligibly, as she'd learned to do from her partner, the Master Cusser of the Universe. While she didn't mind running a red light—or two or three—she did mind receiving a moving violation summons. So intent had she been on determining whether the white Range Rover would attempt to follow her through the light that she hadn't understood for several blocks the intent of the blue flashing lights behind her. "Hellfire and damnation!"

The young cop stood outside her car door and leaned slightly into the window, his hands on his hips and his face a road map of displeasure: forehead raised and wrinkled, eyebrows bunched together, lips curved down. "That's how people get killed. You probably didn't see those two vehicles that missed nailing you by inches, did you?"

She shook her head but more in dismay than in response to his question, though his question is what she answered. "No, Officer, I didn't see them." She shook her head again and blew out her frustration through pursed lips in a burst of air. "What do running red light tickets cost these days?" she asked as she leaned over to retrieve her registration and insurance card from the glove box and her license from her purse.

"Depends, Miss Gibson," the young cop replied so dryly that she wondered if he really was as young as he appeared, especially as he proceeded to ignore her with the nonchalance of a cop with Jake Graham's years of experience as he studied the documentation in his hand.

⬤ ⬤

"Why didn't you tell him you were being followed?"

"I don't know for certain that I *was* being followed."

"You just told me you were being followed!"

"Telling you is one thing. Telling the cop who stopped me for running a red light is another thing. And why are you busting my chops about this, Jake?"

"Because, dammit, C.A., I'm pissed that you weren't driving a company vehicle. You could have been in direct and immediate and constant contact with Central Operations the entire time."

"And that would have served what purpose, Jake? GGI vehicles don't have rear-mounted cameras that would have recorded this guy's presence. A GGI vehicle wouldn't have run undetected through that red light. So being in constant contact with Central would have helped me how, exactly?" She realized that she was sounding slightly whiny, when all she wanted was not to sound as irritated as she felt. Surely there was some middle ground between whiny and irritated.

"You're a partner in this corporation. There is a vehicle assigned to you . . ." He'd stood to deliver this pronouncement and had begun walking back and forth when suddenly he stopped. "By the way, the company will pay the ticket, you know."

She abandoned all her efforts to manage her frustration and irritation with him and laughed out loud, a joyful noise that tapered off into a giggle as he feigned his own brand of irritation. Jake Graham was unique among men and she'd rather have him as her friend and partner than as her nemesis any day. She also let pass the opportunity to chide him about being such a stickler for rules and protocol, strangely aware that along with the levity of the moment, there remained a sense of unease. Besides, she knew what his response would be: "I'm a cop. I do rules." And it was the cop in him that picked up on the uneasy feeling in her.

"You think this guy was with you when you left the—what is it you call the martial arts studio, in Bethesda?" he asked. "Or before that . . . he followed you there?" He thought for a moment. "Or is this just some horny bastard following a beautiful woman?"

Not only picked up on but zeroed in on. For that was exactly the source of her uneasiness: Had the man in the white Range Rover been waiting for her outside her karate class, and if so, how had he known she'd be there this morning? Or had he followed her to Bethesda from her home in the Foggy Bottom section of downtown D.C.?

She shrugged. "I didn't know until I got up this morning that I felt like working out, and I didn't decide to go until after my second cup of coffee. And it's called a dojo." She shrugged again and unconsciously rubbed the place beneath her left shoulder blade and above her left breast where, six months ago, a bullet had ripped through most of the connective tissue and lodged dangerously near the artery to her heart. She still didn't enjoy full range of motion in her left arm. The diligent practice of the martial arts that she loved would, in time, restore the health and strength of that limb. She hoped that it also would dim the painful memory that she had killed a man. With her bare hands. Because she was a martial arts expert.

"I can't picture anybody associated with that undercover insurance thing being smart enough to figure out that you're not really going to let them reconstruct your knee," Jake said musingly, scratching his head.

She stared blankly at him.

"Jesus, C.A. Get a grip, would you?" he snapped, and his words carried a real hint of a sting. "What we do around here isn't so insignificant that you shouldn't be able to remember your part in it from week to week."

"Ouch," she said with a rueful grin. "Retract claws, please, and make no further attack upon partner."

He narrowed his eyes and peered at her through the squinty slits. "This thing has unnerved you, hasn't it? Why?"

"Yes," she replied. "And I don't know why. But I do know that Mr. White Range Rover was no horny bastard who just happened to choose me to follow on Monday morning after a bad weekend." It was her turn to pace. She stood up and realized that she hadn't finished dressing after her hurried shower—her legs and feet were bare and, she realized, she hadn't yet applied any makeup or combed her hair. And Jake had asked if she was unnerved? She sat back down and, suddenly aware that her legs were chilly without stockings, drew them up into the seat beneath her. "And no, I don't think that an outraged orthopedic surgeon is stalking me, even though we did cost them a few hundred thousand dollars."

She ran her memory over the physical therapists and nurses and surgeons that she'd encountered during the month she pretended to be a patient with hip joint pain, while Surgical Associates, Inc. billed her for thousands of dollars' worth of superfluous diagnostic and therapeutic services before finally recommending a surgical procedure she didn't need. While she ostensibly was seeking a second opinion, they'd sent Jake's wife in with a vague pain in her lower back, with the same results. Their insurance company client was so enthused with their preliminary report that GGI now was on permanent retainer.

Carole Ann slowly shook her head, lips slightly downturned in distaste. "No. None of that bunch would be wary or suspicious of me because first they'd have to believe they were doing something wrong. I don't know that I've ever encountered a more self-righteous, smug collection of unlikable characters." The look of distaste on her face intensified. "I'd really like not to have to subject my body to them again."

"Well, another couple of weeks and we're done with them. At least until the next crooked doc surfaces."

"As long as I don't have be the patient next time. I don't like it, as you know, and I'm also not totally comfortable leaving ourselves open to charges of entrapment. I *was* there under an assumed name, after all."

"You were there undercover, C.A. Big difference between undercover work and entrapment. You didn't ask anybody in that office to do or say anything they wouldn't ordinarily do or say. That's the standard for entrapment. And besides, we've got the records and testimony of other patients, including Grace. You're just the expert icing on the cake."

Carole Ann nodded. "And I'm glad it worked as well as it did, just as long as you keep in mind I don't want to make it a habit. I don't do this cop stuff so well."

He laughed at her. "You do 'this cop stuff' like a pro and you may as well give up whining and complaining about it. But . . ." and he raised his hand to halt her protest before it could erupt, "no more of it for a while," and he slapped the palms of his hands together in an up and down motion, dismissing all thoughts of greedy doctors and vindictive insurance companies. Then he shifted focus and fixed her in his sights, almost exactly as if he were lining up a shot at target practice. "What do you want to do about this business this morning?"

"Nothing we can do, Jake."

"I knew you'd say something like that, so I'm going to tell you what we're going to do. I'm going to follow you home tonight and you're going to park your Saab in your garage, where it belongs. And you're going to park your butt at home tonight, where you belong. And in the morning, I'm going to pick you up and drive you to work and you're going to familiarize yourself with the operation of the specially equipped Explorer that belongs to you."

"None of which will prevent the guy in the white Range Rover from following me again if he wants to."

"That's right," Jake said with a tight grin. "It won't. But because your Explorer *does* have a tracking device—not a rear-mounted camera—it will let me know where you are at all times so I can send somebody to grab him if he does follow you, and I'll have his ass spread-eagle on the pavement, begging for the chance to explain."

Carole Ann had no response to that, even though Jake sat quietly for several long moments, waiting. Finally he began rubbing the palms of his hands back and forth as if warming them.

"So. You ready to do Monday-morning stuff?"

Jacob Graham, a former homicide detective in the Washington, D.C., police department, had been running his own investigative and security consulting business for a little more than two years. For the last year and a half, that business had been called Gibson, Graham International, and Carole Ann Gibson, Esq., had been his full partner. A former criminal defense attorney and partner in one of D.C.'s largest and most prestigious law firms, C.A. was, Jake would tell anybody willing to listen, "the best damn trial lawyer in this town."

She slid an eight-inch stack of deep purple file folders—aubergine, Jake's wife called the color—from the right side of the desk to a position in front of her, and opened the top one. She was as adept as Jake at shifting gears and changing direction. It was, after all, Monday morning and time to review and assess the status of their work.

"I'm recommending that we take a pass on this embassy thing. Too much potential for aggravation with not enough potential for a payoff. Essentially what they want is security guards, and as far as I'm concerned, given their relative proximity to the Israelis, the British, and the Egyptians, security's not that significant a problem for them."

Jake frowned. "Then that's something they already ought to have known. Why bother to call us?"

Carole Ann shuffled the pages of the file and plucked one from the middle. "They called us right after that bomb scare at the Canadian consulate. First they wanted a security evaluation, then—"

"Yeah, yeah, yeah," Jake interrupted with an impatient flick of his wrist. "I remember now. Sent Marshall over there three times and every time he met with somebody different, last time because the guy from the time before had been sent home after his third arrest for drunk driving. You're right. We don't need it. Next one."

Carole Ann opened a second file folder, read for a few seconds, and closed it. "This one's a keeper. AU law school security survey, installation, and maintenance. The contract will all but write itself—it will be almost identical to the Howard University one. And we may owe Warren a finder's fee." Jake snorted and she laughed. Warren Forchette was a New Orleans lawyer and friend to them both. "Come on, Jake. Fair's fair. We got American University because of the work we did at Howard U's law school and the Howard job was a direct referral from Warren."

Jake snorted again, then growled, with absolutely no hint of real malice, "Forchette makes enough money on his own without me passing bucks his way. I'm just a poor homicide detective, not a rich lawyer."

Carole Ann's hoot of derisive, disbelieving laughter broke through her partner's feigned haughtiness, and his face relaxed into a real smile as he sank back into the sofa and crossed his legs, right knee over left. His black Kenneth Cole loafers, black silk socks, and black wool slacks would have put the lie to his "just a poor homicide detective" claim if his totally relaxed demeanor hadn't. He locked his hands behind his head, elbows sticking out like wings. "When do they want us to get started?"

"January first," she replied, closing the folder and setting it aside.

"Good," he said with a satisfied nod of his head. "Keep the bean counters happy. Next one."

She opened a new file and a frown wrinkled her features. "Surveillance. A chain of appliance discounters wants us to establish electronic monitoring of all their warehouses and loading docks. You know how I feel about surveillance, Jake," she said.

"Yeah, C.A., I know how you feel about surveillance. Same way you feel about insurance companies. And I love 'em both for the same reason: big, fat, easy money with little potential for physical danger or lawsuits. Am I right?"

She closed the folder, placed it on top of the New Case Files pile, and shook her head.

"Is there any problem with that case, C.A.? Are there any legal or contractual blips on the screen?"

"Moral blips, Jake. Surveillance is spying."

"It is not!" he snapped. "Any more than working undercover is entrapment. We're watching employees on the loading dock of an appliance company where every week, a couple of washing machines or dryers or big-screen TVs or computers or CD players go missing. Somebody is stealing that stuff, C.A. Somebody who works for that company. The owner knows it, and I know it, and you know it. And the only way to find out who's doing the stealing is to watch them. And then catch them."

"And, during the course of our watching, perhaps see employees using drugs, having sex, gambling, sleeping on the job?"

"That's why you write the kinds of contracts you do, C.A., to guarantee that we're not violating anybody's rights, civil or privacy or otherwise." He smiled a smile at her that was mostly a grimace. "Can we please continue our review of pending cases and contracts so I can get back to work?"

She grimaced back at him before taking up a new file. "This missing person thing I like a lot. There still are some questions that need answering before we finalize the agreement, but I'd sure like to pursue it. It's fascinating."

"That's the Islington girl, right? Yeah, that is real interesting," he agreed, and rubbed the backs of his fingers up and down the side of his face, as if checking to see whether he needed to shave. "It could also be a big waste of time, C.A. In the first place, she's not a minor and he can't make her come back home if she doesn't want to. And in the second place, that girl's been missing for what, five or six months now? If her daddy wanted her back, why didn't he hire somebody to look for her back then? God knows he can afford it."

"That's one of the questions I want answered before we commit, though the man could just have been letting the police do their jobs."

Jake snorted. "Rich people never just let the police do their jobs."

"You understand how these cases work, Jake. The police would have done all the right things, wouldn't they? By the book? Push all the right buttons, look under all the right rocks?"

"Oh, hell, yeah!" he said, rubbing his face again, and she could see him feeling the intensity of such an investigation. "After all, this girl was—still is, I hope—the only daughter of the richest man in D.C. Never mind that he's also the biggest asshole in town and everybody hates his guts. Every cop in D.C. and close-in Maryland and Virginia joined in the hunt. So did the Bureau, which treated it as a kidnapping for a while, until it became clear that nobody took her. This case stayed open and active until a month ago."

"Poor little rich girl, huh?" C.A. mused as she studied, one after another, the photographs, black-and-whites and color, of the missing girl. "These are all current, aren't they? Which suggests that father and daughter were close. And if that's the case, why would she just walk away?"

Jake frowned, stood, ambled over to her desk, and stretched out his hand for the photos. He scrutinized them and frowned some more. "I see a pretty girl who doesn't smile enough. How do you get 'close to her father' out of these?"

"Elementary, my dear Graham. Parents who are close to their children take pictures of them. My mother did and still does, especially when she thinks I'm not looking."

Jake slid the photographs back across the desk toward her and returned to his position on the couch. "Good point."

Carole Ann gazed again at the photographs of Annabelle Islington. "She's a beauty, that's for sure. And if she wasn't kidnapped, then she made a conscious decision to disappear, and I'd really like to know why." She returned the photographs to the folder and closed it. "I met Richard Islington once—"

"Then you know why! The man's a bona-fide jerk. Girl was smart, you know. Cum laude graduate from one of those Seven Sisters schools, and she was—is—very pretty, as you can tell from the photos. Brains *and* looks? Who needs millions?"

"Well," C.A. drawled, stretching out the word as if it had half a dozen syllables, "you should know."

He made a studied point of totally ignoring the comment and

busied himself with unrolling and then rerolling the cuffs of his crisply starched white shirt. He still wasn't looking at her when he said, "This case at least will let us get our money's worth out of Petrocelli for a change." Then he looked up and met her gaze and accurately assessed the degree of self-control involved in keeping her face in check. "You ain't funny, C.A.," he said.

"But you are, Jake," C.A. replied, throwing her head back and laughing. "You're absolutely hilarious. Now. Are you ready to deal with this last case?"

He continued to meet her gaze but something shifted in him. "I don't like the way you said that."

"I don't like this case."

He uncrossed his legs, leaned forward so that he sat on the edge of the sofa, and folded his hands on his knees. "What's not to like?"

Carole Ann opened the bottom folder but didn't look at any of its pages, maintaining eye contact with Jake instead. "It gives me a bad feeling, Jake. Nothing specific. No warning sirens and red flags. Just . . . a general unease. I read the spreadsheets and the business plan and the capitalization plan and the marketing plan and the distribution plan and the sales figures, actual and projected. And it all feels like it was lifted from a textbook or a seminar. It doesn't feel real, Jake—"

He interrupted her and didn't show any signs of being apologetic about it. "Well, it is real, C.A. I saw the place, saw the operation. A plant and a warehouse on five and a half acres in St. Michael's County. A fleet of trucks and three shifts of workers—"

"Hold it, Jake! Of course you did. I know you did a site visit and inspection. I'm not saying that OnShore Manufacturing itself isn't real. I'm saying . . . listen to me carefully, Jake, please. The place that is OnShore Manufacturing seems to have been created to fit the documentation—"

He finally exploded. "Goddammit, C.A.! That's the most farfetched, stupidest thing I think I ever heard! Who in the hell would do such a thing? And why, for Christ's sake? Why would whoever would do such a dumb-fuck thing, do it for us?"

Carole Ann stood up, came from behind the desk, and began to pace. She needed to pace to think. "I don't know. . . ."

"What *do* you know, C.A.? For certain?"

She gave the question several seconds to hang between them, time during which each of them was able to determine how far they were willing to push the other. "I know that I trust my instincts and my intuition."

He nodded. "I trust 'em, too. And I also trust my own and I'm asking that you do the same for me. I met the CEO of OnShore, spent time with him. I know a crook when I smell one, C.A. A con man, a thief, a liar, a killer, any kind of lowlife, and Harry Childress is not any of those things. I know a phony setup when I see one, and OnShore Manufacturing is real."

"And I know cooked books when I see them, Jake, and the On-Shore documentation is cooked. I can't tell you how many sets of backup and phony books I've studied, all of them good enough to be the real thing."

Carole Ann stopped pacing and stood before the wall of east-facing windows that gave her a magnificent view of the winter storm that was brewing, the one that the weather forecasters had been growing more hysterical about every day for almost a week. The sky, even as she watched, was turning from pale blue to gray to, off to the northeast, ominously dark gray, and the clouds were swirling above as furiously as were the leaves below. Were it not for the fact that the glass was triple-hung, glazed, and fronted with a newly developed industrial plastic, the windows would have shivered and rattled and allowed the frigid air to roar in. Winter had just arrived in Washington, courtesy of a fast-moving Arctic air mass.

"We need this job, C.A. It's a really important one. It'll put us on the map as experienced in the area of corporate takeovers, and that's a credential we need in order to compete with the big boys."

She nodded. "I know that, Jake," she said quietly.

"And we have the first shot at it, and I want it, but we've got to move on it and move quickly."

A key component of their partnership was that both of them had to agree to accept or reject a case. A key component of their friendship was a degree of mutual respect so intense as to almost guarantee that neither one would refuse the other in any but the most extraordinary of circumstances.

"Industrial espionage and sabotage and corporate takeovers will be the bread and butter for outfits like ours in the new century, C.A.," Jake said, rising from the sofa and walking to stand next to her at the window. "Companies spying on each other, stealing ingredients and product secrets, sabotaging assembly lines. And companies eating each other to make bigger and badder and greedier companies. That's the way of the world. OnShore Manufacturing knows this. They're a relatively small outfit. And the only thing they want is the opportunity to be safely 'absorbed' by a bigger fish, instead of being gobbled. And they want us to investigate the big fish that's looking to eat them—Seaboard Shipping and Containers, it's called. That's all, C.A. It's simple. They want us to confirm for them that Big Fish Seaboard is capable of taking the big bite. So, maybe they did gussy up the books a little to make themselves look more appealing. What's the harm in that?"

"None, I suppose," she said slowly, "as long as we're not working for Big Fish."

He smiled slightly and looked out, with her, at the weather. "Looks like the prognosticators were right about Ole Man Winter. But I sure hope they're wrong about the snow. I don't mind the cold, but I'm not ready for snow the first week in December. Hell, this is D.C., after all, not Denver."

At that moment a mixture of snow and freezing rain bombarded the window with a fury for several seconds before abating. "Looks like you'd better get ready," Carole Ann said. "And me too, for that matter. I need to finish getting dressed and comb my hair and add a little color to my cheeks. I wouldn't want the subterraneans to think ill of me, you know."

He looked at his watch and nodded. Then he looked at her. "I think they might like it if you showed up looking like one of them for a change. You know. Dressed down, as they say."

Carole Ann snorted, then gave him a pat on the shoulder signaling a release of the tension between them. "I'd show up looking like one of them every day if it would prevent me from thinking that they are some of the strangest people I've ever met!"

"Careful, Counselor. That could be construed to be a statement of bias against that segment of the population which just happens to prefer computers to people," he said in a very lawyer-like tone.

"So, sue me," she said, in a very un-lawyer-like tone. "I've said it before and I'll say it again: they're very weird people, those computer types."

"They're not all weird, C.A. Patty's not that weird."

"All things are relative, Jake," she said, thinking as they walked toward the office door that Patty Baker, aka Patty Bake, the section chief, really wasn't as weird as some of her charges, though she, too, was a bit of an oddball.

"Some people think lawyers are weird. Can you imagine?" Jake laughed as she lowered her eyelids and shot him an evil eye from the remaining slits. "So. Are you OK with the OnShore case, C.A.?"

"I'm fine with it, Jake," she said and opened the door for him and closed it behind him when he left. Still barefoot and bare-legged, she crossed the office to the narrow closet adjacent to her desk. First, she quickly removed from its hanger and slipped her arms into the charcoal gray sweater that completed the knit ensemble she wore; and then, still standing, first on one foot and then on the other, she carefully, though quickly and with practiced perfection, donned opaque black stockings, which provided immediate warmth.

She straightened and faced the mirror mounted on the inside of the closet door. Running her fingers through her hair usually constituted combing it, but today she actually whipped out and employed comb and brush. Quickly and with a practiced hand, she applied eyeliner and shadow and mascara and blush. She would apply fresh lipstick after she ate the yogurt in her gym bag. She stepped, finally, into the black suede flats that she loved. One of the many aspects of the practice of law that she didn't miss was the de rigueur uniform of power suit and high heels. She studied herself in the mirror.

"You do look a tad severe for a meeting with the subterraneans," she muttered to herself. Herself frowned a hint of rebuff, so she reached inside the closet toward a hanger and grabbed a brightly colored, hand-painted silk scarf, which she draped across her shoulders. "A bit better," she told herself with a wry grin, as she realized that the black and gray knit suit was the equivalent of jeans and T-shirt given her former work attire.

Then she realized that she saw reflected in the mirror the face of the corporate lawyer she had been for so many years: the bland, blank visage, devoid of emotion, that most often was described as "pleasant." And she knew that her disagreement with Jake over the OnShore Manufacturing case was the reason for the face. Out of habit and practice she had, unwittingly, assumed it so as not to telegraph to Jake her real, true response to GGI's involvement with whomever or whatever OnShore was. She wished she could have been more definitive, more substantive in her reservations and objections. She knew Jake Graham well enough to know that had she presented solid evidence to support her position, he'd have backed away from his. But she hadn't because she couldn't. Not without a considerable amount of time and work, and she didn't know whether it would be worth the time it would take to uncook—to defrost, as she liked to say—OnShore's books. Though she was certain that, given the time, she could prove her point.

But that would be going behind Jake's back. It would be meddling in his turf: OnShore was his case, as was the Diamond Associates insurance fraud case and the AU law school security survey; just as the missing Islington girl and the electronics warehouse surveillance were her cases. They consulted with each other, constantly and routinely, but they did not meddle in each other's affairs.

She faced the mirror again. The lawyer still gazed back at her. She tried to adjust her face, to rid it of its careful nonexpression. She failed and closed the closet door and concentrated on adjusting her attitude instead. She hadn't gotten very far when a knock on the door interrupted her effort and the door swung open to admit Grace Graham with an armload of picture frames.

Carole Ann hurried toward her, accepting half the burden and a half-hug and a warm kiss. "What are you and Jake fighting about now? All he did was growl when I passed him in the hall."

Carole Ann laughed and felt herself relax. She knew that Grace had no expectation of an answer, that her question merely underscored how well she knew her husband, and how delighted she was that he'd found a partner—another partner—that he could trust well enough to display his true feelings. How delighted she was to be the wife of a man who ran his own business . . . a man whose business no longer was the business of murder.

"Is it as cold as it looks out there?"

Grace shivered. "I just heard on the radio that the temperature is dropping five degrees every hour. I'm going to get these pictures hung as fast as I can and get out of here! I wanted you to see them first, though." And she spread out the collection of turn-of-the-century photographs that would create a gallery effect in the long front hallway of the GGI building.

Grace took care of GGI, the physical entity. She didn't meddle. She wasn't a nuisance. She didn't offend with an air of misplaced proprietary behavior, as did the spouses of some business owners. Grace merely was a warm and loving presence. She visited once a week, though nobody could say for certain on which day, and she brought fruit and flowers and left them in places all over the building, for everyone to enjoy; she sent cards for births and deaths and weddings; she spoke to each employee she encountered, calling him or her by name. She placed a television and a stereo system and a well-stocked bookshelf in the employee lounge, and every month or so, she replaced the books and magazines. There circulated a friendly rumor that GGI really meant "Grace Graham Is."

"These are beautiful, Grace." Carole Ann felt herself transported as she studied the black-and-white and occasional sepia images of a Washington that now existed only in memory.

"I'm going to hang this one in Jake's office," she said, proffering a gilt-framed portrait of a stern-faced man in what was obviously a policeman's uniform. "The first Black policeman in D.C.," she said, her voice full of emotion and pride.

"Jake will love it," Carole Ann said, and knew that he would. In the deepest places of his being, Jake Graham always would be a cop.

"And this one is for you."

Carole Ann's eyes widened in surprise, then filled in gratitude, as Grace offered her an oblong frame, approximately twenty inches in length and half that wide. Matted within were three photographs. "The Howard University women's track team, tennis team, and swim club," Grace said, almost reverently. "From the 1920s," she added, as Carole Ann studied the serious young faces of women who now, if not dead, would be nearing a century old. Who would, for her, forever be young and strong and fit.

"I . . . I'm . . . Grace, I don't know what to say!"

Grace smiled and hugged her. "I'm glad you like it. Now, I'll get out of your hair—I know you have a meeting—and I'll go hang these."

"I think for once the rumor mill got it right," Carole Ann stage-whispered to Grace as she held open the door for her. "GGI really does mean 'Grace Graham Is.' What would we do without you?"

"I hope you don't ever have to find out," the older woman responded with a sly grin, then bustled down the hallway leaving behind a gentle whiff of Chanel No. 5 and enough warmth to alter the climate.

2

GIBSON, GRAHAM INTERNATIONAL WAS HOUSED IN A renovated warehouse in an unfashionable section of northeast Washington, D.C., that had been, before the riots following the murder of Dr. Martin Luther King in 1968, a prosperous zone of light manufacturing, warehouses, and trucking concerns. The area's main thoroughfare then and now was New York Avenue, which, before there were interstate highways, was the route to Baltimore, Wilmington, Philadelphia, New York, and other places of trade on the Eastern seaboard. Going in the opposite direction and following New York Avenue south through downtown D.C., one eventually would have found oneself in Richmond and headed toward the Carolinas.

Washington's short-lived tenure as a mini industrial center came about not because it was the U.S. capital, but because Northeastern concerns that desired a base of operations in the South considered Washington only marginally Southern; and Southeastern industry that required Northern connections thought of D.C. as barely North, being, as it was, next door to Virginia, the seat of the Confederacy. The 1968 riots decimated what was the commercial hub of northeast D.C.—H Street—leaving block after block of burned-out shells. The sight of flames and the scent of smoke wafted quickly toward the industrial hub—New York Avenue; it wasn't long before the warehouses were as empty and hollow as if they, too, had been torched.

Not all of northeast D.C. tucked tail and ran in the face of hard times. The Catholic Cathedral of the Immaculate Conception and the Catholic University of America and Gallaudet University, the only full-fledged university for the hearing impaired in the world, and Providence Hospital have all lived and thrived for generations in northeast D.C. But with the factories and plants long closed, and the people who worked in them long gone, most of the area these days hobbles along, at best, a gentrified section near CU called Brookland, adjacent to the subway stop, being the exception. Most of the neat, quiet row houses are inhabited by residents of long standing, neat and quiet and often hobbled themselves. They are predominately Black, the Irish and Italians and Greeks as long gone as the factories where they once worked.

Because of these factors—and because it's cheaper to manufacture almost anything in faraway places where people work for less than a dollar a day—Jake Graham was able to purchase for a song an abandoned two-story warehouse at the end of a dead-end street. And he also was able to purchase the two and a half acres adjacent to the warehouse for a refrain. Directly behind the building was an endless stretch of land belonging to the U.S. Park Service; endless because the land abuts the Baltimore–Washington Parkway, which is what New York Avenue becomes when it leaves D.C. and enters Maryland.

GGI, which specialized in the business of security, was as secure an entity as it was possible to be without being secretive or paranoid—the very model of practicing what it preached to its clients. GGI employees, by requirement, entered the building from a side door accessible only from the fenced-in parking lot on the southern end of the building. The GGI employee ID card opened and closed the gated access to the parking lot; the same card permitted entry to and exit from the building. The card was recoded every month. Guests of GGI entered the front door into a very nicely appointed, though not plush, lobby. The surveillance cameras and metal detectors were invisible and therefore nonthreatening to nonhostile clients.

Jake and Patty had insisted on a level of security they both considered minimal and which Carole Ann, when she joined the company, found excessive, invasive, and borderline threatening. It actually had been Patty who convinced her that the security business and the intelligence business were information driven: the retrieval and use and storage and compilation of information was essentially what Gibson, Graham International was all about. And to the extent that people pay dearly for information, Patty explained, people also will go to any lengths to steal or co-opt or destroy the information held by others. So it was that "the subterraneans" occupied one end of the belowground floor of the building, and the security monitoring station occupied the other end. Both were staffed twenty-four hours a day.

There were fifteen subterraneans and Patty was their guru; "information specialist" was their official title. When Carole Ann found out what they actually did, she immediately drew up and had Jake sign a document that made her the company's attorney of record as well as a partner, so that her knowledge of the potentially illegal activities of the subterraneans became a client confidentiality issue. The computers—and those who knew and loved them—occupied two cavernous, steel-encased chambers, and only the computer specialists who worked there, Carole Ann, and Jake had access to those two rooms. For the same security-conscious reasons, only the security specialists, Carole Ann, and Jake could access the monitoring stations at the opposite end of the underground corridor.

∽ ∾

The chief of the information retrieval section was a Bonnie Raitt look-alike, a stylish, sixtyish retiree from the federal government who had forgotten more about computers than any of the young Turks ever would know. That's because when Patricia Baker, as a very young and newly married Commerce Department secretary, volunteered in 1960 to take a FORTRAN course in a secret location (the Army's Fort Belvoir in Virginia), nobody but the true visionaries could imagine the importance computers would achieve so quickly; so, aside from the visionaries, only the lowly—clerks, secretaries, and women—were the early beneficiaries of the new knowledge and the new technology. By the time the bureaucrats caught up with the visionaries, former nobodies like Patty Baker had become indispensable; and while her title, her responsibilities, her knowledge—and her importance—grew, her Government Schedule ranking and salary did not. So while she was called, first, a data entry clerk, and then a computer programmer, and finally a computer specialist, Patty Baker earned, until her retirement, the salary of a secretary.

But back then, few men and fewer women walked away from a guaranteed government pension, so the naturally nicknamed Patty Bake put in her twenty-five years, moonlighting as a software designer before that was a profession, and becoming part of the growing underground of government computer hacks. Then, almost overnight, everything changed. Computers no longer were expensive, mysterious, monolithic, government and academic secrets. The gap between hardware and software was narrowing by the second and, with it, the complex nature of computing itself. Accompanying this sea change was the realization that the federal government no longer was pioneering or controlling any aspect of the runaway computer industry; ergo, there no longer existed an insatiable need for government computer specialists. Especially no-longer-young, female ones.

Patty Baker happily ended a boring and humiliating retirement at the age of fifty-three to design, create, and manage Jake Graham's computer operations simply because, as she happily told anybody who'd listen, he said these words to her: "I know I can't pay you what you're worth, so how much will you accept to come work for me?" It was the first time anyone had ever paid homage to her knowledge of computer systems and information storage and retrieval methodology.

They'd met at a physical therapist's office. Patty's husband was recovering from a stroke and Jake was recovering from a yearlong paralysis, the result of a bullet to the back that ended his police career. Jake and Eddie Baker were each other's inspiration and cheering squad, and Patty and Grace Graham united in the wall of support they built for their husbands. By the time the men were able to walk again, the two couples were close friends.

Carole Ann liked, appreciated, respected, and enjoyed the company of Patty Baker. She also was intimidated by her. With no intent on her part to confuse or obfuscate, Patty spoke computerese, a language Carole Ann neither spoke nor understood. And it's not that Carole Ann really objected; after all, she frequently was accused of speaking legalese herself. But two meetings with Patty in as many days taxed her. At least Jake had been present at yesterday's meeting, to interpret Patty's reports. Today, she was on her own, having been summoned by Patty to review information that she, Carole Ann, had requested.

She turned left off the elevator and the soles of her Lands' End boots drug slightly on the carpeted hallway. It had been snowing for the last thirty-six hours—lightly and gently—but enough to coat the streets and create ankle-high drifts on the sidewalks. She was thinking that it would be a good idea to keep a pair of more comfortable shoes in her office closet, when she found herself face-to-face with Patty.

"You're always right on time, C.A.," she said, stepping back, holding the door open. She wore a gray wool jumpsuit and high-heeled boots. Her silver-streaked red hair billowed about her head, and her blue-green eyes glistened with intelligence and humor. She waited for Carole Ann to enter before pulling the door closed again, and making certain that it locked. Then she preceded her down a brief hallway and into the middle of the huge space that was the heart, soul, and brain of Gibson, Graham.

Carole Ann remembered the time when being in the presence of so many computers would have required the use of earplugs, so loud and persistent would have been the hum of the old mainframe motors and clacking keyboards. But this much she knew of current technology: that just one of the svelte, stylish central processing units in this room contained the information it once required a computer the size of a room to accommodate. Here, she knew, there were two dozen CPUs and her head hurt every time she tried to imagine what they all contained and processed. In addition to the CPUs, each workstation contained the requisite keyboard, mouse, and monitor, and a high-speed laser printer. The workstations were arranged into six separate pods of four each, and she knew that each pod specialized in something different. She just didn't remember what. Two people were at work in each of the pods; that was the case on every shift, every day.

Patty's private office was in the right rear corner of the room, a cubicle with a front panel of bulletproof glass and walls of steel-enforced concrete. Four chairs encircled a round table in one corner of the office. Three computer screens were arrayed along an L-shaped desktop across the left-side and back wall, one screen in the short angle by itself, the other two side by side on the long arm of the L. There was a chair before each screen. A long, three-shelf bookcase occupied the other wall, on top of which was an impressive array of photographs, proof that Patty Baker enjoyed a full, rich life with human beings.

With a wave of one arm, she directed Carole Ann into the cubicle as she extended the other arm in the direction of a programmer who was walking toward her. Carole Ann groaned at the size of the file Patty brought into the office with her, and sank down into one of the chairs at the table.

Patty sat down next to her and dumped the fat file on the table. It was the size of the combined volumes of the D.C. Yellow Pages. "I know how much you don't like this," she said with a grin and slid her half-glasses even farther down her nose, "and I promise I won't tell you what's on every one of these pages."

"I don't mean to seem ungrateful, Patty, but, quite frankly, sometimes you and your crew intimidate me. Like now. That just seems like too much information."

"Anything I can do to help smooth the way for you, C.A., you know I will." She said "anythang" and "hep," and Carole Ann was reminded again how many of D.C.'s longer-term residents were true Southerners: Patty was from West Virginia and Jake himself was a North Carolinian.

She pointed to the file. "Tell me something that I don't know about Richard Islington."

"That's not his given name."

Carole Ann knew that she failed in her effort to keep Patty from seeing the home run she'd just scored. "What do you mean, not his given name? You're saying it's an alias?"

The older woman shook her head and the thick mane of silver-streaked red hair flicked against her shoulders. "He changed it. He started life as Dicky Rae Waters in Scenic View, Ohio, fifty-six years ago. He started using the name Islington when he was eighteen or nineteen, and changed it legally when he was twenty-one."

Carole Ann also was shaking her head. "I've been reading and hearing about Richard Islington for more than twenty years and I've never once heard it mentioned that it wasn't the man's true name. How could a person of such prominence—and one who is, according to Jake, so universally disliked—maintain such a crucial secret?"

"I don't think it's supposed to be a secret, C.A. There's two big *Washington Post* stories about him that mention his name change, one from September of 1968 and the other from June of 1974."

"But what about after that, Patty? There must have been a hundred stories about Richard Islington in the *Post* since 1974. You're telling me that not a single one of them reported that the richest man in town isn't who he says he is?"

"There are eighty-five mentions of him since 1974, and three more profiles. And no, not another mention of his other name."

"What about the *Journal*, the *Times*, Crain's?"

"Crain's never mentions the name change, and the other two mention it just once, both times in the late 1960s."

"Television? Magazine articles?" Carole Ann felt as if she were grasping, but everything she'd experienced of the media's fascination with the tidbits of human life—especially the lives of prominent humans—suggested that Richard Islington's name change would have merited at least a mention in every mention of him.

Still without opening the file or checking a date, Patty said, "Ed Bradley did a *60 Minutes* story on him ten years ago, and it was Islington who brought up the name change. Same thing in a *Regardie's* story the next year."

"*He* brought up the name change? Islington himself?"

She nodded. "And he gave the same reason both times: said he decided when he was fourteen that he didn't want to be a coal miner or a poor man, so he started reading every book he could get his hands on, to learn what else he could do. He decided when he was eighteen that he wanted to be rich, and he legally changed his name when he was twenty-one because, he said, no rich man he'd ever read about had a poor man's name. And Dicky Rae Waters, he'd said, was a poor man's name."

Carole Ann leaned back in her chair. Jake had said the man was widely despised, and indeed, she'd heard as much herself; but based on information supplied by Patty so far, Richard Raymond Islington sounded like a man one could envy and perhaps even distrust, if changing one's name could be considered deceitful. But the brand of intense dislike that breeds hatred? "Is the man a thief, Patty? A corporate raider? Does he intentionally ruin competitors or their businesses?"

Patty shook her head and pointed to the intimidating file. "He's a hard man, and maybe not always a hundred percent fair, you know what I mean? But he's not sneaky. Anybody he beat out or brought down knew he was coming. Either he told 'em right up front, or he made enough noise comin' through the brush that anybody with ears knew it was an elephant and not a puppy dog."

Carole Ann grinned at the imagery. And immediately she could imagine and understand how a Richard Islington generated feelings of extreme dislike bordering on hatred: a beast of that size, even moving slowly, tramples everything in its path. Only a beast of similar stature—a rhino, for example—could afford to stand and hold its ground. "Anything else I need to know?"

"Umhumm," Patty said with a sly little smile, the kind that says, "I thought you'd never ask." "His wife left him when their daughter was just two years old and nobody's heard a peep out of her since. And the daughter disappeared twenty years to the day after the mother left."

❧ ❧

Paolo Petrocelli came to work for Jake Graham on the Monday following the Friday that was his last day of work for the FBI, where he'd spent eleven years developing an expertise as a missing persons investigator, specializing in missing children. He'd quit, he told Jake and anybody who asked, because he thought it more efficient and effective to follow his own investigative instincts rather than the FBI's bureaucratic handbook. He also didn't like how it felt to find a subject a month or a week or a day or an hour too late. To the FBI, what mattered was that the subject was located and the abductors apprehended. To Paolo, it mattered whether the subject was found alive or dead, tortured or whole.

Jake Graham didn't promise Paolo that Paolo would locate a subject any sooner or any more alive working for him than for the FBI, but he did promise that GGI didn't have a rule book for him to follow. In fact, Paolo Petrocelli would be GGI's new missing persons unit all by himself until Jake hired someone to work with him, missing persons being a significant profit center for a business like GGI. And furthermore, he could be as unorthodox and unbureaucratic as he liked. Both of which he proved to be during the satisfactory resolution of his first three, very high profile cases. Then came a string of duds—rejected cases—borne in on the wave of his quick and early success: two cases in which the victim had been missing for several years; one in which the parents refused to believe that the body recovered from the rocks and boulders of Great Falls was that of their son; another in which the husband's tale of his wife's disappearance rang hollow, especially in light of the fact that he'd made no report to the police. So, Paolo Petrocelli hadn't been very busy in the last couple of months. Then came Richard Islington.

Hunched over on the love seat in Carole Ann's office with his elbows planted on his knees and his face nestled in the palms of his hands, he stared balefully at the pile of papers on the coffee table before him. He listened to everything she said without ever removing his eyes from the file. "What's the first thing we're gonna do?" he asked when she finished briefing him.

"Have a heart-to-heart with Richard Islington," she replied, thrown off guard by his question and his demeanor. She'd met Petrocelli when he was hired, of course, and had exchanged greetings with him in the hallway and in the employee lounge, but this was her first extensive encounter with him and she marveled that he'd survived as long as he had within a government agency as autocratic as the FBI.

"I hear you know this Islington guy."

She shrugged, now not only thrown off by him but put off as well. "I've met him."

"And?" he queried.

"And what?" she snapped.

"If you were his daughter, would you disappear without a trace or a word, of your own volition?"

She studied him for a long moment, which didn't seem to faze him in the least, intrigued enough by the question to take the time to contemplate an answer, which she wasn't compelled by intrigue or anything else to give him. Instead she replied dryly, "Our meeting with Islington is at eight tomorrow morning. Unless you get a bad feeling about him or about the case from him, we'll sign the contract, accept his retainer, and you'll go find his daughter."

Paolo sat up straight and looked directly at her for the first time. "You gonna help me look for her?"

"Nope."

He sat up straighter. "You think I'll find her." It was not a question.

"If she's still alive."

He stood and scooped up the file with one hand, something neither C.A. nor Patty nor Jake could manage. "You got any ideas?"

She nodded. "It's a two-fer," she said, and wondered how long it would take him to understand her meaning.

"Twenty years is a long time," he said after barely a beat. Then, "Where would you start?"

"Scenic View," she answered, and reminded him to remember everything he'd learned about mothers while he was learning how to locate missing children.

He raised his hand in a half-salute when he left, and she turned immediately to the contracts before her in various states of completion. One of the objections she'd raised most vociferously when Jake first asked her to join him in business was that she'd been a trial lawyer for too many years; that she didn't remember torts and contracts. She'd been surprised to discover how much she remembered, and didn't know whether to credit the expertise of her law school professors or her own prowess as a student.

She quickly completed the letter to the embassy regretting Gibson, Graham's inability to accept it as a client at the present time, and turned her attention to the electronics warehouse surveillance contract. She intended to make certain that the owner expected to be informed only of that illegal activity relating to the theft of merchandise owned by the electronics company. After struggling with the concepts, both legal and moral, she included language to the effect that GGI would report to the police department any observed evidence of a felony; no other incident or activity would be reported by GGI.

She wrote swiftly, refining and clarifying the language until she was satisfied that the interests of all parties were both met and protected: the interests of the client, the interests of the client's employees, and the interests of GGI. Then she turned to the American

University law school contract, which essentially was a duplicate of the Howard University contract and which, therefore, required little work.

For all the complexity of the matter at hand, the Richard Islington contract was fairly straightforward: GGI would employ any means necessary, possible, and viable in the search for Annabelle Islington, and would not be held responsible or liable for any state or condition or situation in which said subject might be found, including deceased, unless a court of law would rule GGI directly responsible for her death. And she and GGI would guarantee the impossibility of that likelihood. For his part, Richard Islington would agree to make available to GGI and its agents all pertinent documents, records, and information in any form, including the names of persons with direct knowledge of Annabelle Islington. "And that includes you, Dicky Rae," she said to herself.

Carole Ann pushed the chair back, stretched out her legs, and propped them on the desk. She leaned back and allowed free rein to her thoughts about the Islington case, beginning with the man himself. Her lasting impression of him, based on the one time she'd met him, at a reception she and Al had attended at somebody's estate somewhere in Potomac for someone of prominence, was that he seemed detached. Uninterested in anything or anyone and disinclined to feign false interest. The crowd ebbed and flowed around him, moths drawn to the heat and light, but it was clear that nobody dared land on Richard Islington. She recalled with clarity that when she and Al had been introduced to him, he'd said, "Good evening to you both." He had not said, as people are wont to do in such circumstances, that he was pleased to meet them or wasn't it a nice party or that he'd heard or read about them. Then he'd told Carole Ann that the color of her dress—a red coral—was his "most favorite of all the colors." And he'd turned away from them to accept another greeting.

Patty's two-fisted file, which Carole Ann had all but memorized, supplied dozens of instances that demonstrated the accuracy of the information expert's elephant analogy. Time and again Islington had either outbid or outbullied competitors to gain control over projects worth many millions of dollars, often against the wishes of the locals. But as there were few rhinos among the locals, Richard Islington almost always got his way, a notable exception being in Florida, where a local developer whose brother was a city councilman benefitted from a hastily enacted legal requirement with which it was impossible for an outsider to comply on short notice. Carole Ann particularly noted a case in New Mexico, where Islington was widely suspected of being the source of erroneous information about a stretch of land in a remote mountainous area that precipitated the withdrawal of a group of local developers from bidding for it. The misinformation— that a bill was pending in the U.S. Congress that would regulate the use of the land, rendering it useless for commercial development— left Islington with uncontested access. He was able to purchase twenty-five thousand acres of pristine forest land for a relative pittance. Six months later, an international developer announced plans to construct a ski resort on the land.

Carole Ann's assesment of Richard Islington was that he was a gifted businessman who also was an unapologetic bully; that he often was unscrupulous though there was no proof that he was dishonest; that he had no sense of, or need for, social niceties; that he was oblivious to the effect of his behavior on others because it not only didn't occur to him that others were affected by his actions, he also didn't care. Nowhere in the pages and pages of documents in which extraordinary details of Richard Islington's business and professional lives were revealed was there a single mention of family or friends—unless "former wife" counted—besides that of his "only daughter."

None of that helped Carole Ann understand why it was that she believed Annabelle Islington was alive and well and with her mother, but that is what she believed. And so, to a lesser extent, did Paolo Petrocelli, though he knew exactly why he held his belief and he gladly told her: "People either hate or fear this guy, but nobody calls him their best buddy. Why would his wife and daughter be any different? They're also probably the only people in the world capable of hurting him, and what would hurt him worse than to lose the daughter at the hands of the mother?"

Pondering the intricacies of the Islington issue, she thought that Paolo could be correct. Since becoming partners with Jake, she had found that she rarely missed the rigors of being a trial lawyer, but she very often yearned for the feeling of satisfaction that accrued when all the pieces of a case came together. She was experiencing that old, familiar sense of satisfaction around the intrafamilial tensions of the Islingtons when OnShore Manufacturing rudely insinuated itself into her consciousness. "Damn," she muttered to herself, and she lowered her legs, dropped them to the floor, and resumed her upright position at the desk. Back to reality.

She was as uneasy about OnShore as she was energized by Islington. For Jake's sake she would like to be mistaken, but she knew her misgivings were valid. Yet, she also knew and trusted Jake's instincts. So how could they both be correct? She pulled the OnShore file toward her and extracted Jake's report. As usual, it was so thorough and detailed that she could visualize the place. He'd spent the better part of a week at the plant and with the CEO, a fifty-seven-year-old native of Maryland's Eastern Shore named Harry Childress. He was as good an assessor of character as she, and if Jake's take was that Childress was "a stand-up guy," then he was. That meant that there was another player . . . someone Jake hadn't met. But who? She studied the file open on the desk before her. John David MacDonald was the COO counterpart to Harry Childress, and she'd never heard Jake mention him. Was he the rotten apple? And how to find out without risking her partner's wrath?

She closed the OnShore file and shoved it away with a gesture of impatience and anger. Anyway, it was too late now to worry about it. It was a done deal: signed, sealed, and delivered even if she had agonized over the contract so long that Jake finally had snatched it away from her and sent it off to OnShore for signature, over her objections. "Dammit, C.A.," he'd fumed, "we've already done half the work and you're still diddling with the contract. They've paid us a retainer—on trust—and you're still looking for something to be wrong! Stop acting like a lawyer!" And he'd stormed out of her office—contract in hand—really and truly angry with her for the first time in their often stormy but always friendly association. Why couldn't she let go of whatever was gnawing at her about OnShore and trust Jake? She had enough of her own business to worry about: Suppose Annabelle Islington *wasn't* hiding out with her mother?

She looked up at the square chrome clock that had been a present from her friend Lillian Gailliard in New Orleans: barely eight o'clock, though it felt like hours later. It always did when darkness came at four-thirty or five o'clock in the afternoon. She reopened and reread the work before her, making changes and adjustments, refining and clarifying language, until she was satisfied. Then she turned her thoughts to herself and what was still too long a stretch of night ahead.

Carole Ann's husband, Al Crandall, had been murdered two and a half years ago, and while she thought herself well along the road to healing, being home alone for too long a time still presented emotional traumas that she didn't manage very well. Usually she ran at night after work, even in the winter. But not in the ice and snow; that was much too treacherous. She was, she realized, hungry, and certainly she could go to dinner. But dining out had been a favorite enjoyment of hers and Al's, and her favorite restaurants also were his. . . . Then she remembered the new Cajun place in Georgetown. She'd eaten there with Jake and Grace and had enjoyed the food—after she'd admonished herself to stop comparing it with the "real thing," that being the almost indescribably magnificent food prepared for her by her Cajun and Creole friends in Louisiana.

She gazed again at the clock. Lillian Gailliard and her brother, Warren Forchette, and their relatives: their great-aunt Sadie Cord and her grandson, Herve; their uncle and his wife, Eldon and Merle Warmsley; Ella Mae Forchette, Warren and Lil's mother. These people, who now were her family, too, had helped to uncover the horrible truth of her husband's murder, and then had helped her heal and recover from the trauma of that ordeal. And throughout, they had fed her. The food of the people of the bayous of Louisiana. Nothing in a restaurant ever could approximate the beauty of the real thing. But the food at Bayou North—that was the name of the place in George-town—was a noble and worthy effort.

An hour later, after having talked, via conference call, to all the Louisianans, and after a hiliarious and heartwarming conversation with her mother in Los Angeles, she felt ready to spend an evening amusing herself, wrapped as she was in the good humor and goodwill of the people who loved her. And armed with the good advice from Eldon Warmsley to "drink enough beer that it don't matter what the food tastes like," she cleared off her desk, packed her briefcase, and began plotting the fastest way across town.

3

RICHARD ISLINGTON WAS STANDING BESIDE HIS DESK waiting for them. He walked forward several paces and met them in the center of the large room in his home that was his office. He shook both their hands, greeting them by name. Then he faced Carole Ann. "That still is one of my most favorite colors," he said, before he instructed them to have a seat wherever they were most comfortable. They chose a grouping of chairs before the stone fireplace that occupied an entire wall of the room and which was adjacent to a wall of French doors through which the snow-laden woods that comprised Islington's backyard could be appreciated. It was a majestic sight and feeling, the combination of the huge, crackling fire and the vast iciness.

These powerful visuals were the only obvious symbols—aside from the man himself—that true wealth was on display. Although Islington did possess and display the aura of one accustomed not only to having his way, but to taking it if it was not freely given—and taking it without fear of consequence or retribution—his home would have been considered modest by those of comparable wealth. It was a stunning, breathtaking house, but it was a house and not a mansion, and so positioned within the forest as to appear to be one with it. The architectural harmony of the place reminded her of the house of a smuggler of illegal Mexicans in the southern California desert, an adobe and tile and log structure that appeared to have risen from the sand and cactus rather than having been constructed upon it.

Within moments of their seating themselves, there was a quick knock on the door and it opened to admit a tall, thin man in his mid-thirties pushing a serving cart. He was dressed in much the same way as Islington himself—neat wool slacks and a shirt open at the collar, sleeves rolled to midarm. He, too, reflected a higher than average degree of wealth and comfort, and looked nothing like a servant.

"There's coffee, tea, soda, beer, wine," Islington said, waving toward the cart and saying nothing to the man who brought it. No one said anything else until coffee was poured all around—into thick mugs and not puny little teacups—and the man with the cart had left, still without uttering a word.

"You think you can find my daughter," Islington said into a silence that they knew he reserved the right to break.

"We think it's reasonable to look for her," Carole Ann replied.

"Means the same thing to me," Islington shot back. "Y'all ain't the kind of people who'd take a man's money just for the pleasure of taking it. I know who you are, Miz Gibson, and I know about Graham. Know about you, too, Petrocelli. And I know you know all about me."

Carole Ann didn't really believe that Islington was the kind of man who would feel the need to rely on his poor-country-boy, idiosyncratic dialect to put them off balance; she believed that his idiomatic manner of speaking was genuine. But she was not willing to give him the benefit of the doubt, so she put him on the defensive.

"Not enough, Mr. Islington. We'd like to know why you think your daughter left, and whether that had anything to do with your wife's disappearance."

Aside from first sipping at his coffee, then slowly and deliberately placing his coffee cup on the table next to him, Islington exhibited no sign that he'd been affected by the intended sting of her words. Petrocelli, making no effort to subvert his reaction, shifted in his seat and angled his body just slightly so that he could see her as well as Islington. Then he took a noisy sip of his coffee and swallowed audibly. Carole Ann understood his warning: don't turn off Islington! But she ignored him and calmly watched and waited.

He appeared so ordinary: average height and build with the average amount of thinning, graying hair for a man in his middle fifties, with the ruddy complexion of someone who spends significant time out of doors. His clothes—herringbone tweed slacks, pale yellow silk shirt, loafers—were expensive and of good quality though not in the least ostentatious. But he was uncannily, eerily still. He sat without moving or speaking, barely blinking and breathing, and it was, ultimately, unnerving.

Carole Ann, too, sat silently with her legs crossed, right knee over left, between the two men, but angled toward her host. She, too, wore expensive and well-tailored wool slacks and a silk blouse and slip-on loafers. She cradled her coffee cup in her palms, a caress, almost, in appearance, but in reality an occupation for her hands.

"My wife left because she didn't like it here. She missed her home. She didn't share my need to be wealthy. She felt uncomfortable in the presence of educated people, especially other women, who made a game of looking down on her—she wasn't very... smart. And I claimed Annabelle as mine. I took her with me everywhere I went, kept her close to me. I had my money and I had my daughter and I didn't need more."

"That explains why your wife left, but presumably your daughter didn't feel unwanted?" Carole Ann deliberately made it a question. She wanted to elicit some degree of emotion from the man, and almost succeeded.

"I don't know what Annabelle felt," he replied in a tight voice. "She didn't talk to people, she read books."

"What's her name, Mr. Islington? What's your wife's name?" she asked quickly, deliberately too close on the words out of his mouth.

He didn't answer for a moment, in which he appeared to be trying to remember. "Eve," he replied finally, in a flat tone.

She shifted gears. "Why do people dislike you so, Mr. Islington? I'm certain that you don't care why; I just wonder if you know why."

For the first time he smiled. It was small, and brief, but it was there, and it was real. "Because I don't respond or react to things or events or people or circumstances. Not the way they want me to or think I should. And you know very well, Miz Gibson, that folks don't like what they don't understand."

She met and held his gaze, wondering what, exactly, he meant. She did, indeed, know very well the extent to which people distrusted and disliked that which they didn't understand, that which was different. She'd been different from the majority of the people in her surroundings for the majority of her life. But then, she was Black and female. Surely Richard Islington wasn't equating his preference for rudeness and people's reaction to his behavior with . . . but of course he was. The cocky set of his head and his steady, level meeting of her gaze indicated that.

"Anybody mind if I jump in here?" Petrocelli looked from one to the other of them, aware that he was interrupting something intense, something potentially explosive. "Did your daughter ever tell you that she wanted to leave or that she planned to leave or did she ever threaten to leave?"

"No," Islington replied dryly and then stood abruptly.

Petrocelli followed suit, getting to his feet as abruptly, and clearly creating a brief moment of unbalance for Islington. "I know your daughter has her own place, Mr. Islington, but does she still have a room here?"

"Why?"

"Because I'd like to see it," Petrocelli responded in a calm tone.

"Why?" Islington asked again, the challenge undisguised.

"We need your complete cooperation, Mr. Islington, if we're to have a successful working relationship." Carole Ann rose to her feet as she was speaking, placing her cup on the table and turning to face the two men in a single, fluid movement. "It should be obvious to you why we need to learn as much as possible about Annabelle. But even if it isn't, please accept that it is."

Islington opened, then closed his mouth, and turned away from his guests and strode over to his desk. He touched a button on the telephone and then crossed to the door and opened it. "My associate, Jack, will show you Annabelle's rooms. He will also have for you the signed contracts and a retainer. I know you'll contact me when you have something to say." And he turned away from them and returned to his desk, leaving them alone in the hallway just as the tall man who'd wheeled in the drinks cart appeared.

"Miss Gibson," he said in a deep and melodious voice. "Is there something I can do for you?"

"If your name is Jack, there is," she replied, and told him and he nodded and led the way down the plushly carpeted hall to a rear staircase that seemed to lead to heaven. They climbed the open-plank staircase, mesmerized by the outside world: the wall of glass at the rear of the house seemed to lead not only upward but out, to eternity. Once again, Carole Ann marveled at the warmth she felt in this house, for as they reached the landing and turned in toward the center of the house, recessed lighting and rich Oriental and kelim rugs scattered on top of the Berber carpeting enveloped her. She turned her head and yes! the snow-covered outside still was within her grasp. She was wondering how somebody could live in such an environment and make a hobby of being unpleasant when the man named Jack stopped at a doorway.

"This is—was—Annabelle's suite," he said, and Carole Ann strained to identify the undercurrent of emotion she detected in his voice. It seemed to have deepened and trembled slightly on the "was." He stood away from the door and Paolo entered first. Carole Ann followed, expecting their guide to follow; when he didn't, she turned and caught a definite though fleeting glimmer of something in his expression before he closed it off and nodded politely at her.

Carole Ann turned her attention back to Paolo and his prowling of the main room of Annabelle Islington's suite. It was a sitting room/den/library, longer than it was wide, with floor-to-ceiling book shelves on two walls and the outlines of where at least a dozen frames once had hung on the other walls. A matching sofa and arm chair were the only furniture, though a television and VCR remained in the shelf facing the sofa. Otherwise, the shelves were empty.

Paolo walked around the room twice, touching each piece of furniture and the appliances, and tracing the outlines of several of the phantom frames. Carole Ann followed him through to the bedroom. A much smaller room. Two twin beds on low platforms at right angles to each other, both covered with batik-print bedspreads. Just as she was wondering at the lack of additional furniture, Paolo slid open a mirrored door to reveal a walk-in-closet-size room. Built-in drawers and cabinets and shelves. He began opening and closing drawers and running his hand over shelves. He shook his head slightly, then turned suddenly. "Sir? Jack?"

"Yes?" the man answered, his lovely, deep voice now completely composed.

"Did Annabelle do this?"

"Do what?" he asked, puzzled.

"Clear out. Leave nothing of herself here."

There was a slight pause before the answer: "This is how Annabelle left her rooms," he said. And since there was nothing more to be seen or said, they followed him back down the stairs and down the hallway to the front door, where he helped them into their coats and boots and, as promised, presented them with an enevelope containing contracts and payment.

"If that guy's the butler, I'm the Duchess of York," Paolo snorted in a stage whisper. They were barely out of the house and down the walkway to the drive, both of them charged by their encounter with Islington and their tour of Annabelle's suite, though manifesting their energy differently. Carole Ann shrugged off the need for a reply and turned to look back at the house, to admire it again, perhaps even to covet it momentarily, to imagine it in the spring and summer. And she saw, reflected in one of the glass panels, standing paralyzingly still, sadness etched in his face, Jack, the "associate." When he realized he was being observed, he backed quickly away.

"Islington called him his 'associate,' " Carole Ann reminded Petrocelli.

"And I'm the King of Siam," he replied with total irreverence. "By the way, you poked ol' Dicky Rae pretty good. Did he tell you anything you didn't know?" Petrocelli asked as he wheeled the GGI-issue Ford Explorer down Islington's winding drive toward the street. The roadway was as clear and dry as if it were June, and only the deep drifts of snow, stark against the blackness of the barren trees, validated the need for the four-wheel-drive vehicle. Until, that is, they reached the main road, which had yet to be paid a visit by the city's snow-removal team.

"Don't know," Carole Ann answered, looking out the window and reveling in the scenery. She truly loved winter and especially days like this one. The sky was brilliantly blue and cloudless, as often happens following a snowfall, and it was bitterly cold. The warmth they'd garnered beside Islington's fire dissipated the moment they walked out of his front door.

"Still think we can find the daughter?"

"Don't know that, either. And right now, I'm not at all sure he wants us to find her, though if that's not what he wants, then what does he want? Because judging by the look and feel of Annabelle's room, she certainly doesn't want any part of dear old Dad."

"I had that exact same fee—oh shit!" Petrocelli began whipping the steering wheel back and forth as the big vehicle spun around in the middle of the road. "Oh shit!" he said again when he'd regained control of the vehicle. "It's all ice. The little melt that the sun is producing is turning to ice."

Washington harbored several different kinds of exclusive neighborhoods. There were the Federalist front houses of Georgetown and DuPont Circle and Foggy Bottom and Embassy Row. Some of these were enormous in size, and all of them were old and expensive and too close together for nonnatives from the upper East Coast who equate physical proximity to one's neighbors with poverty. Then there were neighborhoods like Cleveland Park and the Gold Coast and Tilden Park, where the streets were wide, the houses large, and there was enough land to require professional landscaping and a gardener. Then there were those enclaves of exclusivity that bore no names, just addresses on streets unknown to common citizens; the street names that only those who'd been invited had ever heard of. That's where Richard Islington lived—on one of the streets cut into the cliffs overlooking the Potomac River. The streets were narrow and winding—some of them little more than lanes—and all of them too narrow for the municipal snow-removal equipment. But then people who lived on streets with secret names weren't required to explain to bosses why an icy hill prevented their presence at work.

"Four-wheel drive ain't worth diddly on ice," Petrocelli said with a relieved exhale of breath when they finally wound their way out of the hills and were back on the properly plowed Foxhall Road.

"Paolo, be careful, OK?"

He bristled. "What the hell do you think I was being? If I'd been anything else, we'd be belly-up in the woods."

"No, no, no!" She raised her hand and reached across the wide expanse of the vehicle toward him. "That's not what I mean. I'm not talking about your driving, Paolo!"

"What, then? You're making about as much sense as Mr. Islington, and that's no compliment, I gotta tell ya."

Carole Ann grinned at him. He sounded every bit the south Philadelphia native that he was in that moment. "I mean watch yourself, watch your back, cover your tracks as you're searching for Annabelle. At least until we have a better fix on what he wants with her."

He nodded. "It did occur to me that Dicky Rae would be the kind of guy to hire watchers to watch the watcher. But how are you going to find out what he really wants? And what was that business about his favorite color? And what's the real deal with that Jack character? And it's for damn sure it's not just his little girl he's after. Not exactly a Bill Cosby kind of dad, our Dicky Rae."

She grinned at the Bill Cosby analogy, then asked, "Were you able to get anything at all from that room?"

He shook his head. "Zip."

She turned quickly and looked at him. "But what, Paolo?"

He hesitated. "Wherever she is now had nothing to do with the way she left that room."

"What do you mean?" Carole Ann asked, random feelings beginning to connect to one another in a pattern . . . not yet a discernable one, but a pattern nonetheless.

"That room was emptied in anger. Annebelle was—is—angry with her father; so angry that she erased herself out of his life. She intended to hurt him when she left."

Yes, Carole Ann thought; that made sense. She thought of her own room in her mother's house. She still had clothes there, and textbooks from high school and college. And there were photographs of her and mementos, running shoes and shorts in the closet and a toothbrush in the bathroom. She hadn't erased herself from her mother's life when she'd grown up and moved away. Her mother's home still was her home, too. But Paolo was exactly and perfectly correct: Annabelle Islington was angry enough with her father to erase herself from his life. Why?

"That means something to you, doesn't it?" Paolo asked, stumbling around in her thoughts. "What?"

She shook her head. "Don't know."

"Just so you know, Miz Gibson," and he emphasized the words, producing a perfect Islington imitation, "I don't believe you when you say, 'don't know.' I don't ever think you don't know. I think you know plenty, you just don't tell."

She shrugged. "I'm a lawyer behaving like a cop. What do you expect?"

෴ ෴

The Christmas–New Year holiday can be a perfect time to conduct business in Washington, or a perfectly lousy time, which was the case for all open and active GGI investigations. And it perhaps was for the better, since the GGI principals were, in truth, more interested in the festivities of the season than in working. For the first time since her husband's death, Carole Ann remained home for the holidays, and was joined by her mother from Los Angeles and her brother and sister-in-law and their children from Denver. Dave Crandall, Al's father, and his wife, from Atlanta, stopped in for a couple of days en route to New York, and Tommy and Valerie Griffin came home to D.C. from their new home in L.A. for the week between Christmas and the new year. And Warren Forchette came up from New Orleans to celebrate, on New Year's Eve, the fifteenth wedding anniversary of a college and law school classmate and took Carole Ann to the best New Year's Eve party she'd been to in a decade.

And for the first time in anybody's memory, D.C. was presented with a white Christmas. It began snowing on Christmas Eve and continued for the next two days. Thick, heavy, pillowy snow. A relatively small city by most city standards—like Chicago or Los Angeles—D.C. became a village for a week. People walked in the middle of streets, pulling children on sleds. People skied and tobogganed and rode cut-up cardboard boxes down hills. The scent of burning firewood, hot chocolate, and mulled cider hung over the entire city. Overexcited dogs, their tongues lolling sideways and pink, followed perfect strangers home to be fed leftover turkey and ham and duck.

By the time the last glass of Cristal was downed and the final "Auld Lang Syne" sung, everybody was holidayed out and ready to return to the calmer, more restful pace of work. And indeed the first week of the new year was predictable in its ordinariness. Then things changed, beginning with the weather. By the middle of January, D.C. was behaving like the South: temperatures were in the fifties and the elders were sourly predicting that everybody would be sick as dogs before it was over. They were, as usual, correct, despite the continued denials of the medical experts of the existence of a correlation between viruses and the weather. Whatever the cause, Carole Ann and a half-dozen GGI employees were visited by nasty, ugly colds. Jake and another half dozen got the flu. A mean, brutal, kick-ass flu that consigned them to their beds.

Dehydrated and headachey and with a nose worn raw and peeling from repeated blowing, Carole Ann was ending her fifth consecutive sneeze—they came in fives—and was trying to gently blow her nose when she heard a "God bless you" from the doorway. She looked up to see Patty Baker standing there with a box of tissues in one hand and a thick file folder in the other. Patty, too, had wrestled with the cold and, C.A. knew, several of her crew had not been so fortunate, having been felled by the flu.

"Feeling better?" C.A. asked, waving her visitor into the room and toward the sofa.

"Depends" came the nasal reply. "Better than what?"

Carole Ann laughed. "Thanks, Patty, I needed that."

"You're welcome," she said, and dropped wearily down into the couch. "And you needed it more than you know."

Carole Ann looked up at her and pondered the meaning of the words for several long seconds. Then she pondered the true meaning of a visit from Patty, who never voluntarily left her subterranean domain. Then it registered that Patty had tightly and securely closed the door when she came in. She sat up straight, folded her hands on the desktop, and looked steadily at her visitor.

"What is it, Patty?"

"The Islington girl left with close to three million dollars—all of it hers, by the way. And that OnShore thing that Jake is working on? The man who's supposed to be the COO doesn't exist. He's dead. Been dead since 1971."

Carole Ann literally didn't have a single thought for several long seconds. She merely absorbed the information. Then she thought what an effort it must have been for Patty Baker to condense into those few sentences information that it had taken her weeks to retrieve from sources C.A. probably didn't want to know about. Then she thought how good it didn't feel at that moment to be right. Then she smiled at Patty, which completely unnerved the other woman, until she heard the reason for it—Carole Ann, in a complete departure from the norm, actually shared her thoughts and feelings. Then she laughed.

"You're a one, C.A., truly you are." Patty lowered her head and blushed. "You don't give me lawyer-speak, so I can at least try not to give you computer-speak."

Carole Ann smiled grimly. "Well, you can give it to me now. Do your thing, Patty. Tell me how you know what you know."

Patty talked for almost an hour and Carole Ann found herself appreciating the excruciating detail of the discourse. It was clear that the computer expert loved not only information itself, but the pursuit of it: how many places information could be; how many ways it could be stored; how many ways it could be accessed; and how many ways it could be hidden, camouflaged, manipulated, and transformed. But Patty's bottom line was that if it existed, all information could be retrieved and that she, Patty, could retrieve it. To wit: Annabelle Islington inherited a million dollars on her eighteenth birthday, and another million on her twenty-first birthday, and when she graduated from college, which occurred seven and a half months after her twenty-first birthday, she received another eight hundred thousand dollars.

The money, Patty said, came from a fund established by Annabelle's mother, to whom Richard Islington had given one million dollars as an incentive to leave him and their daughter. She hired an Arlington, Virginia, lawyer who had invested the money wisely enough that it almost tripled itself. Richard Islington had had no knowledge of the existence of the fund until Annabelle's eighteenth birthday, when she received the first one million dollars. Patty did not know whether Annabelle had prior knowledge of the money or prior contact with her mother; she knew only that the money remained under the control of the Arlington lawyer until the day that Annabelle left, when she took possession of the money in the form of bearer bonds, securities, certificates of deposit, cashiers' checks, and cash.

"As for this second bit of business," Patty drawled, the South in her voice enhanced by the clogged nasal passages—it came out "bi-niss"; OnShore Manufacturing's chief operating officer, John David MacDonald, was, according to the curriculum vitae attached to the documents that OnShore submitted to GGI, a Canadian by birth and educated at the University of Toronto. And true enough, Patty said, a John David MacDonald did earn a B.S. in business at the University of Toronto. He entered the United States on a work visa more than fifteen years ago and became a naturalized American citizen five years later. The only problem, she said, was that the Social Security number included in the vitae belonged to a John David MacDonald who was a native of Atlanta, Georgia, born there in 1946, and who was killed in a car crash in 1971. "That's where they screwed up," Patty said. "They didn't know that your SSN tells where and when you were born. They thought they'd done their homework with the two John David MacDonalds." She spat the words out, the taste of disdain obvious. "People are so smart they're stupid," she said.

Carole Ann didn't say anything for a long time, which didn't seem to matter to Patty, who sat quietly and comfortably on the sofa, periodically sniffling and blowing her nose. When finally she ordered her thoughts, Carole Ann stood and crossed to sit next to Patty on the couch. "You weren't just a government secretary all those years, were you?"

Patty's raucous hoot of laughter would have sailed up and down the hallway had the door been open; thankfully, it was not. "I see why Jake calls you the best trial lawyer in town. When you ask a question, you leave only enough room for somebody either to tell the truth, tell a lie, or make a fool outta themselves trying not to do one or the other." Then she turned serious. "I won't make a fool outta myself, but I will say that I once heard that a smart lawyer didn't ask a question he—or she—didn't already know the answer to."

Carole Ann accepted the folder that Patty offered and thanked her for her work. She escorted her to the door and then stood for a moment deciding whether to leave it open and thereby signal her accessibility to the staff since Jake was absent, or close it and claim the privacy she needed to read the file and think through all she'd just heard. The ringing of the phone decided for her. And since it was her private line ringing, she knew that she had mere seconds to decide whether to keep what she knew to herself long enough to assess all the potential implications, or to tell Jake immediately, since nobody but Jake ever called her on that line. And instead of the cussing she expected when she told him, there was deadly, unnerving silence. She didn't even bother trying to dissuade him from getting out of bed and coming in. She sat down and began reading so that she could tell him, as succinctly as Patty had told her, everything that there was to know about Annabelle Islington's surprise trust fund and OnShore Manufacturing's bogus chief operating officer.

⁓ ⁓

"So you think Islington's wife has been around all this time, keeping an eye on her daughter from a distance?"

Carole Ann nodded, then shook her head, then shrugged. She didn't know what she thought. The composite picture of Eve Simmons Islington that was emerging was both complex and complimentary: a young and uneducated though highly intelligent girl moves from a small town to the big city with an equally intelligent, tough, and ambitious husband, where she quickly discovers that a shared background of small-town poverty isn't sufficient to sustain a marriage. Not even the birth of a child could produce a spark of warmth between them.

"Islington lied about her leaving him, though. He sent her away. Paid her off and sent her away, probably thinking that a million dollars would buy her permanent absence, though most likely being prepared to pay more later if necessary."

"But she didn't come around asking for more, so he, what, just forgot about her?" The flu bug may have beat up on Jake's body, but his mean streak was still healthy and active. "He thought she sold her kid for a million bucks?"

"It happens. She was a poor country girl, remember. People have done and always will do amazing things for money."

"People suck," he said with more energy than his body had, and he virtually collapsed against the sofa back in a spasm of deep, chest-rattling coughing that brought Carole Ann to her feet. He waved her off. "I'm OK," he managed to wheeze, as he worked to restore his breathing.

"For Richard Islington, money is everything, so even though Eve had let him know she wasn't happy with his pursuit of wealth, it didn't strike him as out of character for her to take his money and quietly vanish."

"But you really don't think she—Eve—was in touch with the girl all along?" Jake's breath still was labored and several deep inhalations were required before he completed the question.

Carole Ann shook her head. "I don't think so. I don't think that would have been possible without Islington's knowledge and it looks like that first million to Annabelle came as a shock to both of them— to Annabelle and to Richard. But I do think that, somehow, she was able to keep track of how and what her daughter was doing all those years."

Jake chuckled, then stopped himself as it turned into a cough. "I'd like to have seen that bastard's face when he found out the girl didn't need him after all."

Carole Ann thought she'd like to have seen that, too, though she believed she had witnessed the aftershock; for that's what she saw in him that day in his house, she realized. His forced self-control was a product of shock and the slow, burning anger it could produce. She recalled Paolo's assessment of Islington as not a Bill Cosby kind of dad, and knew that his search for Annabelle was not motivated by love, but by revenge. Then, she thought: It's not Annabelle he wants but Eve. The force of that realization produced a physical reaction so intense that Jake noticed and queried her, and when she explained he, too, immediately accepted the premise as logical.

"Not a Bill Cosby kind of husband, either," he grumbled through a hacking cough. "What do you want to do about it?" he asked, wheezing and struggling to catch his breath.

"I don't know yet," she replied with a slight impatience, for even though she believed she was correct about Islington's basic motivation—find Annabelle and he'd find Eve—that didn't explain Annabelle's anger at her father.

"So." Jake dropped the word and all its meaning into the silent place created by the end of the Islington discussion and waited for her to answer the unasked question . . . unasked because of his fear of the answer.

She told him what Patty had told her and what she had learned from reading all the information and documentation she had gathered, and then waited for him to digest and process it all; and while she waited, she watched. He looked weak and tired. She knew the worst of what the flu does had passed—the chills and fever and achy joints and searing headache. What's left is a body that has to fight its way back to strength and health, a process that Jake had yet to begin.

"I met MacDonald one time. He was rushing out of the warehouse and into one of the trucks. And I thought at the time that he was avoiding me—that's what it felt like when he brushed past me, claiming he was late for something, I don't remember what. I thought that the COO of a company would want to spend at least a couple of minutes with the guy his partner had hired to do such an important job. That's what I thought at the time. Then I let the thought go so it wouldn't get in the way of a potentially big payday."

He was beating himself up enough, so she didn't reply; she sat and waited for him to continue.

"We're pretty well into the background checks on the top execs at Seaboard, and into the analysis of their finances. One interesting thing: the state AG investigated them four years ago but we can't find out why. They dropped the investigation and put the whole thing

59

under seal. The next year, Seaboard gave the maximum allowed to every Republican running for statewide office. That was the first, last, and only year they made political contributions."

"A sealed investigation by the state attorney general that didn't result in charges?" She sat up straight. That had the odor of the kind of criminal activity she knew all too well. "I'll find out what that's all about, but whatever it is, it won't win the Good Housekeeping Seal of Approval for Seaboard, Jake, and you know that."

He snorted. "Right this minute, I don't care shit about Seaboard, C.A. Wouldn't matter to me if they were making porno movies and selling moonshine whiskey in the basement and charging admission. I care if we've got a bogus client. And I care if it's my fault that we've got a bogus client."

She didn't believe for a second that he didn't care if Seabord was shaky and shady, but she wisely chose not to comment. "Well, perhaps whatever that's about, along with our knowledge of Mac-Donald's phony identity, will push OnShore into being more honest with us."

He sat frowning and thinking for a moment. "You think that's what we're supposed to find out for them? What this whole thing is all about?"

"Could be," she responded, pondering the possibility. "Could also be OnShore doesn't know anything about the attorney general's office looking at Seaboard, and finding out about it could sour the deal for them." She shrugged, as if trying to rid herself of the burden of the tangle of new information. "MacDonald, or whoever he really is, travels extensively out of the country, according to the information Patty compiled, and the reason given on his visas and declaration forms is always 'business.' " She picked up a page from among those scattered about on her desk and scanned it quickly, looking for something. "Here it is: he lists his occupation on his entrance forms as 'development consultant.' " She tossed that paper aside and scooped up another. "Nothing in this vitae points to his having any kind of experience or expertise that would legitimize his calling himself a development consultant. Who is the John MacDonald who's alive? How did they find out about the dead John MacDonald? And who is the On-Shore COO who's using the MacDonald name?"

Jake stood up, shakily, and walked slowly toward the door. "Guess I'd better get busy finding those answers."

She stood, too, and followed him to the door. "You don't have to do it today, Jake. Go back home, go back to bed, and start fresh in the morning, OK?"

He sighed and nodded. "I don't have enough lung power to argue with you, C.A." He opened the door and was in the hallway when he turned back to her. "C.A.? Thanks for not being the kind of person to say you told me so."

"You're welcome, Jake," she said, and watched his slow progress down the hall to his own office. She stood there, watching, while he entered his office, and watched as, just moments later, he emerged, bundled in scarf and overcoat, closed and locked the door, and headed, hunched over and moving slowly, toward the elevator. Without turning to look at her, he raised his hand and gave a backward wave good-bye, and disappeared around the corner.

Back at her desk, she took up the folder presented to her by Patty a short four hours ago. She separated the OnShore pages from the Islington pages. OnShore was Jake's case, Jake's business, Jake's problem. Eve and Annabelle Islington were her problems, and she was beginning to feel that that was a very apt description for them.

⋘ ⋙

Bill Williams. She almost didn't believe the name, and had it not come directly from Patty, she perhaps would have spent time and energy verifying the likelihood of a lawyer named Bill Williams. But that's what Patty said was the name of the lawyer Eve Islington hired twenty years ago to create and manage her daughter's trust fund; and she recognized the address, knew the approximate location of Bill Williams's office in Arlington. And, she thought, if he'd been there for twenty years or more, and if he'd been forward-thinking enough to have bought the building back then, he was sitting on a gold mine now. And anybody competent enough to triple a one-million-dollar investment could be considered forward-thinking. At the very least.

Bill Williams's office was exactly where Carole Ann thought it was: one of the first exits off Interstate 95 South in Virginia, after the monuments and the Potomac River and the Pentagon have been left behind. When she moved to D.C., that area was beginning its transformation into an enclave of trendy exclusivity, though enough of old Arlington remained that it was readily and easily identifiable as a convenient and affordable home base for the thousands of mid- and low-level government workers and military women and men who called it home. Now, it was home to lawyers and lobbyists and association executives and journalists—people who could afford to live close to downtown D.C. and work.

The building was a one-level brick square on a corner lot. The other three corners were anchored by a twenty-four-hour, glass-enclosed gym that provided a constant view of fit and trim young men and women stepping and pumping and sweating; an elegant country French restaurant that looked as if it had been transported that day directly from Avignon; and a trendy, *très chic* combination coffee shop/juice bar. As she traversed the perfectly manicured brick walkway to Williams's building, Carole Ann called to memory everything about the man from Patty's report; and remembering that he was seventy-plus years old, pondered the nature of his relationship with his neighbors.

There were four names on the building directory, all of them lawyers, Williams's the last. But his office was the first to the right off the foyer. She opened the door and entered.

"If that's Miss Gibson, come on in," a booming bass voice called out, and she followed it through an empty though well-equipped reception area to a surprisingly large and very inviting office. One wall of the room was taken up by a floor-to-ceiling bookshelf, completely filled. On another wall was a built-in entertainment center, the focal point of which was a gigantic television screen but which also contained a VCR and CD player, and dozens of videocassettes and compact discs. Directly across from the entertainment center was a long burgundy leather sofa, two leather club chairs, and three tables. And, facing her, a desk the size of a football field and, behind it, a man the size of a couple of linebackers.

Bill Williams heaved himself to his feet and Carole Ann winced at the obvious effort. The man was simply enormous. Not like a football player at all, she thought; more like a sumo wrestler. And he didn't appear to be seventy-three years old, which, according to his date of birth, he certainly was. He had a head full of sandy hair, bright blue eyes, and, when he shook her hand, a dry, firm grip.

"I don't know why you want to see me, Miss Gibson, but I couldn't contemplate saying no," he said, indicating that she should take the seat across from the massive desk, and dropping himself down into a leather rocking chair.

"I appreciate your generosity, Mr. Williams, and I'll try not to take up too much of your time."

He said something that sounded like "pshaw," and shared the information that he was essentially retired and that it was only fifty years' worth of habit that brought him to the office every day. "I still do some estate work for a few clients of long standing. But," and he chuckled, "those any more long standing than me are all dead. So I watch TV and old movies and listen to music and read."

Carole Ann studied the room and, taking in his words, realized that it was as much home as office. "It's a wonderful room, Mr. Williams, and I envy you the luxury of testing yourself by having books and music and movies in your office. I dare not." And she meant it; she was not merely making conversation, though she was quickly forming an opinion of Bill Williams that ran counter to his courtly presentation.

He chuckled deeply and acknowledged her compliment with a nod of his head. Then he got down to business. "You've got quite a reputation, young woman, and it amuses and amazes an old-timer like myself. Could you possibly understand my fascination with the fact that you and I are both called lawyers? Like the GP of my day and the nuclear surgeon of today are both doctors. The same way, I guess, that watermelons and grapes are both fruits with seeds. Amazing. And amusing if you're inclined toward the pursuit of humor. Which I am." Then the old man wheezed another chuckle and settled back in his chair, double chins resting on his chest, hands folded across his enormous belly, and waited for her.

A perfect portrait of a caricature pretending to be a caricature, Carole Ann thought, and realized what it was about the man she found off-putting: he was patronizing. He was a member of that class in the old school that didn't welcome women to his world, and most certainly not Black ones. She'd encountered more than a few like him over the years.

"You're very good at what you do, Mr. Williams, even though you may not do very much of it these days. But I suspect that one of the things you're still very good at is lulling people into believing you're a dithering old has-been. A guy just like you handed me my butt on a platter early in my career as a trial lawyer. It was a good lesson."

"And you're obviously a good student. What can I do for you, Miss Gibson?" The chuckling, country lawyer had evaporated, to be replaced by the shrewd, calculating street lawyer Carole Ann was convinced he was. One who didn't like or trust women.

"Richard Islington hired my firm to find his daughter. We want to be certain that locating her won't put her—or her mother—in danger."

The old man didn't move a muscle. The only hint that he'd reacted to what she said was a subtle change in his breathing. Because he was so large, his normal breathing was audible; under stress, it became louder. "Why are you talking to me about Richard Islington's daughter?"

"Because several months ago, you conveyed two point eight million dollars to her in negotiable funds and I thought she might be grateful enough to keep in touch."

He heaved himself up from the chair and supported his bulk by leaning on the edge of the desk. His breath was coming rapidly now, as well as noisily. "I don't know how you know what you know, Miss Gibson, but it strikes me that illegality entered the equation somewhere. We're definitely different kinds of lawyers. I don't believe in breaking, bending, or twisting the law to suit my own purposes. And I don't believe in working for the client with the most money."

"You also probably don't believe in vodoun, the Buddha, or the benefits of exercise and a vegetarian diet," she snapped at him. "But that doesn't make me respect you any less, and since you've obviously lived a long if not necessarily healthy life, it really doesn't matter to me. What does matter is whether I can locate Annabelle Islington and her mother before harm comes to them, or at least warn them of the potential for danger. You'd do them a great service by delivering that message."

"And why should I—or they—believe you, Miss Gibson?"

She'd already turned away from him to leave, but she turned back to face him. "No reason at all, Mr. Williams," she said in an almost airy tone but with a look that contradicted it. She held his steely gaze with her own and became instantly aware that he'd had more practice at this than she, and therefore was better at it. "Thanks for your time, and you have a good day." She turned quickly away again. She needed to break eye contact with him.

"Hold on, now, Miss Gibson," he said in a wheedling voice, signaling the return of the good ol' country lawyer. "I'm trying to work with you here, if you'd just give me a minute. I want to believe what you're saying—"

She whipped around, not making any effort to conceal her dislike and growing distrust of the man. "I don't need you to do me any favors. I came here to do you one, and you can accept it or reject it. Your choice." And before he could reply, she stalked out of the office, omitting to close the door behind her.

4

HOURS LATER, SHE WAS STILL WORKING TO UNDER-
stand the basis for her almost instant dislike of the old Arlington
lawyer. It wasn't simply that he'd hauled out his country bumpkin
routine and tried it on her; practically every lawyer she knew, herself
included, employed a fake persona, a facade, for dealing with the
public—clients, juries, other lawyers, cops. It was standard and acceptable. Nor was it the underlying hostility to her gender and her
race; that, too, was as commonplace as suspenders and bow ties.
There was something else, some intangible thing, that raised her
hackles and primed her for the attack. She wished Jake were around;
he could provide an accurate assessment of her reaction to Williams,
could help her identify the source of her hostility. And could tell her
whether she owed the man an apology.

But Jake wasn't around . . . hadn't been around for several days.
He was somewhere on Maryland's Eastern Shore, like one of the wa-
termen famous in the region, casting his own nets, hoping to catch
something to help unravel the mess that was OnShore and Seaboard.

She heard something that caused her to look up, and she did a
double-take at the figure leaning against the doorjamb. Recognition

dawned slowly, but finally she discerned that the grungy-looking specimen grinning laconically at her was Paolo Petrocelli. She'd always had difficulty imagining him conforming to the strict dress code of the FBI—dark suit, white shirt, conservative tie, wing tips—but neither did he project the bearded, blue-jeaned, sneakered, rough-and-ready street cop of film and television. He was partial to chinos and bucks and denim shirts and knit ties. And he wore his dark, reddish-brown hair in a neat and stylish ponytail.

"What happened to you?" she asked with a bemused grin, taking in the ACE Hardware cap with the bill turned up, the plaid work shirt, the khaki slacks, and the steel-toed boots favored by construction workers. And these boots had seen work.

"Scenic View, Ohio, is what happened to me," he said with an exaggerated curtsey, and ambled into her office and over to the love seat, a bag in each hand.

"You had to look like that to go to Ohio?"

"To go to the part of Ohio that was the birthplace of Dicky Rae Waters and Ruthie Eva Simmons, yes, indeed, I had to look like this. If I wanted anybody to talk to me, that is."

"And did they talk to you?"

He grinned, removed the cap, and released his long hair from the barrette that secured it in place on top of his head. "Yes, they did. Nice people, too," he said as he took an elastic band from his wrist and deftly wrapped it around his hair. "That was one of the things that always pissed me off about the Feds, going into some place and demanding things of people and scaring and intimidating them. We usually got what we wanted, but we never got handshakes and smiles, you know?"

She stood and came from behind the desk and sat in the rocking chair across the table from the love seat, facing him. "And you got smiles and handshakes in Scenic View?" she asked.

He nodded. "I did. I also got"—he opened the larger of the two bags he'd brought in with him—"this. The 1972 Scenic View *Miner.*" He opened the book, turned a few pages, and passed it to her. "Right side, bottom row."

Carole Ann studied the almost thirty-year-old photograph of Ruthie Eva Simmons. She—and all of her classmates—looked impossibly young. And she knew that being eighteen in the early 1970s was, indeed, younger than being eighteen in the early days of the new, twenty-first century. She studied the legend beside Ruthie Eva's name: Debate Club, French Club, Honor Society, newspaper staff, Girl Most Likely to Succeed. She looked up at Petrocelli and he nodded, knowing exactly what she was thinking. "Islington made her sound backwards and ignorant, like a country bumpkin. 'Most likely to succeed'? And she didn't want to live in Washington and be the wife of the richest man in town?"

Instead of responding, he withdrew several sheets of paper from the bag and passed them across the table to her and watched her as she read the documents, turning them over, peering closely, he knew, at dates and signatures. And as she read, he opened the second bag he'd brought with him and withdrew a cup of Starbucks coffee. He removed the top, gently blew on the black liquid from which steam rose, and took a satisfying—and noisy—sip.

"Well, I'll be damned," she said finally. "Everything he said or implied about her was a lie."

He nodded. "She spent two years running up the road to Athens, home of Ohio University, to get herself licensed as a cosmetologist, then came home and opened her own beauty salon, bought herself a car, and was taking care of her parents when ol' Dicky Rae came along and swept her off her feet. She gave him the money to buy his first piece of real estate. She's the one who put him on the map."

Carole Ann leaned toward him. "And this was common knowledge around town? That Eve gave Islington his start?"

He nodded. "I heard it more than once."

"What else did people say about her? Do people like her? Respect her?"

He was nodding vigorously. "Oh, yeah. She was a fairy-tale hometown girl. Shy but popular, smart, a good daughter to her parents, a good friend. Determined to make something of herself, something better than the wife of a coal miner and the mother of too many children too soon. She didn't go out much with guys and hadn't had a serious love interest until Dicky Rae popped into her life. And the residents of Scenic View are not impressed with Dicky Rae—and they still call him that, just like they call her Ruthie Eva—and a good number of them believe that he's done something bad to her. Otherwise, they say she'd have come back, at least to visit."

"And she hasn't been back? Ever?"

"Nope. Never. And they think he's done something to her to prevent her return."

Carole Ann thumbed through the papers again. "They got married in 1975. She was twenty-one and he was thirty-one. And it looks like they left Scenic View in . . . what? Seventy-seven?"

"Yep. Dicky Rae had bought and sold land in Ohio and in West Virginia and had made a pretty decent profit and could talk about nothing but moving to Washington, D.C. Everybody I talked to remembered that: Dicky Rae talking about what Richard Islington was going to do when he got to Washington, D.C."

"Certainly appears that he was a man of his word," Carole Ann said, dropping the papers on the table. "And less than two years into D.C., Annabelle is born and Eve is gone." She rubbed her hands together as if for warmth and looked across the table at Petrocelli. "How much help do you need, Paolo?" and she dreaded his answer because given the number of people out sick and the number of people already assigned to cases, there wasn't a single extra body available to give him. It would mean shifting one of the investigators to the Islington case from something else.

He was grinning slyly. "Right now, I need only you, C.A., and I need only for you to take Ruthie Eva's Social Security number off that piece of paper there and walk it underground to Patty Bake. We all know what Patty can do with a Social Security number." He was laughing out loud by now, and she joined him. The news of Patty's discovery of the bogus OnShore number had spread quickly through GGI, further enhancing the walk-on-water reputation of Patty and the subterraneans, as they now were called, as if they were a 1960s Motown group.

Carole Ann wrote down Eve Islington's Social Security number and they took a few moments to discuss the virtual obsolescence of the flat-footed, gumshoe investigator in the modern world, and the importance of computers and those who know how to manage them. Paolo took his papers and his coffee and departed. C.A. called Patty and gave her Eve's Social Security number. Then she got busy proving to herself that she could be as valuable to GGI as any computer.

⁓ ⁓

The call came exactly thirty minutes into their regular Monday-morning staff meeting, as if the caller knew that the first fifteen minutes were spent telling jokes and tall tales while fixing their coffee and bagels. Then the five of them—Carole Ann, Jake, Patty, Donald Smith, the business manager, and Carla Thompkins, executive assistant to all four of them by title and who, in addition to overseeing the activities of all the GGI staff assistants (Patty had requested that nobody at GGI be called a secretary), actually ran the place.

A hasty and loud knock on the conference door preceded the entry of one of the young security specialists.

"What is it, Bob?" Carla asked him, frowning.

"I'm sorry, Mrs. Thompkins, everybody, but there's this guy on the phone demanding to speak to Mr. Graham right now. He says if you know what's good for you, sir, you'll take the call."

Without comment or hesitation, Jake pushed back his chair, stood up, and strode to the phone. He looked down at the several blinking lights on the display and then up at Bob, who was still standing in the doorway.

"Sorry, sir. He's on thirty-six," Bob said, and closed the door.

Jake picked up the handset and pressed a button. "This is Jake Graham," he said into the mouthpiece. "Who are you and what do you want?" He'd spoken matter-of-factly and with more impatience than hostility in his voice. Therefore the change in him was startling and everyone at the table stood, almost in unison, and began to move toward him.

Carole Ann reached him first and, standing very closely to him, put a hand on his arm. It felt like a rock. He gripped the telephone so tightly that the veins in the back of his hand seemed on the verge of rupturing. The muscles in his jaw clenched and beads of sweat appeared on his forehead. He squeezed his eyes shut and then reopened them. "Yeah. It's all clear," he said in a tight voice. "When . . ." he began, and then held the receiver away from his face, staring at it. Then he replaced it gently and again closed his eyes, this time as if in prayer.

"What was that, Jake?" Carole Ann asked.

"Grace has been abducted and she will be held until we turn over every piece of information and documentation we have on On-Shore Manufacturing and Seaboard Shipping and Containers. We are to turn over *everything*. We are to retain *nothing*." He was like a zombie—totally lifeless and inanimated—and his speech sounded computerized or digitized.

Nobody moved or spoke, everybody waiting for somebody else to be able to think of something to say or do. Carole Ann acted first. She reached around Jake and picked up the phone. She punched a button. "Find Petrocelli now and tell him to call me," and then, still holding the phone to her ear with one hand, she depressed the button with the other. "They'll release Grace in exchange for our On-Shore and Seaboard files. When?"

He shook his head then shrugged his shoulders. "They'll call again in an hour."

Everybody except Jake jumped when the phone rang in that moment, and Carole Ann lifted her finger from the button and spoke. "Paolo? Stop whatever you're doing and go immediately to four thirty-five Oakview Road in Silver Spring. That's in the Georgia Avenue-Colesville Road-Sixteenth Street triangle. That's Jake Graham's home. His wife's been abducted. Get there, now, Paolo. We're on our way."

She hung up the phone. "Come on, Jake. Patty, start collecting that stuff and stay by the phone. You, too, Carla, and put everybody who isn't on a job on standby."

She turned to leave, expecting Jake to follow. Instead he stood rooted to the spot on the floor next to the phone. She looked at him and didn't know what to say. Donald Smith came alive. He rushed out of the conference room, taking Carla with him and leaving Carole Ann and Patty to try and rouse Jake.

"They're not going to hurt Grace, Jake. If they were going to hurt her, they wouldn't have called you. You know that.

"Jake, come on. Let's go. Please?" The pleading in Carole Ann's voice barely concealed the tremor. She was almost shaking with fear and very near tears. She took his arm and pulled him toward the door. They met Donald with Jake's overcoat and Carla with Carole Ann's coat and purse.

"Bob's got the truck at the front door. He'll drive you," Carla said.

Patty took Jake's other arm and she and Carole Ann led him to and out the front door, C.A. aware of them breaking the GGI rule about employees using the front door; aware of a swirl of odd and unrelated thoughts: She didn't know Bob's last name or how long he'd worked at GGI; she hadn't remembered that any of the GGI Ford Explorers was green—she'd thought all of them were black; she'd forgotten that it was forecast to turn sharply colder today, with temperatures falling through the morning hours until nightfall would bring single digits; she had never before seen Jake frightened. Not even when there was a bullet in his back and he was paralyzed and facing the prospect of never walking again.

Patty opened the truck door and put Jake in the front and fastened his seat belt around him as if he were a small child, while Carole Ann climbed into the back and Bob shifted into drive and sped off even as the sound of the slamming doors still reverberated in the frigid air. No one spoke on the drive. Carole Ann stilled her thoughts by concentrating on Bob's expert operation of the onboard computer that plotted their route across the top of D.C., from east to west, avoiding a couple of traffic jams along the way. When they screeched to a halt in front of Jake's house, Paolo was there, standing on the front steps. He ran down the walkway to meet Carole Ann as she leapt from the truck and ran toward him.

"Front door was open," he said, leaning in close to her and speaking into her ear, "so I went in and took a look. Nothing out of place except a turned-over chair in the kitchen. Cup of coffee and a muffin on a plate on the table, along with the *Post* and *The New York Times*. I guess she—Mrs. Graham—was sitting there, having her breakfast and reading the papers. Car's still in the garage. At least I suppose it's hers . . . ninety-something Chrysler LeBaron convertible?"

A sick feeling spread through her as full reality set in. She herself had given the car to Grace, who loved it and who never would have left home without it. "Yes, it's hers," she whispered, only because that's the best her voice would do for her.

Paolo was about to speak until he looked up and over her shoulder and at Jake. "Jesus," he whispered, and Carole Ann turned to look. Jake had slumped and Bob was barely holding him upright. Both Carole Ann and Paolo rushed back to the truck. Jake was a small man. Paolo and Bob were not, and they had no difficulty, one on either arm, propelling Jake up the walk and into the house. Once inside, he seemed to return to himself. He ran through the house, from room to room, never speaking but looking, searching, until finally he, too, opened the laundry room door and looked into the garage.

He stumbled back into the kitchen and sank into a chair. "She's gone. They have her."

"What did they say? What do they want?" Paolo asked.

"They apparently want us to back away from Seaboard and On-Shore. Jake, what exactly did they say?"

"I already told you what they said."

She inhaled deeply. "I know you did, Jake, but Paolo needs to hear it so he can make an assessment."

"Then you tell him, C.A.," Jake said, sounding like a total stranger and looking like one, too. He had sagged and was deflated. He was flat.

Carole Ann inhaled again and struggled to remember Jake's words after the phone call: "When he hung up the phone, Jake said, 'We are to turn over every bit of information and documentation we have on OnShore Manufacturing and Seaboard Shipping and Containers. We are to retain nothing.' He said Grace would be returned if we met those conditions, and that the caller would call again in an hour."

She, Paolo, and Bob simultaneously checked their watches. Only Jake remained motionless. Bob picked up the phone on the kitchen wall and punched in some numbers.

"We're at Jake's, Carla. . . . yeah, she's definitely gone. . . . no, not yet . . . it's been almost an hour. . . . OK, I'll tell her." He hung up the phone and turned to Carole Ann. "Patty's got the file ready," he said.

Paolo knelt before Jake. "What was Mrs. Graham wearing when you left her this morning, Jake?"

He raised his eyes and looked across the table at where Grace would have sat that morning, where her abandoned coffee and muffin still sat. "A navy blue sweater, the kind that buttons up the front, and gray slacks and blue suede shoes," he said, and choked on the words. He cleared his throat and continued, "She volunteers at that big senior citizens center on Georgia Avenue a couple of times a month, and one of the old guys there used to be a blues singer. First time Grace wore those shoes there he started singing to her. 'Don't nobody step on my blue suede shoes.' " Jake laughed softly. "He told her how Elvis Presley stole that song from a Black blues man from the Mississippi Delta, a friend of his. Old guy said he'd never seen any blue suede shoes before. So, Grace wore them whenever she went there. Just for him. That's where she was going this morning."

Paolo touched his shoulder. "Did she take a coat? Or a purse?"

Jake shook his head. "Not the purse anyway. It's in the bedroom, and I don't think a coat's missing. . . ." He shook his head and looked past Paolo at Carole Ann. "If I'd listened to you in the first place this wouldn't be happening. You told me not to fool with the OnShore people and I wouldn't listen—"

"Goddammit, Jake Graham, don't you go there. Don't you fucking go there!" she snarled at him through clenched teeth.

"Why not?" he said almost breezily. "It is my fault. I could have backed off after Patty turned up that bogus social, but I didn't. As usual, I just got mad and dug deeper, bound and determined to make them sorry they ever lied to me. Now I'm the one who's sorry. Sorry son of a bitch I am for getting my wife killed. . . ."

Carole Ann shook him hard and his head danced about, back and forth, as if there were no bones in his neck. She stood before him breathing harder than after a five-mile run. He sat at the table looking up at her without expression in his eyes. Bob wore a look of fearful confusion. Paolo tensed, awaiting an eruption or explosion from one of them—he didn't know which—and wishing he didn't have to witness so intimate an exchange.

Then the phone rang.

"It's them," Jake said quietly. "You answer it, C.A. I don't . . . I can't . . ."

Nausea rose in her as she turned in slow motion toward the phone. Paolo brushed past her and picked it up in the middle of the second ring.

"Hello." He quickly reached into his jacket pocket and retrieved his notebook and pen and began writing. "We need to hear from her first. Mr. Graham needs to talk to her and be sure she's all right."

Jake had come alert and was out of the chair and to the phone in one swift motion when Paolo beckoned. "Grace?" he whispered. "I'll do whatever they say, Grace, I prom—" His face tightened, then sagged, and he returned the phone to Paolo.

"Can someone drive her? That's rough country at night. And it'll be icy—" Paolo held the phone away from his face and cursed it before hanging up. Then he turned to Carole Ann. "They want you to make the exchange. You're to deliver the documents and get Mrs. Graham back."

She shook her head back and forth and backed up away from him. "No," she said, shaking her head. "No. I can't. You do it, Paolo."

"This is their game, C.A., not mine, and they asked for you." He tapped his notebook. "I wrote it down. We do it their way, just as they say, and we get Mrs. Graham back."

"*No!*" She shouted. "I can't!" "I can't go back there" is what she wanted to convey to them, but it already was too late. She already was back—the memory crashed in and washed over her: deep night on a Louisiana bayou. Beaten, bound, gagged, tossed into the bottom of a boat. All senses dulled until the only remaining sensation was that of wanting to die. Of believing that death, indeed, was imminent. And not caring. She remembered as if it were now. Terror caused her legs to tremble.

"Please, C.A.," Jake whispered.

"Suppose I do something wrong, Jake?"

"I've already done whatever there was to do wrong. You can only get Grace back for me. Please, C.A."

⌘ ⌘

She couldn't stop shivering. The heat was blowing full blast in the Explorer and she was layered from head to toe. And yet she was freezing. Once again, as they miraculously had been all winter, the weather forecasters were accurate in their predictions and the temperature now hovered at the twenty-degree mark though it was barely six o'clock. But it had been dark since four-thirty. And in the woods of Calvert County, Maryland, dark meant pitch black. It also meant lonely and isolated and roads which, though salted and sanded, still were dangerously icy and required every point of her attention, and she was grateful for the need to focus on something outside herself. To turn inward would be to encounter the fear, the terror—the memory—that roamed there, a marauding bandit capturing all that dared move.

Carole Ann's gaze constantly shifted between the absolute darkness of the night that stretched ahead of the light projected by the
high beams of the truck, and the glow of the onboard computer
screen that confirmed that she was still going in the right direction.
Paolo had programmed the computer from the directions Grace's
kidnappers had given him over the phone. They were, he said, thorough and clever. They had allowed only enough time for their orders
to be followed, and had left no time to put into place a plan of support and protection for the two women. There was a tracking device
connected to the truck, and virtually invisible video and audio recording devices; it would take hours of thorough searching to locate them
and Paolo didn't believe the kidnappers would invest that kind of
time and energy. But there would be no one close enough to help her
if she needed help. There would be backup "nearby," Paolo had said,
people who could get to her in a matter of several minutes. . . .

She refused to allow herself to ponder the things that could happen in several minutes, focusing instead on the ribbon of road that
was winding its way deeper into Washington County and toward the
Pennsylvania state line. She was due to reach her destination at six-
thirty. Normally a drive of less than two hours, they'd allotted three,
given the fact that weather and road conditions were notoriously
treacherous the closer one got to the Allegheny Mountains of western Maryland. It had been a reasonably easy drive out of D.C., given
the normal nature of rush hour traffic. Interstate 270 to Interstate 70
was bumper to bumper but uneventful—no tractor trailer had over-
turned this day and backed up traffic all the way to Richmond. Leaving I-70, however, to access the state road that would deliver her to
her destination, frightened and unnerved her. She fought for control.

Just ahead, according to her instructions, she should expect to
see a signal. She slowed almost to a crawl and looked instinctively
into her rearview mirror. The darkness was complete and overwhelming. No danger of being rear-ended for stopping in the middle of the
road. Impenetrable darkness faced her as she rolled slowly forward.
She glanced again at the computer screen and when she returned her

gaze to the roadway, there was a shadow beckoning her with a high-beam flashlight. She began shivering again.

She followed the beam of light into a turn-off she'd never have noticed otherwise, then followed the poorly plowed road. She stopped and shifted into four-wheel drive and then continued. The snow was heavy and drifting, but at least it was snow and not ice and the Explorer made steady progress. Carole Ann peered ahead. She didn't know what she was looking for so she didn't know what to expect and therefore was startled and unnerved and, finally, terrified by the appearance of three figures in her headlights.

Dressed in solid-black ski clothes and bathed in the high beams of the truck, the three stood still before her and, as she observed them, she felt herself grow calm. If this were a film instead of her life, she'd consider the scene overdramatic and borderline racist: black-clad evil emerges from the sinister darkness—against a backdrop of peaceful, white snow—to terrify the heroine. "Fuck this shit," she muttered to herself and, throwing the truck into park and jamming the emergency brake down with her foot, she opened the door.

"Remain as you are, please," the center figure called out in an almost cheery voice, raising his hand like a school crossing guard to halt her progress, and moving slowly toward her. The other two raised their hands, as well, though in them were weapons she hadn't previously noticed.

She stopped and waited for the man giving the orders to get close enough that she could hear his instructions over the idling roar of the truck's engine and the wail of the winter wind.

"Where are the documents, Miss Gibson?"

"Backseat, passenger side," she answered, her eyes locked on his, the only part of his entire anatomy that was visible. Brown eyes.

"Stand down out of the vehicle, close the door, and turn away from me," he ordered, and she obeyed. "I'm going to blindfold you," he said, removing his gloves as he approached her. "If you leave your hands at your sides, I won't need to handcuff you as well. Understood?"

"Understood," she replied, and turned her back to him and stood with clenched fists while he covered her eyes. She heard the back door of the truck open and close and nothing more for several seconds. Then there was the sound of a zipper and the rustling of papers. "Where is Mrs. Graham?" she asked. "You have what you asked for—"

"Sshh," he almost whispered, close to her ear, as if she were a small child he wished would go to sleep.

She whirled around, the terror that had controlled her turned to unbridled fury. "Goddamn you!" Then she stumbled, lost her footing in the drifting snow, and went down on one knee, throwing her arms out before her for support. As she was going down, she angled her head in toward her shoulder and tried to shove up whatever was covering her eyes. At the same time, her—what? captor, tormentor?—reached out to her. To help her, to punish her, she didn't know. But in a flash of a glimpse, she saw his hand. And the ring on his finger . . . Then she took herself all the way forward, down and face first into the snow.

A powerful grip pulled her up then pushed her forward and into the side of the truck and held her there. "Don't move again," he said in the almost-whisper voice. "Not a muscle."

She stood there against the truck feeling the cold creep into her despite her protective covering; and this time, the shivering produced chattering teeth. Her feet and toes were numb and tingling, as were her hands and fingers. She wondered how long it took for frostbite to occur when the temperature was below twenty degrees. Snot was running from her nose and, she could tell, freezing on her mouth and chin. She was about to ask for permission to wipe her face—the bile rising to her throat at the necessity—when she heard the door to the truck open and then slam shut.

"Get in, Miss Gibson, and sit for exactly five minutes before departing." He no longer was near her—in fact, he was himself departing as he said the word.

She heard nothing more so she fumbled around, trying to locate the door handle. The combination of the blindfold, gloves, and frozen fingers impeded her progress. Using her left hand, she removed the glove from her right hand and with that hand, the covering over her eyes. She quickly opened the truck door and climbed in. A blindfolded Grace was sitting in the passenger seat.

"Grace."

"C.A.?"

Carole Ann reached over and removed Grace's blindfold and hugged her briefly.

"Are you hurt, Grace? Did they hurt you?"

She was shaking her head. "No. They didn't bother me. Where's Jake, C.A.? Is he all right?" All the panic she must have held in all day released itself on those words and she wept. It was a helpless, pitiful sound that Carole Ann wished she had not had to hear. She slid across the seat and gathered the older woman in her arms and held her and searched for words of comfort and consolation. As that comfort and consolation had been provided for her when she needed it . . . She pushed away those memories. With everything in her being she had resisted them; she would not permit their intrusion now, when the task almost was completed.

"Can you hang on for just a few moments longer, Grace, until we get out of here?"

She released Carole Ann and nodded and, leaning forward, opened the glove box and pulled out a handful of tissues, half of which she offered to C.A. They both blew their noses and wiped their eyes. Then Carole Ann looked around, not that she could see much beyond the headlights in front of her, and nothing to the rear. She released the emergency brake, put the truck in reverse, and began to back out the way she'd come in, only then remembering the admonition to wait five minutes.

"Fuck you," she muttered to herself. Then, "I can't see a thing," and she tried to recall how long it had taken her to get up the drive from the main roadway. She did know, though, that it had been a straight shot, so she continued to back up slowly and in a straight line, shifting her eyes from the rearview mirror to the front and back again and keeping the steering wheel steady. She didn't know that she reached the main road until she felt the shift in the terrain, felt the smoothness of the blacktop highway. She stopped, shifted out of four-wheel drive, and gunned the engine. She had to keep reminding herself to slow down, that there were icy patches on the road.

Her heart was racing and instead of shivering, she now was hot and sweating. She gripped the steering wheel so tightly her hands hurt; so did her shoulders from being hunched up around her ears. Ahead she saw the familiar red, white, and blue shield that signaled the approach of I-70. She heard Grace whisper, "Thank God," and she increased the pressure on the gas pedal. The truck shimmied just a bit on the entrance ramp to the highway and she rotated the steering wheel to compensate and, to regain complete control, she entered the freeway slowly even though there was little traffic. Then, suddenly, behind her, there was the unmistakable flash of red and blue lights.

First there were too many thoughts in her head. Then there were none. Fear overcame her as one police vehicle sped up to get in front of her, while another pulled up close on her rear. She stopped and waited. Not thinking, not feeling. Terror again was in control and her senses had shut down. So it did not immediately register that there were faces at the windows and that those faces belonged to four Maryland state troopers and to Jake Graham and Paolo Petrocelli. Until Grace screamed out her husband's name.

⌾⌾ ⌾⌾

One good thing about the Hagerstown Barracks of the Maryland State Police, Carole Ann thought, was that it was warm. Another good thing was that it was near an all-night Dunkin Donuts and one of the troopers had fetched a dozen fresh, warm ones. The barracks coffee, however, was disgusting. She drank it anyway. It was, in its way, preferable to the prodding by the police and the investigator from the state attorney general's office, all of whom were more than a little angry to realize that a former D.C. homicide detective, a former agent of the FBI, and a member in good standing with all the local bar associations, had failed to notify authorities of a kidnapping, and who, for a while, threatened to bring several levels of charges. Until enough of the lawyer was roused within Carole Ann that she put a stop to those threats. It was not illegal to not report a kidnapping, and none of them had broken any laws in procuring the safe release of Grace Graham.

Carole Ann's willing return to the lonely stretch of road to search for the exchange point before more snow could fall and eradicate tracks did a lot to ameliorate the hostility that was fueling the police, and finding the spot produced a moment of true euphoria. The investigators would have, she thought, jumped for joy, had they been standing instead of sitting in the cramped trooper vehicle. But they pumped their fists in the air and one of them gave her a hearty "atta girl." She appreciated what they were feeling but didn't share it and was relieved when a trooper in a backup car sped her back to the barracks and warmth.

The young trooper quickly spread the good news and his barracks mates re-created the euphoric feeling. It was quickly destroyed by the news that the OnShore Manufacturing buildings were, at that moment, burning to the ground. The Jake Graham who still was a cop emerged from his shell long enough to rattle off a series of questions, which were transmitted from their location at the Hagerstown Barracks to state troopers from the Waldorf Barracks a hundred miles away, on the scene of the blaze: no, there were no vehicles on the premises—no trailers, no cabs, no cars—which led Jake to speculate that the fleet of trucks he'd seen there were rentals. No, there was no danger from the gas pumps—they were dry and had been for years; and no, the fire wasn't burning so hot because of stacks of cardboard boxes and paper products, but because of the accelerant that was used to set it.

With every response, Jake caved in on himself a little more, until he resembled a flat tire. No vestiges of the cop remained. All the joy he'd exhibited at Grace's return had dissipated. He sat hunched over, elbows on his knees, hands folded between them, shaking his head back and forth, oblivious to all sight and sound. "They got me good," he said once, to nobody in particular. He displayed emotion only once, when the AG investigator questioned his assertion that GGI no longer had any files pertaining or relating to OnShore Manufacturing or Seaboard Shipping and Containers. "I told you we gave 'em everything. We kept nothing, just like they said. And see," he pointed toward Grace. "I got my wife back. Just like they said."

"You wouldn't mind, then, would you, if we checked your computers? Just to be sure?"

The real Jake Graham surfaced for a brief though impressive moment. "Goddamn right I mind. You're calling me a liar, you slimy son of a bitch, and I don't like it when scumbags call me names. You think I'd play games with my wife's life! They said delete the file, we deleted the file. They said don't try to find them, we're not gonna try to find them. They can burn down the whole damn Eastern Shore if they want to. I got my wife back and that's all I care about, you got that?"

Then he sagged again, out of breath and energy and fire and anger. Grace sat close to him, her arm around his shoulders, and she was as energized and animated as he was apathetic, despite her obvious physical exhaustion. She wanted to cooperate with the police. She wanted to tell them everything she saw and heard and remembered, and the more she talked, the angrier she became. The only problem was that she hadn't seen or heard very much. She never saw the faces of her abductors, and all she heard were their demands: over and over they told her that if Jake relinquished the complete OnShore and Seaboard files, she'd be released unharmed. They emphasized *complete*, Grace said, and implied that they would know if any information was retained. They also made very clear—no implication here—that if GGI made any attempt to trace or locate them, they would know about it. "They said to tell you not to doubt them or underestimate them. They said that would be a fatal mistake. Those were their exact words: 'fatal mistake.' "

Carole Ann told them almost everything she saw and knew: three black-clad, ski-masked figures standing at the end of a driveway in a discreet clearing in the woods, two of them pointing automatic weapons at her. She made the decision to withhold the one thing she did see and the one impression she formed until she felt more rational. And since no one asked him, Petrocelli didn't mention the secreted recording devices in the Explorer.

༄ ༄

It was near dawn when she got home, and she had no words to describe how she felt. More than fatigued or exhausted; more than angry and frustrated; she had been more than frightened and terrified. The only sensation that she could adequately and accurately define was the nature of the interaction with the law enforcement officials. She'd been a criminal defense attorney for a good number of years and had cautioned enough defendants to know how to traverse that terrain. As an experience, it already was dimming in her memory, barely a blip on the screen of the horrible days and nights she'd known.

She undressed and uncharacteristically left the pile of clothing in the middle of the bedroom floor. She stood for a long while in the shower, wondering whether she was merely numbed by the events of the day, or whether all her senses had short-circuited from overload and that's why she had no feeling. She had promised never to place herself in danger again after having been shot and nearly dying in Los Angeles, after having been abducted and beaten nearly to death the year before that in New Orleans. Her promise made after her own mother had accused her of deliberately trying to get herself killed in some kind of bizarre atonement for Al's death.

Carole Ann, perhaps, at one time, had wanted to die, but no longer; she could live without Al, after all, she had discovered. Not only could, wanted to. Yet she could have been killed tonight and there was nothing she could have done to prevent it. She'd had no choice. She could not have refused to rescue Grace Graham. She thought of what Al would say, of what her therapist would say. Of course she had a choice, they would declare. Why wasn't she as certain?

Wrapped in a warm wool and cashmere robe, she lay across the bed. No point in getting under the covers. She didn't think it possible to sleep—too many thoughts were speeding out of control in her head. She tried to slow them, to focus them. Pick one thought: the ring she'd seen on the hand of the man she believed to be the leader of the group. And his voice. Something about it was important but she couldn't remember what it was. She yawned.

The sun was fully up and so bright she knew it was frigid out—it always was coldest when it was brightest. She shivered, recalling how cold she'd been last night, especially standing outside the truck. She considered the nature of terror: freezing and shaking one moment, dripping sweat the next. How different the body's response to the same stimulus. She was still shivering but her body was back in Louisiana, battered and bruised in the bottom of a boat. She pulled back the covers and crawled underneath, seeking warmth. It had been warm—hot and muggy—on the bayou, yet she had shivered. And she had slept . . . perhaps she would sleep now, for a few hours, and then go to work.

5

SINCE COLLEGE, CAROLE ANN HAD SOUGHT REFUGE
in her work. No matter what was happening in her life, she could
avoid or evade or escape or dismiss it simply by turning to work.
When she was younger, she'd had to work at shifting the gears. By
the time she became an accomplished legal practitioner, it was
habit. She had work to do this morning. Yesterday didn't exist. So
engrossed was she in reviewing the surveillance reports from the
electronics warehouse that she jumped slightly, startled by the gentle tapping at her office door. She looked up, still writing on the yellow legal pad with one hand, flipping a page of the report with the
other.

"Give me two minutes, Paolo," she said, waving him in and toward the sofa. "I'm almost done here," she added, speaking more to
the papers on the desk than to him. In slightly less than the two minutes she'd asked for, she dropped her pen and looked up at him.
"Sorry about that. So. What's up?"

"Should you be here?"

"Where else would I be?"

"Can we talk about yesterday?" he asked, altering his tone.

She frowned slightly, as if, perhaps, there really had been no yesterday. "What about it?"

He inhaled deeply. "If there's anything that you know that you didn't tell the cops, anything you heard or saw or felt or thought that's surfaced since last night, I'd like to know it, C.A. You know, it often happens that when a stressful situation ends, the mind releases little bits and pieces of things."

She folded her hands, interlocking her fingers, and studied him, thinking that he was very good at his job. He'd actually made his comment sound like a question that required an answer. A tactic from hostage-release training.

"I've got work to do, Paolo—"

"You can't pretend that yesterday didn't happen, C.A."

She rose swiftly to her feet, the motion so sudden and sharp that it was cutting. "—and so do you. I suggest you get to it." She walked around the desk and stood before it and watched him tense but remain seated. And she realized that some kind of change had occurred within him; something to do with her and yesterday. His next words proved her correct.

"I've seen a few situations like this, and few people have managed as well as you did. I admire your courage and your strength. But the aftermath of this kind of thing—"

She cut him off by moving toward him, which quickly forced him to his feet; she knew he couldn't remain seated on the low-slung couch with her towering over him. "I don't need a protector, Paolo, or an advisor, or anybody telling me what or how I feel. Is that clear?" The words were volatile but there was no emotion in her voice. Her tone was cold and flat and had the intended effect on him.

He dipped his head and squared his shoulders and stuffed his hands into his pockets. "We've still got to find out who did this."

"No, we don't," she replied. And not allowing him time to reply, she shifted gears. "What are you doing on Annabelle?"

He blew out a long, slow breath, and inhaled deeply to replace it. "I'm flying up to Boston tomorrow. I've got an interview at her alma mater."

"Good," she said, turning away from him and toward her desk. "Make sure you get a letter from Islington authorizing the release of her transcripts and giving permission for the school to talk to us. And see me as soon as you get back." She was back at her desk, seated and working before he was out of the door. But there was a sound and she looked up to see Paolo backing into the room to allow Jake to enter, then exiting the office.

Jake was as visibly upset and rattled as his partner was tightly contained. Though he was cleanly and neatly dressed—he, too, had gone home for several hours before coming in to work—his aura was rumpled. His eyes were puffy and red, as if he'd wept for a long time. He walked slowly and hunched over like a shuffling old man, hands shoved into his pockets.

"Hey, Paolo," he said, barely raising his head. Then he stopped suddenly and both men had to turn back toward each other in order to speak. "I just want you to know how much I appreciate what you did yesterday."

"I'm glad it turned out the way it did, Jake," Paolo said, towering over his boss as they stood framed in the doorway.

"Yeah," the ex-cop replied, sounding not at all like a cop and every bit like a man who'd allowed himself to believe that he was about to be a widower.

"Jake," Paolo began, and got no farther.

"It's over, Paolo. Finished. There ain't nothing more to be said or done. Let it go. Let it be." And he turned away and Paolo disappeared and Jake closed the office door and shuffled toward Carole Ann.

She met him midpoint between the office door and the desk and they shared a brief but fierce embrace. They released each other and crossed the office and dropped wearily down, Jake on the sofa where Paolo had sat, Carole Ann into the rocking chair across the table from him. "You look like shit, by the way," she said to him.

Something that two days ago would have been his trademark

grin barely lifted a corner of his mouth. "I can always count on you, C.A., to raise my spirits and comfort my ego."

"That's what friends are for, and don't you forget it." The smile she tried was only marginally more successful. "How's Grace this morning?"

The grin worked this time. "Stubborn as ever and still mad as hell. Refused to let me stay home with her, claiming I'd be more on her nerves than the damn kidnappers. Said I kept her awake with my tossing and turning and getting up every five minutes to check the doors and windows." Then the humor faded and he wiped his eyes with the back of his hand. "I don't think I can live there anymore, C.A. Somebody broke into my home and stole my wife. How can I live there and be happy again? Especially since I don't know who did it or even why?"

Helpless anger rolled off him in waves and he clenched and un-clenched his fists and pounded the tops of legs, just as he'd done when he was paralyzed and the legs didn't function. She studied him quietly, watching his mind work. She knew how he thought, and she could almost hear his internal dialogue.

"So, should we find out who and why?" she asked.

"I don't know, C.A. For the first time in my life I'm more scared than mad. And I'm plenty mad."

She'd said all she wanted or needed to say. She'd given him the window; it was up to him to open it and climb through. She, too, was more frightened than angry, and was content to let the fear rule. But of course, no one had invaded her sanctuary and stolen what she val-ued most.

"Let me think about it for a while. In the meantime, I need a favor."

She looked at him with raised eyebrows and waited.

"Oh, relax. You'll be doing yourself a favor at the same time," he said, and explained that he wanted her to replace him in two days' time at the signing of a major security contract in Los Angeles, busi-ness that Tommy Griffin and Anthony Killian, the principals in the

GGI West Coast office, had initiated. Jake had done the survey four months earlier, and submitted the GGI bid, and they'd received word two weeks ago of their selection. The project involved the total renovation of a number of warehouses on the pier at Long Beach, with state-of-the-art security and surveillance equipment installed during construction, and constant GGI monitoring once the construction was completed and the trucking operation was under way. It was a lucrative, long-term contract.

"Sure, I'll go, Jake. After all, it hasn't been two whole months since I've seen my mother," she said dryly, and with a hint of pain. Her mother still was angry with her for the events that led to her being shot the previous year, and she still was angry with her mother for not understanding that she'd had to rescue Tommy back then, just as she'd had to rescue Jake's wife yesterday.

"It didn't really register until this morning, C.A., what it must have taken for you to go after Grace," he said, apropos of nothing except the ability to wander around her thoughts.

She held up a hand to stop him. "It's over now, Jake. Let's let it be, all right? If I'm going to L.A. in two days, I've got a load of paperwork to complete, two cases to shove off on you, and a lot to learn about the installation, maintenance, and monitoring of security and surveillance systems in warehouses."

He stood up and shoved his hands deeply into his pockets. "The up side is that you get out of D.C. during the shittiest time of year. Who was it that said February and March are the cruelest months?"

She giggled. "It was only one month, Jake, and I think it was April. And the weather in L.A. in February and March can be pretty ugly. Gray and rainy and chilly . . ."

"It doesn't rain in L.A.!" he snorted, sounding almost like himself. "It's always warm and sunny."

After he left, she succumbed to the exhaustion she'd been fighting. She closed the office door and lay down on the love seat, her long legs dangling over the side. As she lay there, she realized that what she'd thought was fatigue really was the return of feeling—all of it. The fear and the anger and the resentment and the resignation all came flooding back at once. She lay there, eyes closed, and allowed it to happen. Then she allowed herself to remember the real reasons why she hadn't wanted to remember.

Anger and grief had driven her to New Orleans to avenge her husband's murder, and she paid a terrible price for unveiling a murderer: she was abducted and brutally beaten. Jake Graham, at the time paralyzed and confined to a wheelchair, sent Tommy Griffin, then a D.C. cop, to find and save her. And a year later, because she'd gotten him into danger, Carole Ann believed herself obligated to save and rescue Tommy from a gang of smugglers of human cargo operating out of a desert compound on the California-Mexico border. She got shot that time, and almost died.

She sat up, rubbing the place between her left breast and shoulder blade that was a bullet wound. Despondent as she was over Al's death, she hadn't wanted the physical or emotional pain from either of those encounters. She had done only what she'd believed to be right and necessary at the time. But she never wanted to experience that degree of fear again. Yet she had. And so now what? Another pledge to never again knowingly or willingly place herself in danger? Until yesterday, she'd thought it possible to make and keep such a pledge.

She lay back down, still massaging the soreness that held on and wondering if she'd notice when it went away or if, one day, it just wouldn't be there and all she'd have left would be the scar and the memory. And her life. She had her life. Twice she'd almost died and twice she'd lived. Close calls. But close only counts in horseshoes. Somebody used to say that all the time . . . she didn't recall who and it didn't matter. Almost dead was not the same thing as alive and she was alive. And being alive meant living. And living sometimes would result in painful or even dangerous situations. And sometimes, like yesterday, it could result in doing good for another person who would appreciate the deed. Most of the time, she thought, days and deeds done in them would be basic and ordinary. And safe. Like life.

Tommy scooped her up and wrapped her in a bear hug when finally she emerged from the plane, one of the last passengers. "Welcome home! And the first order of business is to brown you up a bit. You got that East Coast, winter-time pale look about yourself."

"And you look positively Hollywood," she beamed at him, ignoring the paleness crack. "It would appear that we've switched hometowns." Indeed, in his cream-colored silk shirt, tan slacks, and dark brown slip-ons, he bore no resemblance to the former D.C. beat cop that he once was.

"Just call me Angeleno," he said with a wide grin and another big hug. "So what's up with Jake that he couldn't come? Not that I don't appreciate your company," he amended quickly.

"Yeah, yeah, yeah," she teased back, feigning hurt feelings.

He placed one gigantic palm across his chest and gave her a wounded, hangdog look. "You know, Carole Ann Gibson, that after my wife, my mother, and my grandmother, I love you more than any woman alive."

She giggled and playfully punched him on one of his massive, muscular shoulders, and knew that through the silliness he was being completely honest. They shared a very special bond. "I'll tell you all about it over lunch. I'm three hours past hungry. My body thinks it's three o'clock in the afternoon."

A Los Angeles native, Carole Ann routinely experienced intense longings for the things and places and people that had tempered and textured her growing up, and ever since Jake had asked her to make this trip in his stead, she'd been imagining a burger, fries and a chocolate milkshake from Fatburger—the original one—and Tommy's wide grin when she announced her lunch preference bespoke his approval. By the time they were seated and eating, and Carole Ann was explaining why she was in L.A. instead of Jake, Tommy's face had creased into a deep frown and his fingers kept up a steady drumbeat on the table.

He made her tell him everything a second time and then he asked enough nitpicking questions to make her truly annoyed with him. "You're sounding and acting like a cop, Tommy," she hissed at him, usually enough to make him stop. Not this time. He idolized Jake Graham. Jake was the kind of cop Tommy always wanted to be, would have been, had he not been dismissed from the D.C. police department. Dismissed because, at Jake Graham's request, he had traveled to New Orleans to rescue Carole Ann from a murderer.

"Damn, C.A.," he said over and over. "That's some really scary shit."

"Yeah, Tommy, it is," she agreed.

"And you all are just gonna drop it? Just like that?"

"What else can we do, Tommy? We don't know who those people are or where to look for them, even if we wanted to look for them, which we don't."

Tommy slapped the table with his palm, making a loud, cracking noise, attracting the subversive attention of nearby diners. Then he rubbed his hands together. Then he began cracking his knuckles.

"Stop that!"

He ducked his head, blushing, and grinned, and she was reminded how young he was—not yet thirty—and how vulnerable. He totally and completely trusted her and Jake, would do whatever they asked without question. "I would just feel . . . I can't tell you how I would feel if something happened to Jake or Miss Grace and I'm all the way over here . . ."

"Tommy." She reached across the table and took his hand. "No one could have prevented what happened. You think Jake and I haven't beat ourselves up for not realizing that there was something shaky about that outfit? We were just so pleased to have business walk in the door that we didn't notice the muddy footprints on the welcome mat." She hadn't told him, and didn't think it necessary to tell him, about the disagreement that she and Jake had about the OnShore contract.

He sat back, a quizzical look on his face, his hand still nestled in hers. Then he leaned forward again and placed his other hand on top of hers. "Is this going to hurt business? I mean, will people find out about it and think we somehow did something wrong? You know how easy it is these days to blame the victim."

She smiled at him, then half stood and leaned across the table and kissed him. "You are good to the core, Tommy Griffin. Do you know that nobody has verbalized that fear? We've all been walking around with it, praying that whatever this mess is, it won't double back around and bite us on the butt. But not one of us has had the courage to voice it. And the answer is, I don't know. Because nobody really knows what it's all about."

He frowned, his thoughts playing out on his face. "But isn't that too risky? Not to know? If we don't ever know what this is all about, what's to say it can't or won't happen again?"

Her warm fuzzies for Tommy were beginning to fade. He was raising every issue she'd ducked for days; issues she knew that Jake was ducking as well, the both of them hiding behind their fear. Fear as a shield . . . She shook her head to shake off the discomfort of that thought. "You're right, Tommy, and I don't have an answer. We haven't discussed it. We need to and we will as soon as I'm back in Washington, that's a promise."

"Unless there's something even uglier about those OnShore and Seabord folks you haven't found out about yet . . ."

She raised her hand to stop him. "Let it go for now, Tommy. No point in pursuing this line of questioning. I told you there are no answers. Not yet."

Tommy stood up. "So what do you want to do?"

She, too, stood. "I want to see our warehouses, then I want to go sit in the sun and forget how cold it is in D.C., and then I want to go see Valerie and the little Griffin-to-be."

"Well, what are you standing there for?" he growled in perfect Jake Graham imitation. "Let's roll."

The drive out to Long Beach was relaxed because they simply ignored the traffic and talked the entire way, Tommy answering all of

Carole Ann's questions about Valerie—Tommy's wife and soon-to-be mother of their child—and Anthony, the other GGI Los Angeles operative, and Anthony's mother, whom she had known in another lifetime. Yes, Tommy said, he kept tabs on Grayce Gibson, Carole Ann's own mother, and on Roberta and Angie, her mother's best friends and neighbors. Addie Allen, a local lawyer, kept the GGI operatives busy with investigative work of her own, and with referrals from other law firms in town.

He told her several Addie Allen stories that made her laugh until tears ran down her face. Addie was five feet tall in her stocking feet and weighed barely one hundred pounds and Warren Forchette called her the West Coast version of Carole Ann herself, "only meaner." She was the best lawyer Carole Ann knew; after all, she'd successfully defended Carole Ann against a murder charge and had fought for over a year to restore her status with the California bar. Yes, Carole Ann thought, wiping her eyes and agreeing with Tommy, "Addie Allen, Esquire, definitely is a piece of work."

༄ ༄

They arrived at the Long Beach pier in the midst of a flurry of activity. Cranes and backhoes and Caterpillars crisscrossed the beat-up pavement of the pier with such frequency that the area almost needed traffic signals. Buildings were being torn down and buildings were under construction and already renovated structures brimmed with activity. Carole Ann shaded her eyes with her hand and peered south, the sun bouncing off the pale blue of the Pacific making it difficult to see. Like the true Angeleno he had become, Tommy wore sunglasses. Like the true Easterner she had become, her sunglasses had been put away with the first frost. "What's that down there, Tommy? Is that really a ship's mast?"

"You better believe it," he said with feeling. "That's what they're calling the 'upscale' end of the pier. There's a restaurant going in there to rival anything in Bel Air or Beverly Hills. And that schooner is part of the dining pleasure. Weather permitting, those with the most money can dine al fresco, attended by stewards from Queen Elizabeth's yacht."

"You're kidding!"

He raised his right hand. "Swear to God! I'm telling you, this area is so hot even the real estate developers can't keep up with what's going on." He made a three-hundred-and-sixty-degree turn and pointed north. "You see that crane? The tallest one? That's the site of a loft renovation—"

"Loft renovation?" she interrupted with a skeptical frown. "In Long Beach, California?"

"And it was sold out before the ink was dry on the offering. Do you know how many Hollywood actors are transplanted New Yorkers? And most of them homesick? That woman, what's her name, the one they keep calling a young Katharine Hepburn?"

Carole Ann nodded. "I know who you mean. What about her?"

"She bought *three* of 'em. Two to live in and one to use as guest housing when her New York friends and family come visit," he relayed with a wide grin.

"Amazing," she said with a grin of her own. "Absolutely amazing."

"And," he said with a flourish, dragging the word out into several syllables, "I've been courting the developer harder than I courted my wife and I think we've got the inside track on their security." The pride spread all over his face.

"Way to go, Fish!" she said, clapping him on the back and calling him the not exactly complimentary nickname he'd left behind in D.C. when he moved permanently to L.A. "How does the title Vice President of Sales sound to you?"

He groaned through his grin. "You really know how to spoil a guy's fun. Quickest way to ruin somebody is to give them a title, C.A. You know that!"

She gave him a gentle pat on the arm and wondered aloud whether GGI could manage a job the size of the loft conversion at the same time as the warehouse installation. He shrugged off her concern with an airy wave of his hand. "Let's go see our client," she said to him.

"And after that, let's go see our client-to-be," he said smugly.

⋘ ⋙

David Tyrone gave her an expansive if dusty welcome to his office in the rear of the warehouse, and told her he'd already signed the contracts and written the check; indeed, they were stacked in the center of his desk in the distinctive though dust-covered GGI aubergine folder, check-containing window envelope on top. Tyrone, too, was covered in dust and Carole Ann wondered how it had had a chance to settle on him. The man was motion itself, electrically charged and wired and pulsating with energy.

"We're happy to be doing business with GGI, Miss Gibson, and more so now that I've met you. I rely a lot on my feelings about people, and both you and Mr. Graham, not to mention my buddy Tommy here, give me a real good feeling."

She accepted his compliment then turned serious so quickly that it startled him and he dropped down on the edge of the metal desk.

"Well, yeah," he said hesitantly, answering the question she'd abruptly put to him. "We outbid a few boys for this spot, and it was pretty intense there for a while. Why?"

She chose her words carefully. "I wonder if your bidding success resulted in any long-lasting hard feelings among your competitors, Mr. Tyrone? And whether those hard feelings could manifest themselves unpleasantly?"

His eyes narrowed and he squinted at her. "You're talking about sabotage, Miss Gibson. You're asking me if anybody was a sore enough loser to sabotage my project." He made them statements and not questions, so she didn't attempt to answer the questions he hadn't asked. She sat and waited and watched him turn over the possibility in his mind. And she watched him slow down physically—as if the power to his body had been shut off.

"I know all the developers who bid against us except one and those I know would never stoop so low. And what I can tell you about the one guy I don't know is that he was a mighty sore loser. Downright nasty, as a matter of fact. And now that you mention it, yeah, I could stretch my mind wide enough to picture him sabotaging my site." He reached behind him and grabbed up the GGI folder. "I guess you'd better amend this contract to provide us with some on-site security and surveillance starting yesterday, Miss Gibson." And he extended the folder to her.

Taking it, she asked, "Do you remember, Mr. Tyrone, the name of the sore loser's company? And would there be a way to take a look at their bid?"

"Outfit called OffShore Manufacturing," he said with a crooked grin, missing Carole Ann's hastily covered-up reaction. "We had ourselves a good chuckle about the name. They're based in Ohio or some place like that. Waaayyyy off shore," he said with a laugh. "And yeah, I'm sure I can lay hands on that bid. Can't do it 'til tomorrow, though," he said.

She stood up. "Tomorrow's fine, Mr. Tyrone. By that time, I'll have your amended contracts ready to sign."

They shook hands and he thanked her for thinking of something he said he wouldn't have considered. "This is a risky business," he said, pumping her hand. "Everybody who does it knows that and nobody bothers getting mad at the other guy. Hell, I'd have been disappointed to lose this bid. But mad?" He shook his head. "No way. I'd have been too busy looking for my next opportunity."

She left him, she and Tommy as covered in dust as he was, and thinking of one of the first lessons she'd learned from Jake Graham: "Don't get mad, lady, get even," he'd growled at her as he was sending her on her way to find her husband's killer.

"What the hell was that all about?" Tommy demanded as soon as they were outside. "How did you get from not having any answers to my questions to knowing that there was a connection? And what's with this 'OnShore-OffShore' business?" He was waving his arms back and forth and breathing hard and looking mean and mad. Several hard-hatted men slowed to observe them, to be certain, Carole Ann knew, that she was in no danger.

She took Tommy's arm and steered him toward the truck. "Will you calm down? It was a hunch, Tommy, that's all. You made me think. There had to be a reason GGI was singled out, something we don't understand. But for some reason, OnShore or Seaboard or both wanted us involved."

"And they're the same? OnShore and OffShore?"

She squeezed her eyes shut and shook her head. "I don't know," she replied, remembering that Richard Islington was an Ohio native but that he had nothing to do with this case. "I just asked a couple of questions, Tommy, and instead of answers I got more questions. So there still are no answers."

"But what made you ask the questions in the first place? You had to be thinking something, you had to know something—"

"I was," she said wearily but hastily, needing to halt his intense, attacking barrage. "I was remembering something you said, actually, about OnShore and Seaboard being uglier than we knew. What could be uglier than what they've already done? Except, perhaps, to use GGI to hurt somebody else. Now don't ask me anything else, Tommy, because I don't have any answers."

Tommy was silent and reflective on the brief drive down the pier to the lofts-to-be, an unimpressive site in its present state: four three-level concrete squares single file along the pier's edge, and not even the vastness of the Pacific spread out before them could mitigate their unattractiveness.

"Wait 'til you see the architect's drawings," Tommy said, reading her thoughts. "They're gonna be Moorish on the outside, and the Village on the inside."

She raised an eyebrow at him and looked again at the four ugly squares. "Don't believe everything you hear, Fish."

He laughed and accused her of having lost all traces of her California dreamin' nature. She acknowledged that he might have a point, and followed him into a double-wide construction trailer.

Three men were inside: two of them, seated side by side on a well-used couch, looked stereotypically like construction workers, from hard-hatted heads to steel-toed shoe tips. They halted their conversation, looked up at the new arrivals, nodded identical greetings, and returned to their conversation. The third man was seated behind a metal desk—obviously the best kind for a construction site, Carole Ann thought—holding a phone to his ear. Carole Ann's first impression was that he appeared too young to be managing a multimillion-dollar construction job: he was about Tommy's age, not yet thirty. Her second impression was that he looked more like a graduate student than a builder. He also looked annoyed, though he was working hard to keep his face expressionless. "I'll give him the message but I don't think it'll change his mind," he said, barely concealing the annoyance. He listened for another moment before ending the one-way conversation. "Look, I've got people here and work to do. If Dad wants to talk to you, he'll call you." And with exaggerated gentleness, he returned the phone to the cradle and looked up at Tommy and Carole Ann. His expression changed from pained to welcoming.

"Sorry to barge in like this, Mr. Wainwright."

"No problem," the man said, standing and extending his hand to Carole Ann. "Pleased to meet you, Miss Gibson, and I look forward to meeting Mr. Graham, since your glue stick here isn't gonna leave me alone until I hire you folks."

Carole Ann laughed out loud. "Glue stick," she repeated looking at Tommy. "I'm afraid he's stuck with that one, Mr. Wainwright."

Tommy blushed as Wainwright and the two other men joined in the laughter. They were introduced to her as the architect and the construction superintendent and, after a hurried and low-volume conversation with Wainwright, they left and he waved them onto the now vacant sofa.

"Are you a New Yorker, Mr. Wainwright, or merely a brilliant visionary?" Carole Ann asked.

He laughed. "My wife is a New Yorker *and* a brilliant visionary. This was her idea," he said, pointing in the direction of the empty blocks out on the pier. "She sold my dad first, and I ultimately—and wisely—saw the light. These days my new mantra is 'Yes, dear, whatever you say, dear.' "

"Well, GGI would be delighted to work with you, Mr. Wainwright, should you decide you want to work with us."

"I'm sold, Miss Gibson. I talked to Tyrone the other day and even sneaked a peek at your contract—" He held up his hand at the look on her face. "Not to worry! I'm not focused on the numbers, just on the service, and we want everything he's got *plus* on-site security during construction. I don't trust that damn Islington as far as I can throw him, though that MacDonald is a much more decent fellow."

Carole Ann felt like the butt of a joke everybody knew but her, as if she had a "kick me" bull's-eye pinned to her back. First David Tyrone tosses out "OffShore" with unknowing casualness and now here was Wainwright dropping Islington's name into the mix, in the same breath with MacDonald's. Now they *were* all connected: Seaboard and OnShore and Islington. She was busy navigating the quickly converging paths of her thoughts and feelings and premonitions. There were too many coincidences to ignore. She slowed her mind enough to return it to a single path. "What does Richard Islington have to do with this project?"

"Not a damn thing!" Wainwright exploded in exasperation. "He didn't even bid it. He was a Johnny-come-lately, by way of this MacDonald character, who, it seems, he partners with on a project-by-project basis. MacDonald tried to butt in and when he got the brush-off, he called in Islington, like that should make a difference!" Wainwright seemed genuinely injured by the thought.

Carole Ann frowned. She'd learned from Patty Baker's thorough research that Richard Islington was a tough competitor, and a ruthless one, given to bullying to get his way. She also recalled Patty saying that Islington bought land, not buildings; nor did he himself own a construction company. His business was acquisition and development of land. She raised this point with Wainwright, allowing her confusion to show through.

"That's what this MacDonald does," he said, nodding his head up and down. "You're right about Islington but this is new territory for him and I don't mind telling you, I wish he'd stick to land acquisition. He'll be a hell of a competitor if he turns developer." And he shook his head at the thought.

"What do you remember about MacDonald?" Carole Ann asked. "Do you recall his first name? What he looked like?"

"Sure. John, and he was tall and thin and a few years older than me, maybe even forty. And kind of a nice guy. But next to Islington, Attila the Hun could seem like a nice guy."

On the drive from Long Beach to GGI headquarters in south-central L.A., C.A. filled Tommy in on the Islington case and what she knew about the man himself. He listened, asking the periodic question but not poking and prodding as he had earlier. His introspection served to increase her own worry, and by the time they'd inched their way up the 405 and abandoned it for the thick, late-afternoon traffic of Crenshaw Boulevard, she was anxious and edgy.

The L.A. GGI office also was housed in a warehouse, a smaller one, but the security was just as tight, though here as much out of necessity as good business practice. South-central's reputation as one of the toughest neighborhoods in the U.S. was well deserved. GGI chose the location at Anthony's insistence: it was cheaper to buy the warehouse here than in other locations in the city, and the GGI presence would be an aid to other businesses in the area. Since practically all of GGI's investigators were former LAPD and L.A. Sheriff's Department officers, their presence definitely constituted a deterrent to would-be criminals, and local business owners were grateful.

As with GGI-D.C., employees first entered a card-controlled, gated parking lot; and from there, a card-controlled steel door led into the building. Before she was fully in the lobby, C.A. was met by an operative with a message: she was to call Jake Graham immediately.

"Like that's not what I was about to do," she muttered under her breath, and rushed down the hallway, trailed by a grim-looking Tommy.

She picked up the phone and punched a button—both her direct number and Jake's were programmed into Tommy's phone. It was only after the third ring—Jake always answered on the first—that she looked at her watch. It was after eight in D.C. "It's me and we've got problems," she said when finally he answered. Then she listened rather than talked, her expression growing grimmer. Tommy began rubbing his hands together and cracking his knuckles. Carole Ann said he fidgeted when he was nervous or upset, and he was proving the point. She glared at him and he stilled. For a moment.

"What, C.A.?" He jumped up as soon as she cradled the phone. "What?" he said again.

"Marshall's on his way here," she replied quietly. Marshall was their security expert, the one who actually performed the most complex surveys and recommended the most efficient kind of security system for a client's needs and plotted the location of cameras and sensors. "Two bodies were found in what was left of the OnShore warehouse and plant. One of them was Harry Childress, the CEO, the other one's a John Doe."

"And what else?"

He'd spoken quietly, almost reverently, but there was no mistaking the tension beneath his words. Or their prophetic nature. And she managed a real smile for him.

"You're getting good at this, Fish."

He produced his own honest smile through the tight mask of control he wore. "I've got good teachers," he said, and waited for her to answer his question.

"There were bullet holes in their skulls. They didn't just get caught in an out-of-control blaze, they were murdered and, it would seem, the fire was set to cover up the killings." She paused. "Naturally the police want me back in D.C., since what began as an abduction-turned-arson is now a double homicide."

"Naturally," he responded, the attempt at sarcasm falling short and flat. His intense concern made him look frantic and slightly wild-eyed. "What kind of mess is this, C.A.?"

"A big one, Tommy," she answered, forcing more levity than she felt. "Big and smelly and stuck to our shoes."

6

"TELL ME WHAT WE'RE LOOKING FOR, C.A."

"I don't know for sure, Patty."

"Tell me what you *think* we're looking for, then."

"Some tie, some connection between Richard Islington and OnShore, OffShore, Seaboard, Wainwright Construction, Tyrone Construction." She threw up her hands, then brought them down on the desktop with a smack. "And John-damn-MacDonald! The OnShore John MacDonald with the phony Social Security number, who's really dead, is also, according to Jake, a shortish blond guy in his early thirties. Mr. Wainwright's John MacDonald is tall, in his late thirties. The real MacDonald—the dead one—would be about fifty-five if he were alive. And when the hell did Islington become a developer!"

"Shit," Patty whispered. "This could take days, C.A." She closed her eyes, as if tuning in to a computerized brain. "It could take weeks," she said, eyes still closed.

"It's going to take longer than that," Carole Ann said quietly, expecting Patty's eyes to flick open with the rapidity with which they did, before narrowing to slits.

"That means what?" she asked, the West Virginia accent heavy in her voice.

Carole Ann hesitated, choosing her words carefully. It would not do to antagonize Patty Baker, for numerous reasons, the primary one being that Carole Ann didn't want to do that. "They—and whoever they are—seem to have knowledge about us. I want you to run this yourself, Patty."

Patty's lips compressed, creating a thin line of angry disgust. "You're saying I got a traitor working for me?"

"If it turns out that all these things are connected, that means that somebody may be after us, Patty. After Jake or me or GGI or all of us. We don't know the 'who' or the 'why' and Richard Islington is the only apparent link we have. He may not be connected at all, but we need to know that. And we need to protect ourselves."

"Isn't that a bit of a reach, C.A.?" Patty's tone was calm, reasoned, in direct opposition to the tension that practically contorted her body.

Carole Ann nodded. "It is. But that's all I can do, Patty, is reach. Grasp. What I think is that we know something or somebody thinks we know something that we shouldn't. That somebody is connected, without a doubt, to OnShore Manufacturing or Seaboard Shipping and Containers, and possibly to Richard Islington. But if Islington *is* connected, how? And why? And if we have knowledge that threatens somebody, what is it? We need to answer those questions, Patty, and without bringing harm or danger to anybody else. So far, Jake's been the only overt target, but the fewer people we involve the better. And they—whoever they are—did, after all, warn us against looking for them. And I was inclined to believe them when they said they'd know if we violated their orders."

A sly grin lifted one corner of Patty's still-compressed mouth, and she relaxed the hunch of her shoulders and they dropped slightly. "Then they better get ready to come after me 'cause I sure as hell kept me a copy of that OnShore-Seaboard file."

Carole Ann could not prevent surprise from registering on her face, though she did manage not to speak the words.

"Information is too hard to come by, C.A., and I don't believe in destroying it. And I don't like being threatened."

❧ ❧

The Maryland State Police investigators from the Hagerstown Barracks and the investigator from the attorney general's office were in the conference room with Jake waiting for Carole Ann when she came up from her meeting with Patty, and they exchanged the kind of greetings peculiar to people who have shared some kind of intense experience. The men all told Carole Ann again how much they appreciated her assistance on the night of Grace's abduction, and how grateful they were that harm had come to none. For her part, Carole Ann expressed appreciation for the courtesy and professionalism extended to her in the midst of a volatile situation.

Then Carole Ann acknowledged the new player in the group— Sandra Cooper, an assistant state's attorney who was frowning at the display she'd just witnessed: her investigators fraternizing with the other side. Carole Ann always had experienced and therefore expected an adversarial relationship with the police; she had been, after all, a criminal defense attorney, and a good one, to the chagrin of more than a few good cops. But this meeting should not be antagonistic; after all, they were here because the AG's investigator had called and asked, quite politely, if she and Jake would mind if they came to ask a few questions.

They all were aware of the potential jurisdictional problems involved: Grace's abduction took place in one Maryland county, and she had been transported to another. OnShore was located in yet a different Maryland county, and Seaboard in still another one. But GGI was headquartered in D.C., where Maryland authorities had no jurisdiction. A lack of willing cooperation would have benefitted none of them, and could easily create problems for GGI that they didn't need. So why was Sandra Cooper giving attitude?

Everybody else at the table already had a cup of coffee so Carole Ann poured one for herself, as much for the additional time she needed to corral her thoughts, as for the caffeine. She and Jake exchanged a brief, questioning glance as she took a seat at the table, and she wished she could tell him about Patty's secret harboring of the forbidden file. Instead, she offered a slight lifting of her shoulders and slid her gaze away from his.

Though she knew that protocol dictated yielding control and direction of the meeting to the Marylanders, Carole Ann was feeling too off balance to practice good manners. "Have you been able to identify the John Doe yet?" she asked no one in particular, and waited for one of them to answer. That would tell her a great deal about the status of the investigation: if the lawyer answered, progress had been made toward building a case of some kind; and if the cops responded, they were as much in the dark as were she and Jake.

"Not yet," the state police lead investigator answered with a disgusted shake of his bristly blond head. "Talk about charred remains. The only reason we ID'ed Childress as quick as we did was because his wife had reported him missing. We got a dental match on him, and then were able to find his jewelry, which his wife had described for us."

"Were the bodies in the same location?" she asked, and really wanted to know the answer, though she sensed that the lawyer was onto her and was about to put a stop to her questioning.

"Close enough," the state cop, whose name was Teague and who spoke with a true Eastern Shore accent, answered. "John Doe was just outside the warehouse door, in the parking lot. And Childress was just inside. Like they knew they were in trouble and tried to get away. Can't tell yet whether they were running into or away from the building."

Carole Ann was primed to continue her questioning when Sandra Cooper interrupted.

"I want you both to know," she said, looking from Jake to C.A., "that we appreciate your cooperation. And I know I'm about to piss you both off because I'm going to ask you questions you've already answered more than once. But I don't like reading answers, if you know what I mean?"

And it wasn't a rhetorical question. Both C.A. and Jake knew very well what she meant. Words were only part of the answer to a question. The other, sometimes most important part, was tone and inflection; body language; eye contact. What did the respondent do with his or her hands? How long did it take to answer the question? Sandra Cooper was a prosecuting attorney. She would know how to conduct an interview.

"So," she said with a little sigh, "tell me how you came to be involved with OnShore Manufacturing."

Jake leaned back in his chair and crossed his hands behind his head, elbows splayed out sideways. He had no intention of opening his mouth. C.A. was the company attorney; C.A. would do the talking. Which she did for a quarter of an hour, getting to the point of Patty's discovery of the phony Social Security number before the assistant attorney general held up a hand to halt the recitation.

"If I may, Miss Gibson, ask a couple of quick questions here? How did OnShore come to you? Was it a referral?"

Carole Ann looked at Jake. "No," he said. "Childress told me he read about us in *Regardie's* and I accepted that since there was a small mention of us in a big spread on local security companies, about a year ago. We got a mention as an up-and-coming firm, based on a string of successful missing persons cases we resolved, and based on our expertise in security consulting."

She nodded her acceptance of his explanation. "OK. Now if you would, please, tell me again what made you suspicious or wary of the OnShore books?"

C.A. and Jake looked at each other and C.A. seized the lead. "Nothing specific, Miss Cooper. It was more of a feeling we had, you know? After you've seen enough double-kept books and cooked books, you develop a nose, I suppose. Warning bells sound and your nose itches or whatever."

The government lawyer smiled. "So your nose itched. So why didn't you drop OnShore as a client?"

Carole Ann returned the smile. "We had no reason to drop them. We had no proof of anything. All we could do was take a closer look at them, and at Seaboard, which we did, and that's when we found the inconsistency with the Social Security number."

The two lawyers sat smiling at each other and only a pro could detect a difference between them: Jake was a pro and he observed his partner with true admiration. As a cop, he'd known of her legal prowess by reputation, not firsthand experience. Now, he was treated to an up-close demonstration. She was as relaxed in the straight-backed conference table chair as if in the recliner in her living room, legs crossed at the knees, right arm casually draped across the back of the chair. Her smile was relaxed and genuine. She looked as if she could sit that way all day. The young government lawyer could not.

Sandra Cooper's folded arms supported her as she leaned forward toward Carole Ann, across the conference table. Her thin shoulders were hunched toward her ears and the longer she held her smile in place, the more it resembled a grimace. Suddenly she sat back, as if she'd become aware of her unfortunate body language. She took up a pen and began turning it end over end, apparently unconsciously. "And are you going to tell us about that Social Security number, Miss Gibson?"

"Well, of course," C.A. replied languidly, and did so, in what seemed to be great detail, though she omitted any reference to Patty Baker and the subterraneans.

"Detective Graham," Sandra Cooper said, putting a gentle emphasis on "detective," "when you called to confront OnShore about the Social Security number—"

Jake didn't let her finish. "I didn't call to 'confront' anybody about anything, and, for the record, I'm not a detective anymore. 'Mister' is fine with me. I called to schedule a meeting with both the CEO *and* the COO, who was never around when I was there. I told Childress that I had something important to discuss with the both of them and I'd only discuss with the both of them. That was on a Thursday. He—Harry Childress—said MacDonald was on the road, due to return on the weekend. We scheduled the meeting for Monday at noon at OnShore."

"And instead of a meeting that afternoon, you found yourself ne-gotiating for your wife's safe return."

Jake shifted in his chair, giving himself time to make the decision not to respond. What began as a cordial exchange of information ses-sion was rapidly changing character. It was clear that, at least from Sandra Cooper's perspective, this was no friendly exchange of infor-mation; she was exercising her authority and it was a dumb move, Jake thought, and not a little insulting. After all, playing the lawyer-cop intimidation game against a lawyer and a cop was bound to end more like a chess game than one of checkers.

"Since that last comment obviously wasn't a question, do you have any further questions, Miss Cooper?" Carole Ann asked, sarcas-tic emphasis on the second "question," and everyone at the table took note of the fact that the assistant AG blanched.

"I'd like to see your files on OnShore and Seaboard—"

"That's it!" Jake jumped to his feet so quickly and so furiously that his chair tipped over behind him. "You all can find your own way out. We'll cooperate with you people all day long but we don't have to take your insults for a single second! You know good and goddamn well we don't have any OnShore or Seaboard files—"

Paolo Petrocelli's entrance at that moment halted what was promising to be an award-winning Jake Graham performance, and relieved Carole Ann of the responsibility of deciding whether to amend his claim regarding the OnShore-Seaboard files. The Mary-land guests, who had visibly tensed at his abrupt shift of demeanor, had no way of knowing that Jake was just getting primed. They should, thought Carole Ann, thank Paolo, who, after carefully closing the door behind him, approached Jake with a quizzical look on his face. He gave his boss a package, which Jake all but snatched from his hand, then turning toward Carole Ann and taking a seat next to her, he leaned in close to whisper, "Trouble in paradise?"

Jake looked at the package he'd just received from Paolo, then tossed it into the center of the conference table. "We had audio and video surveillance on the truck that night. This is what we got."

Sandra Cooper stood and glared at Jake. "What's on these tapes?"

"They're yours. Take 'em home and find out," Jake snapped at her.

"Why are we just finding out about this surveillance?" Her voice was ice cold and her just-as-frosty gaze traveled from Jake to Teague, her own comrade.

" 'Cause I just decided to tell you about it, that's why, and if you got any sense at all, you'll take it and get outta here before I change my mind. And, lady . . ." he stopped and looked hard at Sandra Cooper, ". . . don't doubt that I can and will change my mind if you keep pushing me." He snapped his mouth closed around the last three words and Teague reached out and snagged the package. The he stood up. His partner quickly followed suit, and after a long moment, so did Sandra Cooper and the AG investigator.

"If we have any questions after we check this out," Teague said, tapping the package he cradled as if it were some fragile thing, "can we call you?"

"You can call her," Jake snapped, gesturing with his head toward Carole Ann, and without another word he turned and stalked out of the room, not bothering to close the door.

"Paolo," Carole Ann said to him, but following Jake's disappearing back with her eyes, and he stood up.

"I'll show you folks out," he said, freeing her to follow her partner.

❧ ❧

She knocked and, without waiting for a reply, opened the door to his office. He was standing in front of the wall of windows identical to those in her office, looking out but seeing nothing. She crossed the room and stood next to him.

"You outlawyered her ass," he said after a moment.

"She's young yet," Carole Ann replied mildly.

"She's arrogant!" Jake snarled.

Carole Ann chuckled. "That's what being young means, isn't it?"

"Doesn't mean you can be insulting, goddammit! Doesn't mean you call somebody a liar!" His hands were fists at his sides and his jaw muscles worked with the effort to control his anger. "She knows full damn well that we don't have those files and her asking for what we already told her we don't have is calling us liars and that's insulting and she'll apologize before I meet with her again voluntarily. Let her subpoena me."

She touched his shoulder and left her hand in place long enough to feel him relax. So determined had she been not to lose control over her own emotions in the wake of Grace Graham's abduction and her involvement in the rescue that she'd never fully considered the impact on Jake. She'd intellectualized his feelings: Of course it had been difficult for him. But it was much more than difficult, she saw. He was close to the breaking point, wracked with guilt and fear and anger—and a palpable vunerability that was painful to observe. She looked at him, into him, and knew that the depth of his emotions in fact exceeded her own. Because he carried the guilt that she did not. He could—and did—blame himself for almost getting his wife killed.

She inhaled deeply. "Jake."

He looked up at her, the question in his eyes.

"We need to talk."

He shook his head slowly. "Not if it's about OnShore we don't. They're deleted, remember? From the computer and from our lives."

Now it was her turn, and the sight of her shaking head caused an upheaval within him that sent a shudder of fear coursing through his body.

"Patty," he said thickly.

"She doesn't believe in the destruction of information. It's too hard to come by, you know?"

"Life's pretty hard to come by, too," he spat out with great bitterness. "She's gonna get somebody killed."

"You've got to stop thinking like that, Jake, and we both have got to dig out of this pit we're in. I've got to stop being so afraid that I'm going to get killed, and you've got to stop blaming yourself for what happened to Grace. She wasn't killed by the kidnappers, and I wasn't killed going to get her and I don't want to live the rest of my life being afraid that something terrifying will happen to me. And I don't want you to live the rest of your life cowering—"

"I'm not cowering, goddammit!" he thundered.

"Yes, goddammit, you are!" she flung back at him. "Listen to yourself. You sound more like the Duke of Earl than the Lion King." Jake was a cat lover and the Duke of Earl was one of his household felines. "You couldn't even properly cuss out little Miss Cooper. If she'd been one of those grizzly courthouse-square lawyers instead of an office lawyer, she never would have even flinched at your little whine."

He whipped around and fixed her in an angry stare.

"See what I mean?" she said off-handedly. "You ain't scaring me, and I know what a mean son of a bitch you are."

He blew breath out through his teeth and lips, making a sound like air escaping a balloon. "What do you want me to do, C.A.?"

She stood close to him, speaking in a low voice. "I want you to send Grace to her sister's. I want you to move into Tommy and Valerie's old place. And I want us to figure out what kind of mess we're in and why."

⊷ ⊷

Carole Ann owned two units in the highrise building in the Foggy Bottom section of D.C., on the banks of the Potomac River. Foggy Bottom was just south of Pennsylvania Avenue. George Washington University and Hospital and the Watergate Hotel and Apartment Complex and the Kennedy Center for the Performing Arts and the State Department and the Vietnam Memorial were a few of her near neighbors. She continued to live in the penthouse unit that she'd shared with Al; until they moved to Los Angeles, Tommy and Valerie Griffin had rented the one-bedroom six floors down, which had remained vacant because she hadn't had the energy to seek new tenants. Jake moved in and immediately began grumbling about how unnatural it was to live off the ground, and so closely surrounded by other people.

Carole Ann cheerfully withstood all the grumbling and complaining because it sounded like vintage Jake. And when he gave Paolo two pages of typed, single-spaced instructions on how to care for his home in his absence, she knew the real Jake was back. "He's doing you a favor, Jake," she reminded him as he sat perched on the edge of her desk.

"I didn't say he wasn't," Jake retorted. "I just want to make sure he takes proper care of my house."

Paolo lived in a tiny Maryland town on the Delaware border because he returned to his Philadelphia hometown as often as possible, and he had a better head start from Delaware, he reasoned, than from D.C. It had been his idea to move into Jake and Grace's, just so it would continue to have a lived-in look. "Though I don't guess I'll be fooling anybody who's paying attention," he said wryly. "Tall white guy with a ponytail. I look a lot like Jake, don't I?"

"You should be so good-looking," Jake muttered, rubbing his sparsely covered dome, and they all laughed.

Carole Ann's office was the meeting place of choice because of the sofa and the rocking chair. And because she'd finally given in and bought a coffeepot and a seemingly endless supply of specialty coffees. Since Paolo shared her passion for good coffee, freshly made, he gravitated to her office like migrating birds to warmth in the winter.

"All we have to go on," she said, "is Jake's one-second look at whoever was masquerading as John David MacDonald, Grace's description of the men who held her, and my impressions of them."

They rehashed the details of their tiny store of actual knowledge until each of them was as familiar with each aspect as its originator: Carole Ann and Paolo could visualize the OnShore COO as easily as Jake and all three had the same picture of the abductors—three black-clad figures bathed in a circle of light against a backdrop of thick, dark forest. That image was retrieved from the hidden camera in the truck. The audio, however, was useless. The howling of the wind that night obliterated any sound.

Looking at the tape, and listening to it, Carole Ann found that she didn't recall the sound of the wind. She remembered being cold, the feeling of her nose running unchecked and of the frozen mucus on her face. But she had no memory of the howling of the wind.

"What?" Jake asked her, head cocked to the side, a look of quizzical concern on his face as he studied her reaction to the video-tape.

She told him and was surprised when Paolo pounced on her. "You don't remember sound?" His words almost were accusatory.

She shook her head. "No, I don't. I don't think I remember hearing anything at all."

"But you did hear the lead guy tell you to get out of the truck?" Paolo was pushing hard, and she felt it. "That's what you said."

"I heard that," she replied, struggling to call up memory of the sound of those words. "I opened the door to the truck . . ." She could feel the wind slice through her clothing as if it were made of summer-weight stuff. And she could feel the fear that was causing her to tremble more than the cold. But she could not hear, had no memory of hearing words. Or the howling wind. She shook her head. "I'm sorry, Paolo. I don't remember hearing."

He waved off her apology. "We'll go back out there tomorrow," he said, as if he were suggesting they take in a film that night. "Sometimes a return to an environment can produce the lost details."

"And sometimes not," she replied quickly and with a sense of unease; she had no desire to revisit the site.

"And sometimes it can get your ass locked up," Jake said with heavy sarcasm, looking from one to the other of them, incredulity filling his face. "Have you two forgotten that we have sworn to the Maryland State Police and the Maryland State Attorney General's Office that we're no longer working this case? And, that being true, what reason would we have to be wandering around a crime scene— *their* crime scene?"

"They're finished out there," Paolo said in his off-hand way, again waving away an objection or a concern.

"How do you know?" Jake and Carole Ann asked simultaneously.

"I've kept the lines of communication open with Teague," he answered carefully, no longer nonchalant. "He's not a bad guy and his back's against the wall."

"And ours isn't?" Jake asked.

"What have you told him?" Carole Ann asked.

"I haven't told him anything you haven't told him. And it's because we're up against it that I'm talking to this guy." He sat calmly in the rocking chair and waited for their response.

"All right," Jake said finally.

"Where are you with Islington?" Carole Ann asked, deftly switching gears and shifting focus.

"He's cramped my style a little bit. You were right on the money, C.A., he does have somebody watching me. So I have to spend a little extra time covering my tracks. A couple of times I've deliberately led them down the wrong path, let them think I was pursuing something I wasn't, just to spend some of Islington's money. I think I'm getting close to his wife's trail—people wanting to disappear should take lessons from this lady—but so far, no trace of the girl. Like mother, like daughter, you know?"

"Have you seen or heard anything that smells like it could connect Islington to OnShore and Seaboard?"

"*Nada,*" he said with a vigorous shake of his head. "The guy's an asshole, for sure. Most people dislike him, and more than a few are afraid of him. He's a bully, and generally just a rude son of a bitch, but not, so far as I can tell, an arsonist. Or a killer. And like the guy in L.A. told you, some people are nervous about him thinking he wants to be a developer, but—get this—everybody I've talked to, including those who actively hate the man, comment on how crazy he is about his daughter. From when she was a little kid, he bragged about how pretty she was and how smart, and most of the time he hauled her around with him. And until recently, her friends say she was on good terms with him."

"So how come she left him?" Jake's growled question was a demand for an answer.

"He did something . . . or she *thinks* he did something that was awful enough to alter her entire opinion of him."

Paolo nodded. "That's what I think, too, C.A."

"Then find out what it is!" Jake snapped at him.

༄ ༄

Carole Ann felt strangely detached from herself and her mission on the drive to Washington County. On her first journey to this destination—an impossibly short thirteen days ago—she'd been so terrified that she shook uncontrollably the entire way. The second trip, later that same night, she'd been too numb to feel fear or any other emotion; and perhaps the fact that on that return trip she'd been surrounded by state troopers had mitigated the need for fear. And now, in the company of Jake and Paolo, both of whom were armed and grim in the front seat of the truck, she felt like an observer; felt like she was watching an event unfold rather than being a participant in it.

Because they were cops and knew how cops operated, they weren't really looking for or expecting to find clues; if there were clues to be found in those woods, the Maryland State Police investigators would have found them. What Jake and Paolo were in search of was less tangible: a reason for events. Why, for instance, bring Grace Graham to Washington County, when all the other business of OnShore and Seaboard was conducted well south, in a completely different part of the state? Was that, in and of itself, the reason? Was there any way to tie any of the OnShore or Seaboard principals to Washington County? If so, then, again, surely the police would have discovered that fact. A records check already had revealed that the land where the exchange was made was in a state forest and so close to the Pennsylvania state line that Grace's abduction smelled like transport across a state line—a major felony if it had occurred.

Carole Ann stiffened. Even though it was full daylight, she knew they were approaching the turnoff: that invisible pathway off the two-lane blacktop indicated by a shadow in the night waving a torch. It looked different in the light, yet it felt very much the same. It remained isolated and desolate and dangerous even without armed kidnappers hidden within the forest, for the snow still was more than a foot deep and it still was bitterly cold and there still was no house or barn or place of safety within eyesight.

Paolo, who was driving, slowed at her direction, and turned when she said. He bumped and slid forward on the icy ruts until, without the need of direction from her, he stopped in a clearing. "Wonder what's through those trees?" he said.

"Why don't we go find out?" Jake replied in a tight voice, opening his door. He turned toward the backseat and Carole Ann. "You coming?"

She shook her head and they exited the truck, the doors slamming shut in unison. She sat there, eyes closed, reliving the experience of that night. Suddenly her eyes flicked open and she squeezed across the center console and into the driver's seat of the truck. Her hands gripped the steering wheel. She could see everything clearly in her memory. And hear it. "Remain as you are," he'd said. And "Stand down out of the vehicle." The language had been precise and clear, clipped, almost; and while it had been unaccented, it was, she realized, spoken by one for whom American English was not his native language. And the way he pronounced "out." It was the way Tidewater Virginians pronounced the "ou" sound . . . *the way Canadians pronounced it.* She thought of Peter Jennings, the television news anchor, and how it still was possible to discern his Canadian roots after more than a quarter century on American television when he said the words "out" and "about." And if the kidnapper was Canadian, that made J. D. MacDonald the most likely suspect, which then made it most unlikely that he had perished in the warehouse blaze—a theory that she'd been trying out.

She was wondering whether this unearthed memory really held any value when Jake and Paolo emerged from the thicket of snowdrifts, struggling to maintain balance on the icy terrain. She climbed through the middle and to the backseat. She could tell by the look on Jake's face that he'd clamber in cussing.

"Crafty sons of bitches they are, you have to give them that," he said, breathing heavily. He still carried significant lung congestion from the flu, not helped by his hasty return to his full workload. "Nothing in there but a trail leading to another trail leading to a rutted road like this one, which leads right back to the main road. They drove in and drove out. You were probably right on their tails and didn't even know it." Bitterness was heavy in his voice.

She told them what she'd remembered of the voice of the kidnapper.

"The bastard kidnaps my wife just to avoid having a meeting with me?"

"To avoid having you see him or know anything about him. Without those files, you never met a man calling himself J. D. MacDonald," she said.

"But if that *was* MacDonald, C.A., then who's the crispy critter in the warehouse?" Paolo asked.

She winced. She knew that firefighters and cops and paramedics—even some nurses and doctors—often adopted callous terminology to help shield them from the gruesome and horrible realities they confronted daily. She knew and she understood but still found it jarring. "Who says 'stand down'?" she asked. "The British and the Canadians"—

"The military," Paolo interjected quickly. "Soldiers say 'stand down.' "

They all contemplated that possibility in silence for a few long moments, and they were well down the road to the I-70 freeway entrance before Carole Ann spoke. "American soldiers?"

"Yeah," Paolo replied, "I think all soldiers. I think that's fairly standard military terminology. So nobody is confused about what's meant."

"Oh, lovely," Jake snarled. "As if this whole thing isn't a big enough mess, we got some Bruce Willis kind of fool wanting to make sure nobody's confused about what's meant." He cussed some under his breath and both passengers—Carole Ann from experience and

Paolo from intuition— knew better than to interrupt. "Well, I've got a message I don't want *him* to be confused about: he can kiss my black ass! C.A., give me that bag on the floor back there," and without turning around, he stuck his hand toward the backseat and reached for the Starbucks bag with the handles that contained Jake's street shoes.

"That ring! He was wearing a woman's ring!" she exclaimed and Jake whipped his body around so that he was facing her.

"Who was wearing a woman's ring?"

"The kidnapper. On the baby finger of his . . ." She squeezed her eyes shut and called up the memory of the ungloved hand reaching for her, pulling her up out of the snow. ". . . of his right hand." She recalled vividly the hurried glimpse she'd gotten of a definitely masculine hand, the baby finger of which was adorned by a decidely feminine ring—a thin platinum or white gold circle of diamonds . . . a ring that could have been a woman's wedding band and a source of fond memory or grief for the current wearer.

"Or he's a fuckin' thief," Jake snarled, "who robbed a woman and took her wedding ring and wears it like some kind of trophy. This bastard is making me sick to my stomach and the more I know about him, the sicker I get."

"Jake, we don't have to pursue this," she said quietly.

"The hell we don't! And anyway, you're the one who told me it was dangerous to let ourselves be victims. Isn't that what you said?" It was more challenge than question but it required an answer.

She nodded. "That's what I said and that's what I believe."

"Then what do you mean, 'we don't have to do this'?" He said it in a simpering tone, designed to irritate her, and snatched the bag that held his street shoes from her grasp.

Deciding not to take the bait, she shifted gears—and tactics. "How are we going to approach Mrs. Childress?"

They had decided to pay a courtesy visit to the widow of Harry Childress. A condolence call to the wife of a client, they would say by way of explanation should they be required to explain their visit to the Maryland police or AG investigators. But they needed to know what, if anything, Beth Childress knew of her husband's last days; whether she knew of the Monday meeting with Jake and what his reaction to it was; what she knew of John David MacDonald.

OnShore, according to its financial statements, had been a reasonably successful manufacturer of paper and plastic containers for shipping. It had been a small company, noted for its aggressive efforts to modernize its plant while remaining competitive in the field—a major reason the larger Seaboard would want to absorb the smaller company. Harry Childress had started OnShore more than twenty years ago, and had taken on MacDonald as a partner two years ago, after his original partner died after being struck by lightning on the golf course. The Childress home, on a quarter acre of well-manicured and carefully landscaped turf in Montgomery County's Kensington community, was impressive though not palatial; a home reflective of success, not rampant wealth. If Harry Childress had been engaged in any kind of fraudulent activity that netted him extra income, it wasn't evidenced by his living quarters.

There was nothing fraudulent about Beth Childress's distress, of that Carole Ann was certain. As a woman who'd lost her own husband suddenly and violently, she knew that what she saw and felt in the older woman was the real thing. She was in her mid-fifties and had her eyes not been red-rimmed and puffy, and had she had the slightest desire to maintain her normal ritual of self-care, she would have epitomized the attractive middle-aged wife of a successful businessman: she was about five-and-a-half-feet tall and of average weight for a woman her age. That meant she didn't appear to be anorexic or the recipient of annual liposuction, nor had she succumbed helplessly to the natural weight gain that was the bane of the fifty-plus woman. She looked as if she exercised regularly, and out of doors—when, that is, she wasn't overcome with grief. Her hair was obviously lightened and pulled back into a short ponytail. She wore red University of Maryland sweatpants and a zippered jacket.

Her eyes registered recognition when they introduced themselves, and she invited them in. They followed her down a long, car-peted hallway, past well-appointed living and dining rooms, through a state-of-the-art kitchen, and into a comfortable sitting room that obviously hadn't been cleaned in several days, though the blazing gas fire gave the room a cozy glow. The blanket and pillows on the couch spoke poignantly and dramatically of the woman's inability to sleep in the bed she'd shared with her husband of, Carole Ann imagined, probably more than a quarter of a century.

Beth Childress dropped down onto the sofa and invited Carole Ann and Jake to take the wing chairs on either side of the fireplace. Instead of sitting immediately, Carole Ann knelt down before the new widow, took her hands, and spoke quietly to her for several mo-ments while Jake observed, astounded at the change that took place almost immediately in the other woman. Tears filled her eyes but she did not weep; instead she smiled, a real smile, and embraced Carole Ann. Then she pulled several tissues from a box on the floor at her feet, blew her nose and wiped her eyes, and faced them squarely.

"It was very generous of you to come, Mr. Graham, Miss Gib-son, and I appreciate it. I know you're busy people."

"I barely knew your husband, Mrs. Childress, as I'm sure you're aware. But what I saw, and what I knew, I respected, and I am ap-palled at what has happened," Jake said.

"I don't know what help we could be," Carole Ann said, "but if there's anything you think we can do, we'll be happy to be of assis-tance."

"You already have helped," the woman said. "It is amazing how many people in our society don't know what to say in the face of death. You two strangers have helped me feel better than all my friends and family just by treating me like I'm still alive and not likely to die anytime soon. And maybe you can do that because you both understand death," she said pensively, then added, "as much as any living human being can understand death." She got very quiet and seemed to go within, and so they sat quietly, unwilling to disturb her. She took a deep breath, wiped at her eyes, then looked from one to the other of them. "I suppose you want to know all about Harry's battles with J.D.," she said resignedly.

⁂

What they had to tell Paolo instantly mitigated his annoyance at having sat in the truck waiting for them for ninety minutes. They had, they told him while profusely apologizing, forgotten that he was waiting for them. So shocked had they been at Beth Childress's willingness to open up and share information with them, they'd forgotten practically everything else.

J. D. MacDonald was a Canadian, Beth Childress told them, and his real name was Jimmy Sanderson—he'd confessed that soon after finalizing the partnership. He had an arrest record in Canada, he said—he'd embezzled funds from the trucking company where he'd been a vice president—and hadn't wanted to risk losing the chance to partner OnShore. Harry had met him on a fishing trip just after his partner of twenty years had been killed.

"Hold it a second." Jake had raised his hand. "This guy admits he lied about something as serious as his identity and your husband didn't kick him out the door then?"

She smile ruefully. "To Harry, that was a sign of true honesty, of integrity. The man 'fessed up, owned his mistakes, and was just hoping for a new chance. Harry believed everybody deserves a second chance." Besides, she'd added, J.D. was a lot younger than Harry, who thought that was a key benefit.

But Harry hadn't liked J.D. initially, Beth said, because he was a braggart and Harry was anything but. However, beneath the braggadocio was an astute businessman, despite his youth, with a knowledge of trucking and a willingness to make a cash infusion into a going concern. "That was one of J.D.'s favorite phrases: 'going concern.' And he seemed to know quite a lot about the packaging industry, which I thought odd but which didn't bother Harry."

"Why did you think it odd, Mrs. Childress?" Carole Ann had asked, and had been rendered speechless by the answer.

"What do *you* know about the packaging industry, Miss Gibson?" And when no reply was forthcoming, the woman had nodded her head in a confirming manner. "My point exactly: nobody outside the industry knows anything about it and J.D.'s expertise was trucking. And I guess I'd better tell you the other half of why I was a little put out with Harry: right after he loses Gordy, who'd been his partner for all those years, he's ready to take up with this J.D. character. 'That's what you'll do if something happens to me,' I told him. 'Take up with some other woman before I'm cold in the ground.' "

"So you think," Carole Ann had asked, "that the meeting between your husband and J. D. MacDonald—or Sanderson—was no accident?"

"Harry went out on the bay every chance he got. He'd play hooky from work if he heard the blues were biting. J.D. not only would refuse to go with him, he never went fishing again as far as I could tell."

Additionally, said Beth Childress, the sudden interest of Seaboard in the affairs of OnShore rang hollow. Seaboard was a big company and had been in business longer than OnShore and had never even acknowledged the existence of the smaller company, and didn't need to. Then, within six months of J. D. MacDonald's arrival, Seaboard wanted to merge with OnShore and MacDonald was so supportive of the plan that Harry Childress started looking for the money to pay back his partner's investment and get rid of him.

Carole Ann and Jake had always believed that Jake's insistence on John MacDonald's presence at the ill-fated Monday meeting had somehow triggered Grace's kidnapping; now they had something solid to hang that belief on. Childress himself was suspicious of MacDonald, enough that he was angling to be rid of him.

Who was John David MacDonald aka Jimmy Sanderson and what was the reason for his interest in OnShore? And what was his relationship to Seaboard? And where was he, the man calling himself J. D. MacDonald, because he hadn't been seen since the Monday morning that all hell had broken loose? Harry's widow had managed to locate one photograph of her husband's partner, taken at a company picnic, and the attempt by MacDonald to avoid the camera was obvious: just as he realized the camera was aimed his way, he'd turned aside, so that only half of his face was visible. But it was enough. It was a clear, close-up shot that showed Harry Childress, half of Sanderson's face, and another man whom Beth identified as the shipping supervisor, seated at a table before a Monopoly board. Sanderson was young, with a thin, angular face and light brown, almost blond hair.

Carole Ann studied the photograph, thinking that there was something familiar about that profile, then chastised herself for wishful thinking. Jake had looked at it, and while he readily identified it as the man who'd brushed past him on the loading dock at OnShore, he didn't place him in any other context. He didn't look to Jake like anybody but J. D. MacDonald. Or Jimmy Sanderson.

Paolo let them off at the door of the office building and drove the truck around to the service bay. They stood on the steps, neither of them reaching for the card that was required for entry. Carole Ann inhaled deeply several times, taking the cold air into her lungs and feeling it clear her head. Jake watched her, waiting for her to tell him what was on her mind.

"Jake?"

"I'm listening."

"Since there's no longer an OnShore, we're going to have to go after Seaboard, to find out who and what they are. Maybe if we know that, we can know—"

He patted her shoulder like he was an old man and she a young child; it was awkward but gentle and kind and loving. "We're gonna know all there is to know, kiddo," he said, a strange new note in his voice. "And you wanna know how I know this?"

"I'm listening," she said, in perfect imitation of him.

" 'Cause we're a couple of bad asses who don't scare easy and who don't take shit off nobody. That's how I know."

"Thanks for sharing," she said dryly, and reached into her pocket for the coded security card that would open the door.

7

CAROLE ANN AND JAKE HAD DIFFERENT RESPONSES to the reaction of the Maryland authorities to their visit to Harry Childress's widow. Sandra Cooper expressed blatant disbelief that the two of them were just paying a condolence visit to the grieving widow of a corporate client. She pointed out that a condolence call to a perfect stranger doesn't take an hour and a half. Jake, as usual, bristled and took offense, especially at the veiled threat of some kind of legal action. But Carole Ann viewed the threats, veiled and otherwise, as posturing—standard blow-hard lawyer stuff—and swatted them away much as she would a swarm of gnats.

Paolo's give-and-get relationship with the state investigator named Teague was proving beneficial. In exchange for the information that the man calling himself John MacDonald was a Canadian named Sanderson and that, according to Beth Childress, he was unmarried, that he was allergic to bee stings, that his birthday was July first—Canada Day—and that he was thirty-three years old, they learned that the three top officers of Seaboard had been charged under the RICO statute with money laundering, but that the charges had been dropped—that was the sealed indictment that had showed up in Patty's research.

Carole Ann pondered the possibilities. There was a time when a RICO charge, almost by definition, signaled an organized crime connection; in fact, the Racketeer Influences and Corrupt Organizations Act had come about precisely to "provide new weapons of unprecedented scope for an assault upon organized crime and its roots." Currently, however, disorganized crime was more the norm: freelance crooks these days believed themselves crafty enough to devise means and methods of embezzlement or drug trafficking sophisticated enough to escape the notice of the most sophisticated crime-fighting machinery in the world. Granted, that machinery was extraordinarily overworked and grossly underpaid, but often enough the established crime-fighting organizations cast nets wide and deep enough to bring to a bad end the careers of both categories of criminals. And that machinery also was not averse to making short-term deals designed to generate long-term results. Which, to Carole Ann, herself a past broker of many such deals on behalf of several kinds of crooks, was what the Seaboard matter smelled like.

With Jake in pursuit of the three Seaboard execs whose names and addresses had been supplied by Teague, Carole Ann went in search of the deal that had netted Seaboard a sealed indictment. A too expensive dinner at an embarrassingly tacky and overrated restaurant in what was left of the exclusive Maryland hunt country produced the answers that she sought. From a lawyer friend who now was an acquaintance—owing to Carole Ann's diminished status as "some kind of private eye these days, and not a real lawyer"—she learned that Seaboard had been used to launder money for one of the big East Coast drug operations—the organized kind. That operation had tentacles that stretched from New York to Florida and it targeted the small towns of the Eastern Seaboard, ignoring what was now considered the risky proposition of doing business in Baltimore and Philadelphia and D.C. and Richmond. In exchange for a walk, Seaboard agreed to allow itself to be wired, to have an ATF agent inside on its payroll, and to help the Feds locate the other laundering centers of the drug cartel.

"Is Seaboard that big a player in the organized crime game on the East Coast?" she asked, true astonishment creeping into her voice.

"Look, C.A.," her dinner guest hissed testily—her guest since she was paying for the meal—"this wasn't my case. Why do you think I would know details like that?"

"Because you're the biggest and best and the baddest in this neck of the woods, Ben. And because I was wondering why it wasn't your case, since you are and have been the attorney of choice since forever in these parts. Are these Seaboard guys new in town, that they didn't know to call you?"

The thick lathering on of praise succeeded. After several seconds of preening and puffing, he was ready to get down to business. "Everything about Seaboard is new except the name: it's old and established. These new guys arrived three, four years ago with legit credentials and too much money for it to be legit."

"Did they by any chance come from Canada?"

He looked at her wide-eyed and admiring. "You may not be a lawyer anymore, but you haven't lost your touch. How'd you know they were Canadian? That's supposed to be a deep, dark secret in the souls of the AG staff."

So that's why Teague is so willing to deal, she thought, shrugging off her annoyance at the crack about her no longer being a lawyer. "It's the missing piece of the puzzle, the upside-down question mark that's been staring us in the face for weeks." She could see him winding up to probe her about her case, and she handily deflected him. "But that doesn't explain why they didn't come to you. If they've got money and smarts, wouldn't it be smart to hire the best and brightest from the local talent pool?"

He shot her a lazy half-grin, the kind that indicates recognition of bullshit, then shook his head in resignation. He'd been bested. He acknowledged it and allowed it. "They did hire locally, in a manner of speaking. And given the deal the old bastard worked out, he couldn't be too dumb. Though there's no question that I would have loved to bill that one to my account."

She shared his chagrin, imagining the potential in legal fees for such a case: Ben billed in the five hundred dollar an hour neighborhood. "So, who was the lawyer? Somebody you know?"

He shook his head. "Nope. Some old geezer from out in Alexandria or Arlington, name of Archibald Wilson."

… …

"Damn!" Jake whispered after Carole Ann filled him in on the results of her dinner meeting. "So it looks like our ol' buddy J.D. for certain set out to get his hooks into OnShore once Seaboard was closed down by the AG."

She nodded. "That's what it looks like. But it still doesn't explain what they wanted with us. What were we supposed to tell them about Seaboard that they didn't already know? After all, Sanderson already was partners with—what are their names? The three Seaboard execs."

"Huey, Louie, and Dewey," Jake said with all the bitterness of a hunter whose prey remains elusive. "The way I figure it, Childress's suspicions of Sanderson were growing. Here's this guy pushing for a merger with this big company that couldn't have needed tiny, insignificant OnShore. Childress was a smart guy, C.A. He was doing the math but the numbers weren't adding up."

"And when you insisted on seeing both Childress and MacDonald together—"

"MacDonald panicked, took out Childress, and covered his tracks by burning the whole thing to cinders."

"So who's the John Doe who burned with Childress? And you're assuming, by the way, that Childress was an innocent. Suppose he was part of the scheme, too?"

"And MacDonald killed him why?" Jake posed, sounding like the homicide detective he'd been for two decades. "And who the hell is that John Doe? I think he's important. I think he was the one who was dangerous to MacDonald, not Childress. At least in terms of what he knew, because I don't think Childress knew diddly about money laundering."

"Hmmm," Carole Ann replied, the business of thinking etched in her face. "But he knew something, Jake. Remember what Beth said? They'd argued quite a bit, disagreed on how to handle things. Childress was so displeased with whatever MacDonald was doing that he was looking for the money to buy him out."

It was Jake's turn to ponder. "Yeah, that's true, as far as it goes. But I think Childress was the kind of guy who, if he thought something illegal was going down, would call the cops so fast he'd make himself dizzy."

Carole Ann took that in and accepted it; after all, Jake had met the man, and had responded positively to him. And despite her initial misgivings about the OnShore/Seaboard job, she had never questioned Jake's character assessment abilities. "But why burn down the building?" she asked. "To conceal money laundering, all you have to do is download the computer. What we have here is overkill. Why?" And for an answer, she received a knock on her office door. "Come on in," she called out, and the door opened to admit Paolo Petrocelli looking like the proverbial cat with bird feathers stuck to his whiskers.

"Could you look any more pleased with yourself?"

"I could," he said, expanding his grin, "but it wouldn't be in keeping with my normal humility."

"Jesus, humor from the FBI?" Jake said.

"I don't work for the FBI," Paolo said self-righteously, "I work for funny people."

Jake snorted and Carole Ann laughed and Paolo made for the coffeepot, poured himself a cup of what he knew would be fresh-brewed Ethiopia Sidamo, and took his cup to the sofa.

"Truthfully, as much as I'd like to, I can't take the credit for this one. And I urge you, whatever you pay Patty Baker, she's worth double that! Maybe even triple! The woman is unbelievable. And . . ." he lowered his voice conspiratorially, "the most competent safecracker I've ever met."

Jake adopted his "I don't know what you're talking about and I

don't care anyway" look while Paolo continued to gaze at him pene-
tratingly. Carole Ann looked from one to the other expectantly.
"Safecracker?" she finally asked.

Paolo shook his head and his ponytail flipped back and forth.
"Not that kind. The new kind. The people who break into coded
computer files."

Carole Ann cleared her throat. "Isn't that illegal?"

"Only if you get caught, I think," Paolo responded with a laugh
and a flick of his hand that dismissed his employers with an "I don't
want to know" message. "Anyway. As I was saying, Patty found Eve
Islington for me. She's calling herself Ruth Simmons, which, I suppose, isn't technically a pseudonym, though she's never officially
been divorced from Dicky Rae."

Carole Ann sat up straight. "She hasn't?" She recalled how much
Patty had said Islington was worth and shuddered at the potential for
disaster. But, she reminded herself, there were no dead bodies connected with the Islington matter. Just a missing one. "Any word on
Annabelle?"

Paolo shook his head again. "Nope. But I figured maybe you
could ask Eve—Ruth—when you see her."

"When *I* see her? Who said I'm seeing her?"

"You ever heard of the Garden of Eden?" Paolo asked.

Her forehead wrinkled in a slight frown. "That beauty salon-spa-
health club place way out in the country somewhere, out Route 66?"
Carole Ann asked, then shock overtook puzzlement as reality
dawned. "That's Ruthie Eva's? From a cosmetology certificate to the
most glamorous day spa in the metropolitan area?" She laughed out
loud.

"And glamorous doesn't begin to tell the truth about the place.
It really is a paradise. And it's out I-81, past 66."

"You've been here?" Jake's eyebrows had inched up to his hair-
line. "On whose budget?"

Paolo grinned and raised his coffee mug toastlike in Jake's direction, then he turned back to business. "Eve sees only a few customers

personally, most of them of long standing. But on occasion she'll see someone new if . . ."

". . . the price is right," Jake completed the sentence. "And how much does it cost to get tended to by Eve herself?"

Paolo shifted his position and turned more toward Carole Ann, hoping that's where he'd find the necessary amount of understanding. "Seven-fifty."

The three of them sat quietly, each imagining what aspect of paradise could be had for seven hundred and fifty dollars. "Do they do mud baths?" Carole Ann asked almost dreamily, and Jake got up and stormed out of the office, closing the door not quietly.

Paolo reported how Patty's exhaustive search finally turned up a fifteen-year-old Virginia driver's license with Eve Islington's name on it. With that license, he'd been able to dig up a fifteen-year-old address. And with that address, he'd been able to backtrack and then track forward to locate the woman who now called herself Ruth Simmons and who had not, since she left her Ohio hometown, used her Social Security number on anything, using, instead, a federal tax ID number. "Shades of difference," C. A. thought to herself. Use of a Social Security number had destroyed Harry Childress and his business; nonuse of her own Social Security number had provided almost two decades of protection for Eve Islington. Then she thought about Bill Williams and what a crafty old guy he was. It was probably on his advice that Ruth Simmons/Eve Islington lived behind the safety of a federal tax ID number. She paid her taxes, like a good citizen, and like most wealthy ones, lived her life under the legal auspices of her business. Not a thing wrong with that. Anybody less skillful than Patty Baker would have lost track of Ruth/Eve fifteen years ago, the last time she existed under her own Social Security number.

"So, Paolo, what do I get for my seven-fifty?"

꿍 꿍

Carole Ann believed in taking good care of herself, in pampering herself, even; she had weekly manicures and pedicures; twice-monthly facials and massages; waxing as needed; and haircuts and coloring when the mood struck her. She just never did them all at once, because she'd never had the time or the desire to spend an entire day in tonsorial pursuits. Paolo had warned her to plan to spend the better part of the day at the Garden of Eden, and when she considered how long it would take her to get there, and the list of pleasures to which she was succumbing, she realized that it would, indeed, take most of the day.

She enjoyed the drive. She enjoyed driving. It was a short hop from her Foggy Bottom neighborhood across the Teddy Roosevelt Bridge and the Potomac, into Virginia and onto Route 66 and points west. The day was cloudless and warmer than it had been in recent weeks—well into the forties, though that didn't exactly constitute warm. Still, Carole Ann said to herself by way of justification, it was warm enough to do it just for a few moments . . . for a few miles. "It" was to lower the top on her ten-year-old Saab convertible and feel the wind. She almost never drove because Al had not enjoyed driving; they had taken monthly excursions into the countryside, choosing a different direction each month, in deference to her California native's love of cars and driving. And they'd often taken this drive, into the lush and exclusive Virginia hunt country, a world of its own and unto itself. But since Al's death, she had taken no such drives and realized how much she'd missed this simple, delightful pleasure.

She knew she was being a little crazy and she already was more than a little cold, and she was acknowledging to herself that it was time to put up the top, when a low-slung red Jaguar convertible passed her as if she were standing still. The top was down on the convertible and the fur-swathed couple within waved at her wildly as the horn sounded, its chime carried back to her on the wind. Kindred spirits! She waved back and pressed her horn, though they were practically out of sight, and punched the button that would lift the top, enclosing her and warming her body. Her soul had been warmed by the whipping, frigid air.

She turned onto I-81 just past Front Royal, and headed toward Winchester. But according to Paolo's directions, she'd never get that far. She counted off the miles as instructed and, as promised, saw on her left a signpost with the word EDEN and an arrow on it. She turned, again following directions, counted off the miles, and, just where he said it would be, another sign and arrow. She turned right this time and almost immediately came face-to-face with paradise. She'd heard about the Garden of Eden. The wives of several of the partners in her former law firm had both the time and the money for monthly visits, as had some of her clients. Several of her friends had the money but rarely the time for more than semiannual visits. But she was not prepared for the sight before her. At the foot of the Appalachian Mountains was a Swiss chalet. Wood and glass and stone nestled in a grove of majestic pines all but winked a welcome. Smoke curled from three chimneys. Though the woods and forests en route still were heavy with drifting snow, the roads to Eden had been perfectly clear, as was the drive up to the building. But there was no parking lot and no cars in the circular drive leading to the front door.

Just as she was wondering whether a mistake had been made, the door to the chalet opened and a smiling young woman clad in white—turtleneck, stretch ski pants, and ski boots—smiled and waved to her. Carole Ann drove up to the door.

"Good morning, Mrs. Crandall," the young woman said, her voice low and extremely pleasant.

Carole Ann exchanged the greeting in what she hoped was as pleasant a manner as the one extended, though she was recovering from being called Mrs. Crandall. She wondered why Paolo made the appointment under that name; but even as she wondered, she realized that she already knew all the answers, and struggled to regain her equilibrium.

"I hope your trip from D.C. was pleasant."

"Magnificent!" Carole Ann replied. "I drove with the top down for as long as I could stand it."

The young woman laughed with real joy, then lowered her already low voice to a whisper. "Mrs. Van der Wal and her sister arrived just a little while ago, and the top was still down."

"Red Jag?" Carole Ann asked with a grin, and they both laughed. Carole Ann relaxed and determined that no matter what Eve Islington said or didn't say, she would enjoy this day. The young woman, whose name was Susan, would park Carole Ann's car in the garage at the rear, and have it ready for her when she was ready to leave.

She was met just inside the door by another young woman, who identified herself as Jasmine and who would, she said, "take care of you for the first part of your visit." Carole Ann followed her across a stone lobby the size of a Caribbean island airport with a wall-length fireplace at one end that was consuming logs the size of small trees. Though people were everywhere, there was no sense of hurry or congestion; there was no noise but the sound of a gentle undercurrent of classical music and the crackling of the wood in the fireplace; there was nothing to feel but luxury and leisure.

Following her manicure, pedicure, and waxing, Carole Ann was led to a grotto from which steam rose as if from a geyser and which was warm and enveloping. She was left to enjoy the hot pool, the sauna, or the steam room, as she chose and for as long as she chose; and her attention was directed to a discreetly positioned buzzer that she was to push when she was ready for her facial and massage. While she was aware of losing track of time, Carole Ann was pledging a monthly return to the Garden of Eden. She didn't know when, if ever, she'd felt as nurtured and relaxed and that included those weeks in Louisiana being cared for by Tante Sadie and Ella Mae and Lil; that time she'd been so ill and so in need of care that it had been more appreciated than enjoyed. This time, in full health, she reveled in the pampering with all of her being. She also acknowledged that it was time to stop wondering who Eve Islington/Ruth Simmons was and find out.

She'd rotated from hot pool to sauna to steam room and back again several times, consuming at least a gallon of water from the strategically placed cooler in the process, and was feeling so languid that she needed to lean against the wall where the buzzer was, and as she pressed it, she peered around the corner of the wall and was startled into a new reality: it was like being outside. The entire back wall of the the room she had thought small was glass, and the snow-laden out-of-doors seemd to be one with the steamy grotto. "This is just like Islington's house!"

"No. His house is just like my paradise."

Carole Ann whipped around to face a woman of eerie and arresting beauty. Not the Hollywood celebrity kind of beauty; the real kind, the kind that emanates from within.

"Who are you?" she asked. "Since you're obviously not Mrs. Crandall."

"Actually, I am," Carole Ann replied with a small smile, "though my husband is dead. Professionally, I'm Carole Ann Gibson and my firm was hired by Richard Islington to locate Annabelle Islington."

The woman studied her intensely. "I'm Ruth Simmons and I like it that you called him by his name—Richard Islington—and you didn't call him my husband, and that you said Annabelle Islington and you didn't refer to her as his daughter—"

She was interrupted by the arrival of several women, whom she greeted by name and with welcoming hugs and whom she bid enjoy themselves. Then she returned her attention to Carole Ann. "Are you ready for your facial and massage, Mrs. Crandall?" And without waiting for a reply she turned away and Carole Ann followed her, aware, only after she'd left the steamy warmth of the grotto, of her nakedness in the chilly hallway.

She gratefully received a thick terry-cloth robe upon entering a small chamber equipped with a reclining chair and a massage table. She sat and knew perfectly well that she was expected to explain herself, which she did in as much detail as she thought necessary to ensure the other woman's cooperation.

"So you think my daughter is in danger?"

"I think *you're* in danger, Miss Simmons. I don't think we were hired to find Annabelle as much as we were hired to have our search for her lead us to you."

"And what will you do?"

Carole Ann shrugged and raised her hands, palms up. "Tell him we haven't found Annabelle. Which we haven't."

She received a smile in return, and a gentle pat on the shoulder that was part push, and the chair in which she sat was lowered and she closed her eyes. Ruthie Eva began applying cooling, soothing creams to her face, and telling her a story. It was very much like the story she'd already imagined: in Ruthie Eva's telling of it, she was a small-town girl who, while she loved her origins, yearned to see more of the world and to be more than the wife of a coal miner and the mother of a coal miner's children. But for Ruthie Eva, "more" didn't mean "better than." Ruthie Eva didn't think there was anything wrong with being a coal miner or a coal miner's wife; she just didn't want to do that. She thought, when she met Dicky Rae Waters, that they shared not only a desire for something different, but a basic belief in the inherent good of all things and all people.

"I never knew he hated our kinfolks or the people we grew up with or our hometown. He didn't tell me any of that until we got to Washington and he wanted me to talk and dress in a different way, to act in a different way."

Dicky Rae also didn't want her to ply her trade. "He called it low-class work, never mind that my low-class work earned the money he bought his first land with, and his first Mercedes Benz."

Ruthie Eva's words were as slow and gentle as the movement of her fingers on Carole Ann's face, smoothing in and then removing the cleansing potions. And as Carole Ann sat with a hot towel wrapped around her face, a steam moisturizer adding intensity to the experience, Ruthie Eva continued to talk. About the baby girl born to her who altered the focus of her life. From that moment on, she wanted only to do for and be with the baby girl. Dicky Rae objected, fearing that she would instill "too much that was common and low class" in the child. "He took her from me. He said she was his and there wasn't anything I could do about it. And there wasn't. I didn't have any friends or people who could help me. I didn't have any money of my own by that time—he'd spent all of mine and everything was in his name. We were rich and I didn't have any money. But when we were poor and low class, I had money all the time. Funny, isn't it, how things change?"

So she'd left. She'd taken the million dollars Dicky Rae gave her and left, relieved to be rid of him, distraught at the loss of her baby girl. Needing a place to live, she answered a newspaper ad for a studio apartment in the Shirlington section of Arlington. It was an apartment in the home of Bill Williams and his wife, who was alive at the time but dying of breast cancer. "I took one look at the two of them and broke down crying. Told them everything. And Bill just about fainted when he looked at that million-dollar check." At the lawyer's insistence, she'd kept one hundred thousand dollars for herself and invested the remainder for her daughter—he'd had to insist that she take some for herself because she'd wanted to invest all of it for Annabelle.

"I used half the money to buy my first shop and half to buy my first condo. In five years, both had doubled in value, so I bought a bigger shop and a bigger condo. In another five years I had investments worth half a million dollars. From doing low-class work. So I took my low-class self to the highest-class place I'd ever heard of— out here to the hunt country. I didn't even know what that meant, 'hunt country.' But I did know that the women who lived out there needed something to do with all their time and money, and I was low class enough to want to give to them."

Ruthie Eva didn't speak during the massage, and Carole Ann was glad of it. With all she'd heard, she had more than enough to contemplate. Ruth was an accomplished masseuse; it was as good a massage as Carole Ann had ever experienced, including the best of what California had to offer. And when it was completed, she sat on the edge of the table wrapped again in the terry-cloth robe, exchanging a look of evaluation with Ruthie Eva. She had pale gray eyes—a rare color, C.A. thought—set far apart and above a straight but not pointy nose and close to perfect lips. She had very dark brown hair in which the gray was just beginning to show, worn not quite shoulder length and with the kind of expensive haircut that looks not styled at all. Her skin was the dark of Jews or Italians or Greeks, though Carole Ann did not think she was any of those. Irish? Scotch? She was not quite as tall as her own five feet nine inches, and her figure was naturally, voluptuously full: no silicone implants there.

"Why didn't you just tell him you'd found me?" she asked finally, and almost sadly.

"I already told you, Miss Simmons. We weren't hired to find you. We were hired to find Annabelle."

"But something turned you against him. What?"

Carole Ann wondered what to tell this woman, then she remembered Paolo's comment: Annabelle wanted to erase herself from her father's life. "We're puzzled, to tell you the truth, but we think that Annabelle is angry with her father and that he may blame you for it."

Ruth made a sound in her throat. "You've got good instincts, you and whoever 'we' is. Annabelle is furious with both of us—Richard and me. She blames him for sending me away and she blames me for going." Tears filled her eyes. "As if I had a choice. Who I am now never would have left Annabelle. But who I was then didn't know what else to do."

Carole Ann frowned. "But if Annabelle is angry with both of you, why is Richard looking for you?"

"He's mad because I filed for divorce. I hadn't wanted to as long as Annabelle needed him. Once she didn't, I didn't."

"But it was because of you that she no longer needed him," Carole Ann replied; it wasn't a question and Ruth nodded and explained that Islington indeed had been angered to learn that his daughter was a millionaire without his assistance. So now he was angry with Ruth, and Annabelle had erased herself from both their lives. Carole Ann was beginning to think that the case had just resolved itself: Annabelle wasn't missing. She just no longer was in contact with her parents, a choice, as a legal adult, that she had a right to make. She was wondering whether GGI would need to refund any of Islington's retainer when they quit his case, when Ruthie Eva reclaimed her attention.

"Miss Gibson. Mrs. Crandall. What should I call you?"

"It doesn't matter."

Ruthie Eva's face was grave and serious. "Did you love your husband?"

"I still love him," she replied quietly.

"Then it matters, Mrs. Crandall. I want to hire you and I'll pay whatever Dicky Rae was paying. More if necessary."

Carole Ann frowned. "Hire me for what purpose, Miss Simmons?"

"To find my daughter. To find Annabelle," she answered, fear showing on her face for the first time. "She's been missing from her home for almost three days."

"Richard hasn't been able to contact her for weeks. Where do you get three days?" Carole Ann's anger, which had been lurking just below the surface for too many days, surfaced. This was the proverbial last straw.

The tears that had been poised and ready overflowed and fell. She wept silently and Carole Ann did not interfere; she was willing to wait for the explanation that she was determined to have. And as she waited, she observed and compared the responses of the parents. Ruth Simmons was both distraught and frightened. Richard Islington had projected concern but not fear for Annabelle, which suggested that Ruth knew something that Richard did not, and she was about to reveal what it was. She took a towel from a cabinet, wet it, wiped her face and blew her nose, and dropped it into a hamper in the corner. She made eye contact with Carole Ann, direct and open, and she began to talk.

Annabelle had driven to Miami, where she boarded a chartered yacht and spent weeks cruising the islands of the Caribbean. She hadn't told her father that she was leaving and she chose her method of escape because she knew that he'd look for her. That's why she drove and why she cruised the Caribbean—no paper trail; friends with island homes eliminated the need for the occasional hotel.

"So how did you know where she was?"

"She called me almost every day, asking over and over how I could have abandoned her. And I think she wanted to believe that I believed that I had no choice. I begged her to give me the chance to prove that I loved her, that I wanted to be a mother. I think it was easier for her to punish Richard than me; she wasn't totally sure that I deserved it. But she also wasn't sure that I deserved forgiveness, either." Ruth shook her head and squeezed her eyes shut and inhaled deeply several times.

Carole Ann allowed the other woman time to compose her emotions, and she utilized the time to compose her own thoughts, one of which was that Richard Islington must have realized at some point that Annabelle was not missing, that she was not in danger. But he was her father and he loved her and he wanted to know where she was; after all, a young, beautiful, wealthy woman is potential prey. And, she continued her musing, he would have, at some point, imagined that if Ruth could contact Annabelle and give her almost three million dollars, Ruth could know Annabelle's whereabouts. But Richard Islington wouldn't hire someone to find the wife that he'd exiled twenty years ago. He'd hire someone to locate his daughter, and follow the trail to his wife. And here was Ruth. And Annabelle really was missing.

As quickly as Carole Ann's anger surfaced, she released it and replaced it with concern for Annabelle Islington. "How do you know, Ruth, that Annabelle is really missing this time, and that it's been three days?"

Ruth hesitated. "I have a . . . somebody who keeps an eye on her for me."

"And this . . . somebody . . . has a key to Annabelle's home?"

Ruth nodded and flushed and ducked her head, but Carole Ann was not interested in the woman's embarrassment at spying on her daughter. She'd been doing her own spying, and knew that Annabelle Islington hadn't been near the town house that she owned in the Virginia suburbs, and she told Ruth as much. Ruth blushed again, then paled. Carole Ann's pulse rate increased.

"She doesn't live in Virginia." It wasn't a question.

Ruth shook her head. "In town. She bought a condo in DuPont Circle, just off Connecticut Avenue. She's lived there for a month."

8

RICHARD ISLINGTON KEPT THEM WAITING FOR TWENTY minutes, a tactic, Carole Ann expected, designed to induce conversation between herself and Paolo, conversation that easily could be monitored from elsewhere in the house; after all, the man had demonstrated his propensity for paranoia, which had given GGI the legitimate excuse to withdraw from the case. So, she and Paolo did chat—about the beauty of Islington's house and the majesty of the view of the woods, and how spectacular they imagined that view would be in the spring and summer. When Islington finally put in an appearance, he was as distantly polite as he'd been on the previous occasion, joining them near the fireplace and, beyond the greeting, not speaking until, almost immediately, the "associate," Jack, wheeling the serving cart, appeared. This time it contained only a coffeepot and three mugs.

As was the case previously, neither man spoke, and just as Carole Ann was deciding to create her own protocol and address the server, he reached across the cart with his left hand, exposing the ring on his little finger. The breath stopped in her chest, constricting it. She didn't dare look at Paolo. She couldn't determine whether he could see the man's hand from his vantage point and she would not risk giving him any signal to do so. She managed to take a deep breath and used some of it to sip the coffee. She looked up at Jack, complimented the coffee and thanked him for it. He nodded, turned, and left.

Carole Ann still found it difficult to speak, and Paolo, she knew, would not until she did. So there was a very long silent interlude, broken ultimately by Richard Islington.

"Have you found my daughter?"

"We have not, Mr. Islington, and because of your actions we won't continue looking."

His eyes narrowed over the rim of his cup, but he took his sip without wavering. He still did not speak and she recalled his statement that the source of people's dislike of him was his refusal to respond to situations and circumstances as they thought he should. Keeping that in mind, she extended a folder to him and held it out toward him until he accepted it.

"This is a detailed record of our activities on your behalf, some of which you're familiar with since you were having Mr. Petrocelli followed. You obviously don't trust us, so, just as obviously, there's no need for us to continue. We did not locate your daughter but we did locate the attorney who managed the trust fund your wife established, and we did ascertain that he met personally with Annabelle. He transferred her inheritance to her. And he hasn't seen her since."

"Then where is Eve?"

"Excuse me?"

"You heard me, Miss Gibson. Where is my wife?"

She paused a moment before answering, enough of a pause to let him know that she knew his true intent. "We weren't looking for your wife, Mr. Islington, we were looking for your daughter." She stood up. "And I had hoped that we would find her. I hope she's well and safe whereever she is." She placed her coffee cup on the adjacent table, picked up her briefcase, and then nodded at Richard Islington. "Good day, sir."

Carole Ann started for the door before Paolo but his long legs provided him a distinct advantage and he reached it before she did, opening it for her. She was in the hall when she was frozen by Islington's voice.

"Mr. Petrocelli!"

It was an order to halt and Carole Ann felt him stiffen behind her, then felt him turn around. But to his credit, he did not speak. They stood staring at each other across the broad expanse of Turkish carpet, Paolo Petrocelli with one hand on the doorknob and Richard Islington still holding his coffee mug in one hand and the GGI file folder in the other, each man scrutinizing the other and neither one hesitant to display the contempt he felt for the other.

"Did you find out anything that you didn't put in this report?" Islington asked, tapping the file against the mug.

Paolo's face became pensive. It was without anger or hostility; his face said that he really was thinking of how to respond. Finally, he spoke in as pensive a tone as his expression conveyed. "It seems that the people you know and do business with feel the need to accept your rudeness. But since I'm lucky enough not to be one of those people, I'll repeat what my boss already said: good day, sir."

That exchange helped Carole Ann continue the effort of calming herself, and by the time they were in the truck and halfway down the winding drive, she felt composed enough to speak. But the moment she opened her mouth, before any sound emerged, Paolo put a finger to his, signaling that she was to remain silent. She understood instinctively and immediately why and was chilled by the thought. A listening device. Attached to their vehicle, or directed toward them? Not an unreasonable speculation given that Paolo already had been followed by someone he believed to be employed by Richard Islington.

Before becoming partners with Jake in GGI, Carole Ann's knowledge of surveillance devices was as good and as current and as accurate as that of any spy- or murder-mystery movie buff: that is to say, woefully inaccurate and inadequate. Partially by osmosis, and partially by design, she had learned quite a bit about security and surveillance, enough to know that it was not difficult to access the lives of others without their knowledge or permission. Expensive, it could be, but it was not difficult. She therefore had not the slightest doubt that Richard Islington could be privy to their conversation in their own truck, now a couple of miles away from his home.

When they drove into the GGI parking lot, Paolo parked the truck at the far end and, when they entered the coded door, asked one of the security specialists to thoroughly check it. Then he asked that both he and Carole Ann be checked. She submitted. She removed and gave the technician her overcoat and scarf and blazer. She relinquished her purse and briefcase. And she stood stark still while a sensor was passed over her body. The entire time her every nerve ending was tingling and pulsating. All the work she'd done in recent days to rid herself of the paralyzing fear that served to remind her of her perilous mortality vanished in a second. She felt stripped and vulnerable. And frightened. And angry. And, finally, relieved not to have been violated and invaded by a hidden recording device.

"Sorry," Paolo said, looking and sounding extremely apologetic, "but better safe than sorry."

She dismissed the apology—and the need for it—with a wave of her hand, left him to deal with the inspection of the truck, and returned alone to her office. It was time to make some sense of this mess, to bring some order. The man who had abducted Grace Graham, the man wearing the woman's ring on the baby finger of his left hand, worked for Richard Islington in some capacity: certainly he did more than pour coffee for guests. She removed from the safe in the floor next to her desk all the files Patty Baker had compiled on On-Shore, OffShore, and Seaboard—the file that was to have been destroyed but which had grown almost daily as information from Patty trickled in from a wide variety of sources.

Carole Ann locked the door to her office, then spread the folders out on the floor. She added the Islington file to the pile, then sat on the floor herself. What, exactly, was she looking for? Did Richard Islington really have anything to do with the murder of Harry Childress and the destruction of OnShore Manufacturing? And if so, why? There was no disputing the man's wealth, next to which OnShore was less than insignificant. And what did Annabelle Islington have to do with any of it? What did Ruthie Eva Simmons have to do with any of it? Where was Annabelle if not with either parent? Who was John MacDonald? Who was Richard Islington's "associate"?

There were too many questions for which there not only were no answers, but for which any feasible or plausible answers made a mockery of reason. And the only available connecting link between and among all the answerless questions was GGI. And since GGI was, essentially, an entity of two, that raised the possibility that she or Jake somehow had something to do with whatever was going on, and that was as absurd as any of the Islingtons having anything to do with OnShore and Seaboard. She surveyed the paper surrounding her, choosing to begin with the most recent addition: the report from the GGI operative reassigned from Annabelle Islington's Falls Church, Virginia, town house to her DuPont Circle condominium.

Carole Ann knew the neighborhood and the elegant turn-of-the-century mansion whose top floor now was Annabelle's new home. Because she'd lived there just a month, she wasn't yet a readily identifiable presence in the area, but the other residents of her building knew her, the occupants of one of the second-floor units better than the others because they, too, were young and single: twenty-three-year-old twins Kim and Kathy Rodgers, grad students at George Washington University.

Carole Ann read quickly through the report, impressed both with the amount of information the operative had gathered in a short period of time, and with the quality of the information: Annabelle was polite and friendly; she was assumed to be wealthy since she didn't work, but she didn't flaunt her wealth; she had walked the first-floor resident's dogs when he was sick with the flu; she frequented a bakery in the neighborhood and always bought cookies or pastries to share with everyone in the building. C.A. was musing over the twins' belief that Annabelle had a boyfriend named Sandy with whom she'd recently argued and skimming over the last few paragraphs of the report when her eyes locked on the words "white Range Rover." She read the paragraph twice before its implications took root.

A tall, thin man whom the twins described as "pretty old," but who was judged to be "probably about my age" by the forty-year-old on the first floor, was a frequent visitor to Annabelle's top-floor condo, whether or not she was home: the man had a key, and several residents, including the twins, thought him related to Annabelle. He often wore dark glasses and he drove a white Range Rover.

Carole Ann felt the fear rise in her but instead of resisting it this time, she allowed herself to feel it and the reasons for it; she pushed herself to see beyond it, to remember that, despite having been terrified, she had actually managed to expose murderers and smugglers. She'd had no plan of action, just instinct and hunches and a burning, seething anger that had masked the fear. She'd also had no support. That is, Jake was at home in D.C. while she was in New Orleans and Los Angeles, and when she found herself in trouble he'd sent Tommy to help her. But she'd been essentially on her own. That no longer was the case. Jake was her partner. Tommy was her partner. And they had resources. She didn't need to fear the man in the white Range Rover, or anyone.

☗ ☘

Jake sat in the chair behind his desk, reclined as far back as possible, black loafer–clad feet crossed at the ankles atop the desk, hands characteristically interlocked behind his head. He watched her pace back and forth before him, speaking clearly and concisely, as if addressing a jury. She enumerated points on the fingers of one hand, using the fingers of the other to do the counting. She stopped and stood still before him to add emphasis to a point. She used her lean, elegant body like an instrument, bending and swaying, shrugging and strutting. He was enthralled and entranced. And appalled. What she was proposing was nothing short of madness and he told her so.

"But brilliant madness, don't you think, Jake?"

They looked at each other for a long time across the desk, she standing there in her black jersey knit, arms crossed over her breasts, and he leaned back, truly relaxed and at ease in the presence of his friend. She was the only person in the world to whom he could admit fear, to whom he *had* admitted fear. And she was the only person in the world whose madness, brilliant or otherwise, he would accept. He grinned at her finally, widely and fully, the grin that transformed his cop's face into a thing of beauty, and picked up the phone on his desk. He sent for Bob, Marshall, Paolo, Patty, and a new hire whom C.A. had met just once, Jocelyn Anderson. Jake had known her as a rookie on the D. C. Police Department. Though she'd worked a variety of assignments, from fugitive squad to bunco, her success, Jake said, hinged on her ability to transform completely her appearance.

"You know how old hat it is to dress a female officer up as a prostitute," he said dismissively. "No big challenge there. But how many female officers have you transformed into pimps? Into Jamaican drug dealers? Into sixty-year-old Georgetown matrons? Into a Wilson High cheerleader?" He chuckled. "Jocelyn Anderson has done that and more. She's amazing. Really amazing."

Within fifteen minutes, they all were assembled in Jake's office and seated around the conference table in front of the window. Jake signaled to Carole Ann, like a stage manager cuing an actor, and she delivered, practically verbatim, the same speech she'd given an hour earlier. When she was finished, there again was a lengthy silence.

"You really think Annabelle Islington is tied up in this somehow?" Paolo asked.

"Strange as it seems, that's what it looks like," Jake responded. "We get this mess untangled and I bet we'll find her. Just keep everything you know about her in your head while you're working with us on this big picture."

"I haven't finished the specs on that L. A. job yet," Marshall said.

"Harvey can finish," Jake snapped. He looked around the table. "Any more questions?"

There were none. But Patty Baker supplied a tension-breaking chuckle. "I thought I had heard of shaking the tree to see what fell out, but y'all are rocking the whole damn orchard."

The laughter quickly spread around the table, like a platter being passed. It was good-natured and tension-releasing. And short-lived. Which suited Jake. He stood up, finally, and came from behind the desk to stand in front of the table. He began talking, not as dramatically or as fluidly as his partner, but with equal intensity. Not that anyone at the table needed to be reminded of the gravity of the situation, but he reminded them anyway. Then he assigned tasks and explored aspects and angles of every task until every person at the table understood not only his or her job, but that of every other person at the table.

Carole Ann listened, impressed by his condensation of her presentation and amazed at how he delineated responsibilities and assigned tasks. And she was humbled by the fact that she was the bottom line. Every operative would report to her every day. She would be the keeper of all information, of all discovery of fact or innuendo or piece of information that didn't yet have a place in the puzzle; and she would be the primary analyzer of it all, the one who would determine whether and where a piece fit. And she knew that this was her job because she was good at it and not because she was the only one of them who was not a trained investigator, who was not a law enforcement officer; the only one of them with only a self-taught experience of working the angles on the street.

Each of them was comfortable with his or her assignment; each of them was ready to get started. But Jake wasn't yet finished with his instructions.

"I want every one of you who's weapons qualified to be armed at all times from now on. You, too, Patty."

"Jake, I haven't used a weapon in I don't know how long," she protested. "I'm too rusty!" Unwittingly, Jake and Patty had just blown her cover and they both realized it in the same instant; and they also realized that it didn't matter.

"Then you'd better grab some WD-40 and head on out to the

range and loosen up," he retorted, utterly humorless. Then he turned toward Carole Ann. "And you go get yourself qualified."

She looked at him, horrified. "I hate guns, Jake. You know that. I won't shoot a gun."

"Then you might as well pack your bags and head on out to L.A. or some place warm until we get this thing finished."

"You can't do that to me!" she hissed at him.

His head snapped a nod. "Watch me! We put this plan in motion—*your plan*—and every one of us is in danger. Two people are already dead, my wife was snatched, a business was destroyed, a girl is missing, and we don't know for sure who the bad guys are or where they are. Any one of us could be ambushed at any time. Being ready, willing, and able to fight back is the only possible defense against an unseen enemy, C.A. And that's not just my opinion. That's fact."

She looked around and received confirming nods from all of them, including, grudgingly, from Patty. She heaved a great sigh. Where would she go to learn to shoot a gun? And who would teach her? With whom would she feel comfortable learning to do something she loathed?

As if her thoughts had been telegraphed, Jake offered, "There's a firing range in Waldorf. I know the owner, former D.C. cop. I'll take you out there myself."

"My partner is a firearms instructor at the Training Academy. She'd be happy to work with you off-hours. And she's really good with people who aren't comfortable with guns." This from Jocelyn Anderson, her first words since entering the room, spoken in such a warm, reasonable tone that one could almost miss the undercurrent of total assurance. No wonder Jake called her a chameleon.

Carole Ann nodded her thanks and asked Jocelyn to make the arrangements. She thought she'd rather learn how to shoot a gun from a woman, if she had to learn at all. And there seemed no doubt about that. She forced herself to swallow the fear that threatened to resurface, and forced her attention outward.

The air in the room was charged. All of them reminded her of

Tommy—of all cops, she supposed, though the only ones she knew well were Tommy and Jake. Tommy loved his work and he positively pulsated when confronted with a job. Bob exhibited the most Tommylike behavior: he was almost twitching, and Jocelyn was running a close second. Though her natural demeanor was relaxed—laid back was putting it quite mildly—her eyes were roaming and flashing and she was opening and closing her hands, as if she literally wanted to get them around the task confronting them. Paolo was tapping his foot and playing with his hair. She'd worked closely enough with him in recent weeks to know the signs: he was deep in thought, shifting and evaluating information. Marshall mirrored Jake's behavior, perhaps because they were approximately the same age. His expression was so serious that it was just shy of grim. He looked as if he wanted to ask why he still was sitting in that room when he should be out and busy.

And he would be soon enough. His work began before that of the others, for it was his job to arrange surveillance and security for Jake's soon-to-be-empty house; for the also-about-to-be-empty home of Beth Childress; for the building that was home to Carole Ann and, temporarily, Jake; for Patty Baker's home; and to install a monitoring surveillance of GGI headquarters. They wanted to be aware of every approach by every possible means, from every possible direction, in the event that GGI itself was the target. From now until resolution of the problem, paranoia would govern their lives.

❧ ❧

Beth Childress arrived precisely on time for their lunch meeting. Carole Ann had arrived ten minutes earlier and was seated comfortably in the window booth when the white Cadillac slid to a stop directly in front of the VALET PARKING sign. The young man who ran out to take the car was still zipping up his jacket, not watching his feet, and slipped on a patch of ice and almost fell, but he steadied himself and offered both a parking ticket and a warm smile as he held the car door open. Beth Childress returned the smile. It was genuine,

Carole Ann noticed, if still full of pain. It would, as she very well knew, be that way for some time to come.

She was well if not elegantly dressed—and there was no call for elegance; their restaurant of choice, while possessor of a Georgetown address, didn't require elegance until dinner. And besides, they were just past the seen-and-be-seen lunch hour and would have a peaceful and quiet meal. Beth Childress had readily agreed to meet Carole Ann; indeed, had not seemed even the slightest bit unnerved or annoyed by the clandestine manner in which the invitation had come, nor frightened by the need for secrecy. Hidden within a basket of fruit delivered by messenger was Carole Ann's letter requesting that they meet on this day and time. She could accept or refuse—her presence denoting the former, her absence the latter.

She took Carole Ann's extended hand when she reached the table and expressed gratitude for the invitation. It was a welcome treat, she said, to have a reason to dress and get out of the house. They both ordered a glass of burgundy and, while they waited for it, talked about Washington's ever-changing weather: it was a sunny day in the mid-fifties, but yesterday had been blustery and snowy, and the forecast for tomorrow promised rain. When it was time to talk, Beth Childress looked expectantly at Carole Ann.

"I contacted you the way I did because we think it's possible that your activities are being monitored and we think it has something to do with your husband's death. We'd like you on record as hiring GGI to find out who killed your husband and why."

"I think J. D. Sanderson killed him," she replied in as quiet and matter-of-fact tone as Carole Ann's.

"So you don't believe that Sanderson is the John Doe, the other man killed in the fire?"

She shook her head. "I never believed that and I told the police that and you better believe I'll hire you to find out who killed Harry because I think the police are barking up the wrong tree."

Carole Ann sat pensively, primarily because she needed to think about the other woman's reaction. She hadn't expected her to be hysterical—her initial meeting of the woman confirmed that she wasn't prone to hysteria. But such clear-eyed, decisive responses in the face of horrible tragedy was unexpected.

"Why do you still call him J.D. when you know that's not his name?" It was a tactic of Carole Ann's, especially when she needed time to think, to shift the focus of a discussion, and to shift the balance of power. It also was rude, and she silently apologized to her companion; the last thing she wanted was to be rude to Beth Childress.

"Habit," she said with a wry grin and no hint of being offended. "After we found out he'd lied about who he was, it didn't feel right calling him by some other name that I wasn't sure was the truth, either; for all I know, his name isn't James or Jimmy any more than it's J.D. So I just kept calling him J.D. Harry called him Sandy, like he wanted."

"You don't think his name really is Jimmy Sanderson?"

She looked exasperated. "I think everything about that man was a lie and that's why it doesn't surprise me that he killed Harry. I think I kind of expected that something awful . . ." Her resolve faltered and her voice wavered. She gulped from her wineglass and the slow burn of the liquid helped her regain control. "We both knew that we were in trouble, but we didn't know exactly what to do about it. So I started backing up the files . . ." and her words trailed off as she bent over, her head disappearing beneath the table. When she reappeared, she was holding a sheaf of papers, which she passed across the table to Carole Ann.

"You kept a backup copy of OnShore's books?" She could not mask the admiring incredulity she felt.

"I've got a business degree from Maryland, Miss Gibson. That's where Harry and I met—in the business school. My family owned several hardware stores on the Eastern Shore and I'd kept the books since I was in high school. When I graduated, I continued working for the family and when Harry started OnShore, I kept his books, too, for years. Then the chain hardware and home improvement stores put my family out of business, and I worked full-time with Harry for a few years. I know everything there is to know about On-Shore."

"This is . . ." Carole Ann found herself speechless. "I don't know what to say, Mrs. Childress."

"It's Beth, and you've already said it: you want to find out who killed my husband." Then the left corner of her mouth lifted in a sly grin. "I think I can trust you, of all people, to do that."

❦ ❦

"Well, I'll be damned," Jake said almost reverently. Then, as he paged through the information his face lit up. "The names, addresses, phone numbers, and job descriptions of every OnShore employee. Including Jimmy Sanderson!" He actually jumped up and raised his fist. "Gotcha, you son of a bitch!"

Carole Ann laughed. "Not quite yet we don't, Jake."

"We got more than we had . . ."

"Which didn't take much," she said dryly, "since we had absolutely nothing. And surely you don't think he's sitting inside wherever it is he told OnShore personnel he lived just waiting for somebody to come find him."

He wagged his finger at her. "I'm not going to let you bust my bubble, C.A. And I don't give a shit whether he's there or not. If ever he *was* there, he left some prints for us to find. He and his low-life buddies." He rubbed his hands together several times, then, with his right hand, created a sliver of space between his thumb and forefinger. "This much is all I need, C.A. Give me this much to go on and I'll nail a perp's ass so fast he'll be doing time before God gets the news he got caught!"

Carole Ann laughed out loud, long and hard, and she was wiping the tears from her eyes as Jake reached for the phone. He punched some buttons and waited. "Tell Jocelyn Anderson I want to see her . . . Oh, hell! Well, tell her I want to see her as soon as she checks in. And tell Bob and Marshall to call me when they can." He hung up the phone and rubbed his hands together again and Carole Ann saw clearly the Jacob Graham that missed being a cop. The steely satisfaction at the prospect of halting criminal activity emanated from him, a palpable thing. The only part of his body that moved were his rubbing hands, but she knew his mind was as active as his body was still.

The phone rang and he snatched it up midring, put it to his ear, and listened. Then he punched a button. "Bob, are you and Marshall together? Good. Temporary change of plans: we've got Sanderson's address . . . damn straight! I'm sending Anderson over to get prints as soon as I can find her. In the meantime, I want you all to secure the place. I don't think Maryland knows about it. . . ." He looked at Carole Ann with raised eyebrows and she shrugged. "Anyway, make sure nobody goes in and make sure you know if anybody comes out." He dropped the handset into the cradle and rubbed his chin.

"Are you thinking that this changes our plans?" she asked, knowing very well that's what he was thinking.

He nodded. "You know we came up with *nada* on those three Seaboard mutts. Saints and angels, the lot of 'em. I'm betting that every set of prints we get from Sanderson's place—and I'm betting we get more than one—will lead us somewhere definite, and that's a hell of a lot better than the shots in the dark we were taking. Now we can rattle some specific cages, instead of waking up all the wild beasts in the jungle."

"Works for me," she said, with a sigh of relief.

He looked at her. "This was your plan."

"I know that," she snapped at him, feigning irritation and making him smile. "But just because it's mine doesn't mean I like it. The whole thing scares me silly, if you want to know the truth. And if it means not having to shoot a gun—"

"Oh, no, you don't! You're going to that firing range, day after tomorrow! And I'll personally deliver you there if I can't trust you to go on your own."

Suddenly, she had no desire for confrontation, no desire to explain the huge resistance within her to perfecting yet another means to kill. She knew that he could never understand and that she could never hold that against him. She looked up at him and saw that he was waiting for her to say something, to do something, to somehow acknowledge that she would accept his dictum. And as she was reaching for a response, the office door swung open and Paolo Petrocelli rushed in, a chill wind.

"What?" Jake said, instantly aware that trouble had just walked in the door.

"Paolo, what is it?" Carole Ann stood up, alarmed at the tightness that contorted his face.

"Fire inspectors found a third body in the OnShore mess," he said, his voice almost too controlled. "A *Jane* Doe," and he allowed time for them to begin to process all the possibilities and arrive at the only logical one. And when he saw that they wouldn't go where he wanted them to go without a nudge, he provided it. "A young Jane Doe."

Carole Ann gasped. "Oh, God, Paolo! You don't think—"

Jake pounded his desktop with his fist. "Dammit! Are you thinking that's the Islington girl? Goddammit! What the hell kind of fucking mess is this! Why would the Islington girl be in that warehouse? What the hell kind of fucking sense does that make? What the hell kind of fucking sense does any of this shit make!"

9

BETH CHILDRESS'S HORROR DIDN'T PREVENT HER from taking Carole Ann's advice and fast-forwarding her packing schedule. She'd agreed to leave by week's end for an extended visit with a college classmate in coastal North Carolina, via a detour to her parents' home on the Eastern Shore, but the grim, new discovery in the OnShore ashes changed all that. She was ready to leave now.

"What would Richard Islington's daughter be doing at On-Shore?" asked the horrified woman over and over, and Carole Ann continued to provide the same answer: they didn't know that it was Annabelle Islington; they did know, however, that Annabelle was missing, and they did know that somehow, Richard Islington and GGI itself were connected to all these strange events.

"We don't want to believe you're in danger, Beth, but we can't risk being mistaken."

"And you really think they might burn my house down?" Carole Ann had asked Beth to remove from the house her most cherished possessions and documents—birth, death, and marriage certificates, family photographs, diplomas, insurance policies, bank books, baby shoes—leaving only those items replaceable by insurance. Two GGI operatives-in-training were on hand to box and seal everything, and to transport the boxes to GGI for safekeeping. "I could kill Sanderson myself!" she exclaimed once in anger, her cheeks flushing.

"We don't know for sure that he has anything—"

"Oh, stop patronizing me! I appreciate everything you all are doing and I'm just grateful to have you to rely on. But I'm not a fool or a shrinking violet. Sanderson's a bastard and I knew that from the moment I saw him and since I can't kill him myself, I want you to do it for me!"

The two operatives stopped packing boxes and looked in shock from Beth Childress to their employer. The first look confirmed that the woman was indeed serious; the second look presented a Carole Ann Gibson they'd never seen before: a hurt, vulnerable, shocked, deflated woman on the verge of a collapse of some kind who literally was saved by the ringing of a bell. The second ring of the phone in her pocket snapped her back and Carole Ann grabbed the instrument, punched a button, listened, and hurriedly shut it off.

"Beth, write a check to GGI, dated yesterday, any amount, and note that it's a retainer for professional services. Maryland State Police are en route and we need to be able to claim client confidentiality if necessary. You two tape up these boxes and get them into the garage."

"Out the patio door would be better," Beth said quickly, writing the check. "There's a toolshed at the end of the yard and no fence." She ripped out the check and gave it to Carole Ann, and then crossed quickly into an adjoining room, followed by the two operatives and their boxes.

Carole Ann retrieved the cell phone, punched a button, and quickly described the location of the toolshed. She punched off the phone as the doorbell chimed. She heard Beth Childress at the door and utilized the few seconds alone to compose herself. She still was badly shaken that someone thought she found killing not only acceptable but easy. The voices approached, one, raised in anger, that of Assistant Attorney General Sandra Cooper. She barreled into the room, two state police officers in her wake.

"Well, Miss Gibson. Still taking time out from your busy schedule to pay condolence calls?" Sandra Cooper's voice was oozing sarcasm.

"Nice to see you, too, Miss Cooper," Carole Ann replied in a light tone.

"I took you at your word, Miss Gibson. I see that was a mistake," the state lawyer said coldly, "but don't think I can't and won't stop you from interfering in this investigation."

"You probably make dozens of mistakes a day, Miss Cooper, but don't let one of them be interfering with my legal and legitimate right to conduct business with my client." Carole Ann had spoken quietly and in a relaxed tone of voice, but it cut as effectively as a weapon and everyone in the room tensed, and one of the young troopers brought his hand to his weapon.

"Your client is dead," Sandra Cooper snapped.

"Not only are you mistaken in calling Beth Childress dead, Miss Cooper, you are extraordinarily insensitive, and I think an apology is in order."

"What are you talking . . ." She shifted her angry and hostile stare from Carole Ann to Beth Childress and her eyes narrowed as understanding took hold. "And you became Miss Gibson's client when, Mrs. Childress?" she asked. "And for what reason?"

Beth Childress swallowed audibly. "In the first place, I'm not Miss Gibson's client—"

"Then she's a liar?"

Beth shook her head and made an exasperated sound. "Why don't you stop attacking people and listen for a minute? I hired the company, GGI, just like Harry did, not a person. I did it at lunch yesterday because I want them to find out what happened to my husband and why. And I don't appreciate your attitude. I didn't invite you into my home—"

"I don't need an invitation, Mrs. Childress."

"As a matter of fact, you do, Miss Cooper. It's called a warrant and unless you've got one with today's date and this address on it, I suggest you get out of here. If you have anything further to say to me, you can reach me at my office. And it would not be advisable for you to appear there without an appointment because I won't see you. Unless, of course, you have an invitation."

Sandra Cooper's exit was hostile, hasty, and welcomed. Carole Ann was anxious to get back to Jake and the office and any information that may have come in during her absence. She was unnerved by the assistant attorney general's visit; not because of the woman's hostility, but because the Childress home still was under surveillance and that suggested that they knew something that hinted at danger. Her concern for Beth Childress increased and she urged the woman to complete her packing quickly.

She was grateful that Beth could load her luggage into her car without being seen—as was the case at Jake's house, the enclosed garage could be entered directly from the house. By the time she aimed the remote opener at the door, the luggage was safely—and secretly—in the trunk. In several days, a GGI operative would pick her up at her parents' and drive her to the airport. The newly installed security system on her home was activated and would scream bloody murder if the wind blew too hard; a camera would record any movement near the house, aided by a motion detector that would pick up anything larger than a dog.

Carole Ann sat in the Explorer, heater blowing not yet warm air, watching Beth Childress's white Cadillac disappear around the curve in the road and wished she'd remembered to tell Beth to call when she reached her parents'. She had too much to think about, she told herself. And too many feelings. She was still feeling the pain from realizing that people thought of her as a killer—or as someone who would kill. Carole Ann knew that her life was public knowledge; after all, there had been literally dozens of newspaper and television stories about her in recent years. But she hadn't considered at all how people perceived her or her actions. Yes, she'd killed the man who was attacking her mother, but that was something she'd regret for the rest of her life, not something she cared to repeat upon request.

"Since I can't kill him myself, I want you to do it for me." That's what Beth Childress had said, as easily as if asking someone to feed the cat or take in the mail.

She turned on the radio; she'd been listening to a Tina Turner CD on the way over and she turned up the volume and began to sing along with the pop diva. Anything but to think. She was halfway down the street, going in the same direction as Beth Childress had done, before she realized she'd arrived from the other direction. She didn't know the neighborhood well enough to risk finding her way out and she wasn't up to fooling with the onboard computer, so she stopped, backed into a driveway, and turned in the other direction. That's when she saw the black car. It had been behind her and she hadn't noticed. She slowed and tried to see the driver but he turned away. That's when she realized that she was being followed. She slammed her foot down on the gas pedal and the Explorer leapt ahead. It was a powerful vehicle, with a powerful engine. The black car was well behind but gaining speed, and she wasn't certain she knew where she was going.

She reached the corner, slowed, and looked both right and left, searching for familiarity. There was none. How had she come here? The directions were on a piece of paper in her pocket but she didn't have time to read them. She made a decision and turned left, gunning the engine. She was halfway down a long, winding street before the nose of the black car appeared behind her. She kept up her speed, tapping the brake as she saw an intersection ahead of her. Then she saw the stop signs. And the two cars approaching from opposite directions. The first car reached the intersection, stopped briefly, and turned left, away from her. She and the second car would reach the crossways simultaneously. She'd determine a direction when she got there.

She screeched to a halt and looked at the other car, a gray hatchback, which had eased out into the intersection. "Move, goddammit!" she yelled and the driver gave her a hard stare. Then he pulled directly in front of her and stopped. The black car was coming up behind her now. She was trapped. The driver of the car in the intersection opened his door and got out, raising his arm as he did so. She leaned on the horn, slammed down on the gas pedal, and turned the steering wheel hard to the right. She heard a series of popping sounds and felt what she was certain was a bullet hit the back of the truck. Then the rear glass shattered. She swerved and lost control of the truck. It careened from side to side in the empty street until she righted it, grateful that people who lived in the suburbs most often had driveways and garages and opted to park their cars in them instead of on the street, as was the case in the city.

A man ran from his neatly trimmed front yard, carrying a pink tricycle in one hand and waving his fist at her, yelling at her to slow down. She did, all but standing on the brake pedal. The tires squealed. She threw the gear into reverse and backed up to him, electronically lowering the passenger window as she did.

"I'm being chased by two men! How do I get out to the main road, to the interstate?"

He didn't hesitate: "Left at the corner, left at the next corner, then right, straight for half a mile. Who's after you?"

She almost answered, then looked behind her. "Him," she said, and screeched off. She was making the first left turn when she saw her savior run into the street just as the black car approached, and hurl the pink tricycle into the windshield.

꿍 꿍

Jake had assumed both their roles: he was pacing back and forth, which Carole Ann usually did, and he was cussing a blue streak, which he usually did. Between streams of cussing he kept asking her if she was sure she was all right. And she kept telling him that since she wasn't dead, she was all right. But she was scared and she was mad and she was confused, and that made her even madder. And furthermore, she added, she was sick to death of this case. Or whatever it was. And that started Jake cussing another blue streak and pacing back and forth in front of the window, which meant he had to walk around the table. It didn't seem to bother him, that constant detour. It would have driven Carole Ann to distraction; watching him was driving her to distraction. She could always retreat to her own office. If Jake ever wound down. But she knew he was just getting cranked up.

Changing tune, Jake alternated between chastising her for not utilizing the emergency call system within the Explorer—all GGI vehicles were so equipped—and reminding her how much better prepared to defend herself she'd have been had she had a weapon and known how to use it.

"Oh, right, Jake!" she snarled, really and truly angry with him. "And I could just careen along a residential street trading shots with some sick degenerate until we killed somebody. And my excuse would have been what? And don't you dare tell me self-defense! That kind of behavior would be indefensible!"

The door exploded open and Paolo Petrocelli blew in, a look of wildness about him. "Are you all right?" he yelled at Carole Ann. "What the hell happened?" he said, still yelling, and getting close enough to her for scrutiny.

She sighed wearily. She had asked the technician to park the damaged truck out of sight, and to keep his mouth shut, until she and Jake could decide how to handle things: meaning until they could decide whether they'd report the incident to the police. And here was Paolo breathing fire. The rest of them would appear momentarily, she knew, a secret being an impossible thing to keep within GGI. And they were in the business of keeping secrets.

"As you can see, Paolo, I'm—"

"Some asshole took a shot at you!" Bob Heller sped into the room, followed by Patty Baker and Jocelyn Anderson in her chameleon manifestation, and Carole Ann had to do a double-take.

She spread her arms wide and performed a slow pirouette. "I'm still all in one piece, folks. No bumps, bruises, or bullet holes. No incontinence or fainting or other loss of bodily control . . ."

"Why didn't you use the emergency call system?" demanded

Paolo, sounding accusatory, and Carole Ann, still wound up from her annoyance with Jake, let him have it.

"I'm not accustomed to being pursued. I'm not accustomed to being victimized. The only thing I was thinking was how to get away. I wasn't thinking about, or remembering, to call somebody on a phone. My priority was to keep from being abducted or being shot or turning over that damn truck and killing myself. I don't need to hear from another soul what I could or should have done differently."

Nobody else moved or spoke, but they all watched her as if expecting a transmogrification.

"Stop watching me. I'm fine. I'm all shook up but I'm fine. And Jake, if you say another word to me about why this proves that I need to be weapons qualified, I'll hit you with something, I swear I will."

"Here," Patty said, and tossed an unopened pack of nuts and raisins at her. She caught it on the fly and, like a shortstop, hurled it at Jake, with more force than Patty had used. Jake caught the pack, tore it open, leaned his head back, and poured in a stream of nuts and raisins. The room broke up in laughter while he chewed. Carole Ann probably was the only one of them who knew that the chewing motion was keeping him from joining in the laughter.

"Did you get a good look at them, C.A.? Could you make an ID if you had to?" asked Jocelyn in her reasonable tone of voice.

She nodded. It would be a good, long while before the faces of those two men faded from her memory, if ever they did. And she knew that she'd forever remember the sensation of a gun aimed directly at her and the realization of mortality that it brings. She'd had that experience once before. . . .

Jake felt the shift in her and quickly turned the focus of the group away from her. "Since you're all here, and uninvited, I might add, we might as well have our daily reporting session. Jocelyn, you can start. What'd you get from Sanderson's place?"

She replied with her usual quiet assurance. "I lifted fingerprints from a dozen surfaces at least, including the phone, fridge, computer mouse, glasses in the sink, light switch plates, and a carton of Chinese food in the refrigerator." She wore a wig of straight, shoulder-length black hair and a makeup job that was Hollywood caliber. Her black Chanel suit and Ferragamo pumps completed the message that translated as "class act" in any language. According to Beth Childress's personnel records, Jimmy Sanderson lived in exclusive Georgetown Park. Jocelyn had arrived at the doorman-controlled entrance in the rear seat of a GGI-driven limousine and had followed a resident into the building and onto the elevator, and not a soul had challenged her; in fact, she said with a grin, the doorman had tipped his hat to her and bid her good day.

In addition to the wealth of fingerprints, Jocelyn's visit had yielded six answering machine messages, which she'd recorded, and dozens of files, which she downloaded from the computer. The micro tape recorder containing the phone messages she passed to Marshall; the stack of computer discs went to Patty.

"Good work, Jocelyn," Jake said. "Marshall, you and Patty get busy. C.A. is waiting to find out what's on those discs, aren't you?"

She rolled her eyes at him. "Any indication, Jocelyn, that the police had been inside Sanderson's?"

She shook her head. "Not at all. The place had a really normal, lived-in look. Not really dirty, but in need of some basic housekeeping. . . ." She hesitated, drawing out the thought behind the words.

"What else, Jocelyn?" C.A. pressed her to continue.

"It feels like more than one person lives there. Or at least has access to the place." She took a moment to order her impressions. "This is the home of a well-to-do, educated man who also is a borderline neat freak. There's a floor-to-ceiling bookshelf on one wall and every book there is perfectly aligned with the edge of the shelf. The books are in alphabetical order by subject. But on the floor next to this recliner, there's a pile of newspapers and magazines all helter-skelter. No neatness or order. Then, in the kitchen, all the food in the cabinets and in the refrigerator—and this is quality food, not junk food—and the plates and glasses, all that stuff is organized, just like the bookshelves, and then there's all these dirty dishes in the sink and these fast-food cartons . . . ?" As she wound down, she left her thought up, hanging on a question mark, wondering whether she was making sense and if her colleagues understood.

Carole Ann nodded. "I'm with you. And you're right: It sounds like either two people live in that apartment, or our guy belongs in a psychiatric casebook."

She looked at Jake and he looked at Paolo, who explained that there were watchers covering every possible entrance to the Georgetown Park building, awaiting Sanderson's return, and a remote camera on the road in the woods going toward Islington's house. "No way to get close enough to that place to really watch it," he said. "You know what it's like up there, C.A. And because it's winter, the woods are naked so there's no place to hide."

She nodded. "When will you see Teague again?" She knew that he'd told the Maryland investigator of their suspicions—fears—regarding the Jane Doe from the OnShore arson, and that a check of Annabelle Islington's dental records was being made. She was dreading the conversation she knew she'd have to have with Ruth Simmons if their worst fears were confirmed.

"You know that kind of analysis can take a while," he began, but was interrupted by Bob, who had replaced Jake as the pacer and was bristling with anger.

"Why the hell are we waiting for those assholes? Why can't we run our own analysis? This Sanderson, whoever he is, has gotten too close, you know? And I'm not liking this shit one goddamn bit! What the hell are you doing, Jake?"

Jake stood up, walked around to the front of the desk, and grabbed Bob's shoulder. "The best I can, Bob," he said with startling simplicity. He released Bob and flicked his wrist at the assemblage and suggested that everybody go do whatever it was they either were doing or should be doing. Then, after the door closed, he turned to face Carole Ann. "Are you sure you're all right? What happened with you when Jocelyn asked if you could ID those suckers?"

She began to explain how, as she recalled the man getting out of the gray hatchback and leveling the gun at her, she realized that it was not his intention to shoot her. "He took too long, Jake. If he'd wanted to kill me, I'd be dead." She faltered then, but waved Jake away as he moved toward her. To be consoled and comforted at this moment would result in a break of her battered composure. "I think it was meant to be another warning. To stay away from Beth Childress, to stay away from OnShore and Seaboard. It keeps coming back to us and them."

"Hold that point," he drawled as he hurried over to his desk to answer the phone. "What?" he demanded of the instrument by way of greeting, then he stood listening, his face changing direction so often that Carole Ann couldn't be sure if the news on the other end was good or bad. Finally he hung up the phone and began rubbing his hands together. "Well, well, well, and well," he said. "Try *this* on for a fit: that Georgetown Park condo belongs to one John David Mac-Donald, a 'development consultant' by profession, president and CEO for the last sixteen years of OffShore Development, a wholly owned subsidiary of Richard Islington Properties, Inc., which is based in Scenic View, Ohio. Oh. And he's a naturalized American citizen. Born in Canada."

She began to pace, allowing the new information to take its place and to settle in. She stopped pacing and stood looking at Jake.

"Beats the shit outta me," he said wearily before she could ask the question.

"We get answers but they don't solve problems, they don't lead us to a common denominator."

"It's got to be us, C.A., GGI. We're the only common denominator in this whole mess."

"If all this was about hurting us, there are dozens of simpler and more effective ways to do it. And do you really believe that the same mind that engineered Grace's kidnapping would also kill three people and then torch a building to hide the murders? Or arrange that Keystone Kops debacle this afternoon? Even though it did scare the crap out of me, those guys weren't trying to kill me. I told you, the one in the intersection with the gun waited until I'd driven away before he fired, and the one behind me—" She stopped suddenly as the realization of what she was about to say took hold: "He wasn't trying to help the guy with the gun, Jake! That's the part that wasn't making sense. Listen: they were too far apart, too far away from each other to be working together. The one with the gun, he wanted to frighten me. The other one, in the black car, he was following me."

"What the hell are you talking about!"

"I think all these pieces are connected but not by design. Somehow things got tangled. I haven't worked it all out yet, but I think we've been going about it all wrong."

"I don't believe in coincidences, and you don't, either. And if this mess really is one big accident, I'd sure as hell hate to be the guy in charge of whatever it was that went wrong. Can you imagine him sitting behind his desk, looking at this pile of shit? Hell, I almost feel sorry for him."

As she often did, Carole Ann found herself amused by her partner; but it was only his manner of speaking that was humorous. "I guess when you put it that way, it's probably a small miracle that only three people are dead. That we know of."

" 'But truly as the Lord lives, and as thy Soul lives, there is but a step between me and death.' "

Carole Ann lowered her head a notch and peered at Jake as if over the rims of eyeglasses. Her determination not to comment or respond produced the desired result: he laughed. "It's from the Old Testament. Samuel."

"I've never heard you quote the Bible. Should I come to expect Scripture from you?"

He was still grinning as he shook his head. "Not from me. Consider this a fluke. Did you know that since I live a more normal life these days, Grace insists that I go to church with her? Most of what I hear goes in one ear and out the other. But Sunday, the minister used that quote in his sermon. I liked it. There's only a step between us and death, C.A."

"And should I be comforted by this revelation? Or scared witless?"

He grinned at her again. "You should make sure you learn how to shoot a gun, and, beginning now, we travel in teams wherever we go. No more of this solo shit."

She was in no frame of mind to argue. In fact, she was in no frame of mind to do anything that required a frame of mind. But there was no choice. She waved Jake good-bye and left his office for the comfort and familiarity of her own, and sought the comfort and familiarity of her former way of life and living: the way of the lawyer. Order. Control. Focus. She sat at her desk and confronted what awaited her. Every piece of information relating to OnShore, Seaboard, and Islington was entered on a separate piece of paper: every name, every date, every incident. A stack of yellow legal pads and a box of green-ink roller-point pens rested on the right side, next to the lamp, which she switched on. By the time she worked her way through every piece of paper, she would have more answers than questions. It would be a long night, but not nearly so long as a life spent living in fear of the unknown.

꿍 꿍

It had been years since she'd slept on the couch at work, and when last she'd done such a thing, it had not produced so disastrous a spinal result, since the couch in her office at the law firm had been a queen-size convertible. Not only did the GGI office sofa not convert, it was not really a sofa to begin with; it was a love seat. Carole Ann stood five feet nine inches tall in her bare feet. She did not compress easily. Nor, it would seem, did she unbend easily.

She had been "up" for forty-five minutes, long enough for a trip to the deserted employee lounge to shower and change clothes, and to return to her office and fold the blanket and return it and the pillow to the closet shelf. But she still was walking like one of her early ancestors. And her head hurt, too, but not from being folded into a too-short sofa; it hurt from her brain having been stretched in too many competing directions. And the pain was being intensified.

"What!" she yelled at the third knock—which now, in her mind, translated as pounding—at the door. "Either come in or go away but stop that damn pounding!"

The door opened and Warren Forchette strolled in, wearing his trademark Xavier University T-shirt and jeans, which fit him like sculpture, and, in deference to the climate, a navy blue wool blazer and a pair of well-worn Doc Martens instead of Converse All Stars on his feet. She eyed him in speechless amazement while still attempting to do in a matter of moments what evolution had required centuries to accomplish: to walk upright. She placed both hands at the small of her back and pushed.

"Well, hi, Warren, how nice to see you," he trilled in a false falsetto. "Hello, C.A. It's nice to see you, too," he replied to himself in an exaggeration of his normally purring bass.

She grinned and shook her head and opened her arms to him. He wrapped her in a warm, tight embrace, which she reveled in until the pain in her back became too uncomfortable and she emitted a slight groan. He released her immediately, holding her at arm's length.

"Are you injured?"

She shook her head. "No, Warren, my back hurts because I slept on the sofa last night."

He looked over at the love seat. "You slept on *that?*" He rolled his eyes heavenward. "You deserve to have a backache. Get down on the floor."

"What?"

"Lay down on the floor on your stomach, C.A.," he said as if speaking to a slow two-year-old, removing his jacket and extending an exaggeratedly polite "thank you" as she complied. He knelt down, straddling her, his knees at her hips, and began massaging her lower back. He was a powerfully built man and all the strength of his hands and arms went into relieving the tension in the muscles of her lower back and spinal column, not all of it caused by her sleepless night on the too-short sofa.

She lay there, unable to speak and instinctively unwilling to release the sounds of relief his ministrations were producing. The opening of the door proved her decision to be a wise one. "What the hell!" said a startled Jake, as he took in the sight before him. Then, recognizing it for what it was rather than what it could have been, exclaimed, "Forchette! What the hell are you doing here?"

Warren repeated his greeting routine: "Hello, Warren, how nice to see you," he said, imitating Jake's growl. "Hey, Jake, it's good to see you, too." And he continued his massage, to Carole Ann's delight. But finally he stopped and sat back on his haunches and looked up at Jake. "I called the both of you until two o'clock this morning. C.A. wasn't home, you weren't home, Grace wasn't home at your house, I got worried, went to the airport, got on a plane, and here I am. You both look like warmed-over death on a rusty plate. Why would that be?"

There was silence while both Carole Ann and Jake pondered how to tell the story without taking too long and having it sound as bizarre to an outsider as it felt to them. They were saved from having to fashion an immediate response by a rapid knocking on the door, which swung open to admit Paolo Petrocelli.

"Good morning, all," he chirped with the brightness of one struggling to remain alert, offering a nod of greeting all around with a slight hesitation at Warren, and heading to the coffeepot. "If you think you can stand the suspense, coffee will be ready and breakfast will be served in a Philadelphia minute." He raised and dangled a bulging brown bag.

Both Carole Ann and Warren knew it was time for her to get up. Though both had ignored it, neither had failed to take in Paolo's startled glance at the scene on the floor. Warren got to his feet and Carole Ann rolled over onto her back, then sat up. Warren extended his hands to her and pulled her to her feet, holding her close for a moment to steady her. She introduced Paolo and Warren to each other and they exchanged a brisk, brief handshake before Warren resumed his position at Carole Ann's side—and his massaging of her neck—and Paolo resumed his duties at the coffee table.

"I know you believe in the early bird and all that, Paolo, but this is pushing it even for you," she said in a joking tone, her voice still containing enough of the pain she felt to not be totally convincing.

"You really did get hurt yesterday," he said accusingly.

"What happened yesterday?" Warren asked quickly.

"Can we tell you later, Warren, please?" she pleaded. "It has to do with why Jake and I both slept here last night and why Paolo's here with breakfast and it's a long story and you need to hear the whole thing."

"Not just the part about her being shot at," Paolo injected and Carole Ann threw him a truly mean look as she felt Warren stiffen beside her.

She changed the subject, and the tone. "What's for breakfast? And how dare you be so chipper."

"Pears and bananas and Nova lox and cream cheese and bagels and fresh grapefruit juice. And I can afford to be chipper. I spent the night with Bob."

"Oooohhh!" she said lasciviously. "I was just thinking to myself yesterday what a fine-looking specimen Bob is, and here you snatch him right from under my nose."

It was pure high camp, not a side of herself she often displayed and which most acquainted with her would have doubted her capable of producing. The three men laughed out loud, all of them releasing the tension they'd been holding. "You should sleep on the couch more often. Pain does wonderful things for your disposition," Paolo said.

"You only *wish* my disposition had improved," she said ominously with a Jake-like growl. Then she shifted her tone and her attention back to Warren. "How did you get here from the airport?" she asked, her voice muffled because her chin was pressed into her chest. She was standing with her back to Warren and her head bent and he was massaging her neck and shoulders.

"I hope you didn't take a taxi all the way out here," Jake said, wrinkling his brow. "One of those guys with larceny in his heart could charge you a small fortune!"

Warren laughed. Having attended Howard University's law school, he was familiar with D.C.'s notoriously primitive taxi system. Instituted to benefit members of Congress who traversed the Capitol Hill-downtown areas, taxis did not have meters, but charged by zones. Naturally, the cheapest zones were those between Capitol Hill and downtown, and the meter, which didn't exist, obviously couldn't run while the taxi was stuck in traffic, which was the norm on a trip from Capitol Hill to downtown. "I took the airport bus to the Convention Center, then a taxi out here. *After* we agreed on the fare."

Carole Ann chose that moment to fully straighten herself and released a loud groan at the effort of accomplishment.

"You don't look much better," Paolo said to Jake. "You don't even have a tiny couch in your office and you look like you slept on one."

"I slept on the one downstairs in the lounge, and it ain't tiny but it sure as hell is hard!"

Carole Ann managed a real laugh as they grouped themselves around the coffee table and actually experienced a few moments of relaxation as they enjoyed the fresh-brewed coffee and fresh fruit and the paper-thin salmon, which Paolo said he got at the Jefferson Hotel.

"I thought I recognized this lox. You have to go to New York to get better. What in the world were you doing all the way downtown at this time of the morning?" Carole Ann queried, talking with a full mouth and without apology.

"Will you tell me first what you meant when you said your disposition really hadn't changed?" He'd asked the question casually and quietly but it was loaded nonetheless.

She nodded. "Sure. I spent the night reaching the conclusion that John D. MacDonald and Jimmy Sanderson can't possibly be the same person. Try this on for size: Our man John is Richard Islington's

Jack . . . personal associate and server of coffee on occasion. Recall the descriptions we've had of an approximately forty-year-old white male, tall, thin, driving a white Range Rover? Fits 'Jack,' and that's a common derivative of John. The only description of Jimmy Sanderson we have comes from Jake and Beth Childress: shorter and younger than MacDonald. *Ergo* they can't be the same person. But I think they know each other."

Paolo nodded, his eyes locked on hers. "Not the same person, but as close as brothers. To be precise, stepbrothers. John David MacDonald and James Daniel Sanderson. Both born in Toronto, Canada, John in 1965, James in 1975." And he explained that he and Bob had spent the night at the FBI lab in the J. Edgar Hoover Building downtown running the prints gathered by Jocelyn in Sanderson's apartment.

Jake frowned. "I thought you were getting them run at the D.C. lab."

Paolo shook his head. "When we got there, they were butt-deep in something to do with a phony ballistics report that was about to surface in the newspaper and all the techs were working triple overtime to clean up the mess so the chief wouldn't look like a complete idiot. Again. So, I took a chance that I could call in a favor from a friend at the Bureau. That and the promise of goodies down the road let us bring home the bacon. Bob's downstairs with the grocery list. Seems look like every set of prints that Jocelyn picked up scored a hit. Talk about a den of thieves!"

Jake slapped the table. "Now we're getting somewhere."

"I'll settle for the condensed version," Warren said with exaggerated politeness, and sat back to listen as he was given anything but. And at the end of the recitation, he agreed that the mess they were in was as murky as one of the bayous and swamps he called home. He expressed a willingness to "stick around, stick my nose in, get in the way. And tonight, C.A., I can take you to your shooting lesson."

10

CHILDREN WHO GROW UP ON THE BAYOU, WARREN explained to her, learned how to fish and shoot in the same day. He compared it to native Angelenos learning to walk and drive and surf in the same week; and when offered that explanation, she understood how and why he didn't share her revulsion for firearms. But she was not ready or willing to embrace a gun as her new best friend.

Sergeant Betty Carpenter was Jocelyn Anderson's exact opposite. Where Jocelyn was quiet and reserved, Betty was the essence of effervescence. Where Jocelyn, nicknamed Chameleon, could blend in, Betty was a standout in every way. She reminded Carole Ann of the singer/actress Queen Latifah: Betty was a big, gorgeous woman with enough personality for half a dozen people. And she could shoot a gun like she was born with it in her hand. But she not only did not belittle Carole Ann for her reticence, the gun expert actually shared the belief that America would have been better off without the bearing of arms as a Constitutional right. Her only objective, she made clear, was to teach Carole Ann how to use the weapon efficiently and effectively and safely. And, she stressed, she could accomplish that task only if Carole Ann was prepared to learn.

Jake had provided her with three of his weapons: two revolvers and a semiautomatic. She could decide which was more comfortable. She immediately rejected the Smith & Wesson .357 as too large for her hand and spent the next hour alternating between the other two, a Smith & Wesson Ladysmith .38 and a Beretta. After another hour, she could fire both weapons without first closing her eyes, and it was agreed that for the next two days Warren would work with her at the private firing range in Waldorf and, when he returned home, she would return to the academy range and work with Betty.

"I wish you'd called me," Warren said to her later that evening, after they'd eaten dinner and washed the dishes and were enjoying one of their favorite snacks: ice-cold beer—her favorite, brought by Warren from New Orleans—and popcorn. "I wish you felt you could have told me all this was going on."

"Actually, I did call you once," she said quietly. "You weren't home."

He sat with that thought for a long moment. "Then I wish you'd left a message. 'Warren, call me as soon as you get home.' I would have . . ." He stopped himself, aware that he sounded recriminating. "How are you getting through all this?"

She looked at him, looked into his eyes and held them, seeking to know if he was asking what she needed him to ask, deciding that he was. "They don't know I'm not like them, Warren. That I don't think like them, don't react like they do, don't feel about these events the way they feel them and feel about them. They forget I'm not a cop, Warren, and I never forget that."

"Couldn't you tell them how you feel?"

She nodded and smiled a little. "Oh, sure. And they'd listen and try to understand. Jake would, I know. And I think Paolo would. And Patty would. But I don't think they'd ever really understand. I'm frightened almost all of the time now, Warren. I'm ready to quit. I don't ever want to think and feel like a cop. I don't ever want to grow accustomed to living with fear. I don't want to know how to kill someone with a gun. I'm a lawyer, Warren. I'm not a cop."

They were seated at opposite ends of the couch in the den, facing each other. The couch where Warren had slept during the Christmas holidays and which he had pronounced every bit as comfortable as a bed. She and Al had had it specially made; it was deep and long, with high arms and a high back and designed to accommodate the special body needs of long people. There was a table at each end of the couch, providing ready and arm's-length access to beer and popcorn. The wide-screen television was across the room, tuned to CNN with no volume. Their focus was each other.

"To tell you the truth, C.A., given what you've been through in the last few weeks, I'm amazed that you're still in one piece. And I think that means you're in better shape than you think you are."

"Explain."

He sat up straight, turned around, and put his feet on the floor. Then he slid himself down the sofa toward her, and looked directly into her eyes. "You can't undo what has happened to you. Nobody can, including your therapist. And you'd be a fool not to have been frightened going after Grace Graham like you did. And nobody but a psychopath enjoys killing people. So don't think for one second, C.A., that there's something wrong with you because you experience fear, or that you experience it in a way that the rest of us don't. Because I'll tell you something, kiddo: I'll bet you that not a single one of your cop buddies has ever endured what you have, in the way you have. Oh, yeah, Jake got shot and he'll never, as long as he lives, forget what that felt like. But he wasn't shot by somebody he'd known and loved all his life, looking him square in the eye when the trigger was pulled. You were. Somebody you loved tried to kill you."

Tears welled up in her eyes and coursed down her face, and she allowed them to fall. She sniffled but did not otherwise move or speak, and he took that as permission to continue.

"And Paolo may have rescued dozens of hostages, but he's never been one and therefore doesn't know that terror firsthand, so Grace is the only one who can feel that feeling with you. But don't underestimate what he knows about how you and Grace feel. And I doubt that any of them, cops though they are, has ever killed another human being. Good cops, C.A., work like hell to avoid taking a life, and they don't take what you did lightly."

Her tears were falling steadily now, as was mucus from her nose, and he got up and strode quickly from the room, returning in seconds with a box of tissues. He offered it to her and she pulled out a handful. She wiped and blew until she'd regained some measure of control.

"I'm almost finished. Can you stand to hear just a few sentences more?"

"Oh, don't stop now," she said, lighthearted sarcasm only partially covered by a sob.

"Because hiding their feelings is something cops do better than even you do," he said, and noticed with a relieved grin that she almost succeeded in shooting him one of her famed evil eyes, "they don't know how to tell you they understand why you're afraid to learn how to shoot a gun. But I believe they do understand, C.A., and I wouldn't bullshit you about something this serious. I also believe they want you to know how to use a gun as a means of protection, not as a tool for death. Jake would die if something happened to you. So would Tommy. They want you to be able to save yourself if ever again you need to. That's all."

He resumed his position of comfort on the end of the couch opposite her, back against the arm, legs stretched out before him, though not touching hers, which were pulled up into her chest. Her head was resting on her knees, but she still was watching him unflinchingly.

She moved suddenly, swinging her legs around and down, and she stood up quickly, drained her beer, and put the bottle on the table. "I'm going to bed. What time do you want to go shoot those damn guns tomorrow?"

"Not too early," he said, releasing the yawn he'd been stifling for the past fifteen minutes. "It is Saturday, after all. And if I may make a tiny suggestion? If you plan to make sleeping at the office a habit, get a real couch."

She laughed and came to stand beside him, placing a hand lightly on his shoulder. "Thank you, Warren," she said in an almost whisper, and left the room, leaving the whispering silence in her wake.

⁓ ⁓

By the time she drove Warren to the airport on Sunday night, Carole Ann had talked through the entire OnShore/Seaboard/Islington mess with him, and had become proficient with both the revolver and the semiautomatic, having a slight preference for the latter. She had evolved to the point that all of her rounds actually pierced the target, though few of them would have resulted in a bullet through the heart. Which was fine with her. She was grateful for Warren's presence and assistance, and she told him as much. She would not have been able to grow as comfortable with the gun or with using it had it not been for him. He disagreed; he told her that she could excel at whatever she tackled. She shrugged.

"Maybe, maybe not," she replied off-handedly; the gun business had taken a backseat in her consciousness to her belief that she knew who was responsible for the turmoil surrounding them, if not exactly why . . . and she thought she knew at least some of the why.

They arrived at his departure gate and found they had time for a cup of coffee—his flight was delayed forty-five minutes. And they used the time, at Carole Ann's suggestion, to discuss Warren's intention to apply for admission to the Bar of the Supreme Court. He wanted her to write a sponsorship letter for him, and when she hesitated, he became visibly upset.

"Oh, for crying out loud, Warren! If you actually can sit here and think I have a single qualm about supporting you, you're a flaming idiot! I'm only wondering whether my trouble with the L.A. Bar Association will look bad for you."

He calmed down immediately and confessed that he'd forgotten about that episode.

"I wish I could," she said with still-painful feelings.

"But you're reinstated, aren't you?"

She shook her head, then shrugged. "I don't know. I'll have to check with Addie. I guess I've been avoiding the issue. Maybe you should ask Addie to write a letter of sponsorship for you."

"I don't want Addie to do it, I want you to do it!"

"And I will, Warren. I'd be honored to do it, and I'm honored that you asked me."

They sat quietly, drinking their coffee and watching the Sunday-night throngs entering and leaving the nation's capital, those returning from getaways to the Caribbean as easily recognizable as those returning from Vail or Aspen; the political types returning to jobs on Capitol Hill from weekends to the home district as definable by their wardrobes as the returnees from a weekend in New York were by theirs. The place was packed, and not only because it was Sunday night. Because of its proximity to residential areas—Washington's airport, located in Virginia—was really right in the middle of things. No matter which way they arrived or departed, even following the path of the Potomac, planes flew over somebody's home. So, flights were halted at ten o'clock every night. Or as close to ten as possible.

Warren looked at his watch. "Guess I'd better mosey on down to the gate and see if they're ready to board me," and they both stood up. They were close enough to the gate that they could see passengers in the boarding line.

"Warren, thank you again. And not just for this business with the gun. Thank you for coming and for knowing what I was feeling and for helping me not fall off the edge."

He put an arm across her shoulders and drew her close. She put an arm around his waist, and they walked down the crowded hall to the departure gate. "I left something for you on your dresser," he said.

"What?"

He laughed. "You'll see when you get home." And then he leaned down and kissed her, and she not only allowed it, she responded, fully, releasing as much of the pent-up emotion as she dared.

Then she broke away and backed up. "I don't know if I'm ready for this. I don't think I am."

"I'm not going anywhere," he said, and turned toward the gate. "Except back to New Orleans. And that's not far."

❧ ❧

On the dresser in her bedroom was a box that was heavier than she expected when she picked it up; and even before she opened it, she knew what it contained. Still, she experienced a strong and confusing mixture of gratitude and sorrow and pleasure when she looked at the gun. She didn't touch it, choosing instead to read the note, which brought tears to her eyes. He really did know what went on inside her. Sometimes with greater clarity than she herself did. She brushed away the tears and checked the clock. She needed to make two phone calls before it got too late, to clarify two points that had been nudging and niggling at her. Carrying the box with the gun nestled inside, she padded down the hallway to her office, wondering which fact surprised her more thoroughly: that she owned a gun, or that she was glad that Warren had given it to her.

❧ ❧

When she arrived at work at seven the next morning, she was the last to arrive. The coffee was made and Jake, Paolo, Patty, Bob, Jocelyn, and Marshall were in her office, waiting.

"Did somebody forget to send me the memo?" she asked, eliciting the laughter she'd hoped for; its absence would have filled her with dread, though their solemn presence could not portend good news. She dropped all of her belongings on top of her desk and pulled the chair from behind it over to the coffee table. When she turned around, Paolo delivered a cup of steaming coffee and she nodded her thanks. His action stirred up the memory of Warren's observation that Paolo "had a thing" for her. She scowled at the thought and he misread it.

"Not strong enough?" he asked, looking worried.

"It's fine, Paolo, and thanks for going to the trouble. And speaking of trouble . . ." She shot Jake a "your ass is grass" look, which made him squirm. She didn't like not having the upper hand and he knew it. His look let her know it couldn't be helped.

Patty, with bags the depth of trenches under her eyes, spoke first and at length. When she was finished, Carole Ann could, for the moment, only sit and wonder, but still not understand. And that is what she said: "But I don't understand how that is possible." And she looked from one to the other of them, feeling as helpless and violated as she knew they all did.

"All telephone lines are vulnerable to those who know how to violate them, C.A. Fortunately, only about a third of our capacity is linked to phone lines, which is why they believed us right away when we said we'd deleted all the OnShore and Seaboard files. But *because* they believed us, just like you said, I knew we had a problem, even though I did *not* want to believe that anybody who worked for me was a traitor. So I knew a line had to have been compromised."

"But *how?* It's not like somebody could call information and ask for the phone numbers to our computers."

"For somebody who knows what they're doing, C.A., it is almost *exactly* like that."

Carole Ann listened to some more of the technology involved and began to get the kind of headache not even a good cup of coffee could ward off, but she got up to pour more anyway, and brought the pot back with her. Jocelyn and Paolo accepted refills. "Bottom line, Patty, how bad have they hurt us? What do they know about our clients' business?"

"Because I don't know how long they've had access, I don't know. I do know that whoever it is knows everything we know about Ruthie Eva Simmons, including her address, the address of her business, her phone numbers, everything."

Carole Ann felt frozen inside. She barely heard Jake when he said he'd had people calling her home and the Garden of Eden every fifteen minutes for the last two hours, to no avail. First Annabelle and now her mother. It was too much. And she was too much of a part of whatever it was that was happening. And being frozen was not being productive. She looked at her watch. It was too early for there to be staff at the Garden of Eden; and it was much too early for Ruthie Eva Simmons not to be home. "Beth!" she said suddenly. "What about Beth Childress?"

"She's fine," Bob replied with as much of a grin as he could muster. "Her daddy cussed me out good when I called for her. Wanted to know who the hell I was calling his daughter when her husband wasn't cold in the ground yet!"

"I'm going to try to see Islington this morning. I think he'll—"

"Islington!" Both Jake and Paolo exploded the word, and Jake jumped to his feet, ready to do battle.

"I don't think he's involved in this. Not directly, anyway."

"MacDonald is involved up to his eyeteeth," Jake exclaimed, "and Islington's not?"

"I don't think so," she insisted. "Islington is a jerk and a bully, but I don't think he's a thief and I don't think he's a murderer. And he's not the kind of man who needs a flunky hanging around all the time. MacDonald's an associate, just like Islington said, and when his job is done, he leaves. He has his own life."

"That's right," Jocelyn said calmly. "MacDonald's apartment is the home of somebody who really lived there."

"But I thought you said it was a mess," chimed in Bob in an accusatory tone. "And anyway, I thought that was Sanderson's place."

"Sanderson didn't have a place," Jake said. "Everything Sanderson said to anybody was a lie. He used MacDonald's address because he didn't have one of his own."

"Yes, he did," Carole Ann said quietly, and they all gave her their full attention. "He lived with Annabelle Islington first in Falls Church, and later, for about a week before she threw him out, in DuPont Circle. Her mother told me this last night. I called her to ask if she knew MacDonald or Sanderson. She knew them both, but even she didn't know until recently that they were brothers. MacDonald has worked for Islington for more than fifteen years. Annabelle brought Sanderson with her the one time she visited her mother, after she received her windfall inheritance. Introduced him as her fiancé."

The silence in the room was deafening and Carole Ann allowed a few seconds for it to settle and lighten before she dropped the other shoe. "I also talked to Beth Childress last night. I wanted to ask her if the partnership agreement between Harry and John David MacDonald still stood, or if they altered it when Sanderson revealed his true identity."

"Well, I'll be damned," Jake whispered through a low whistle. "That makes it sound like the John Doe really is Sanderson and Jane Doe really is Annabelle and we really got ourselves a motive."

"MacDonald killed them all?" asked Patty.

"Then we'd better go find his ass," Marshall said grimly, surprising them all.

"Where do we look?" asked Jocelyn. "Unless you think he'll return to the Georgetown Park place."

"He hasn't been back there, but we'll keep watching it," Jake said. "And the Islington girl's place in Falls Church, too, although nobody's been in or out of there since we've been looking at it. Or the DuPont Circle place."

"Have we been inside there?" Carole Ann asked quickly, rising and striding across the room to her desk.

Jake shook his head. "Hell, no. One B-and-E per week is about my limit. Why? What do you think we might find in there?"

"Probably nothing of interest to us," she said, dialing the phone, "but Islington doesn't know that." She listened and they watched her. "Mr. Islington, this is Carole Ann Gibson. I'd like to see you today. I have information regarding John David MacDonald and your daughter." And she put down the phone.

"If he's not involved, he'll sure as hell call," Jake said with grim satisfaction.

"He'll call, anyway," Carole Ann said with equal gravity and little satisfaction. She asked Marshall to find out what time Islington had left his home that morning and nodded when he asked to use her phone. Then, returning to Jake, she added, "The man is ego driven and events of major proportions that involve him are taking place around him, and without his permission or sanction or knowledge. If Ruthie Eva is any judge . . ." And she stopped herself. Ruthie Eva. She had, that quickly, forgotten about her; they all had. "I'm going to look for her."

Everyone, it seemed, reacted at once and as one, with such overwhelming negativity to the notion that it startled her. But it didn't anger her because, almost as if he were sitting there repeating the words to her, she heard Warren explaining them to her, and she understood. She was thinking of a response when Jocelyn Anderson said, "I'd like to go with you, if that's all right."

"Fine," Carole Ann responded quickly, before anyone could object.

"We need to get somebody over to Islington's!" Marshall said with urgency, hanging up the phone, though keeping his hand on it as if he expected it to ring. "He drives a white Range Rover and that vehicle left the property eighteen hours ago and hasn't returned. Exterior lights that operate on timers didn't function last night—"

Jake pointed at Paolo. "You and Bob—"

"—and . . ." Marshall continued, and all movement ceased. "That gray hatchback, the one that ambushed you, C.A., has made three passes at the Falls Church location since dawn this morning. The driver is a light-skinned Black or Hispanic male in his twenties, no passengers visible."

" 'Somebody done fired up the brimstone, gettin' ready to blow.' " Jake sang the lyrics from the Stevie Wonder hit of another generation, rubbing his hands together the way he did when he was ready for battle, and he executed some kind of little jig or hop that might have been dancing. "Get started," he barked, nodding toward Paolo and Bob. "I'll meet you downstairs in a minute," he said to Marshall, who was already on his way out the door. He turned toward Jocelyn.

"I'm going to get changed," she quickly said to him; and to Carole Ann, "I'll meet you in the parking lot in twenty?" And when she received a confirming nod, she quickly exited.

"I hope you all are finished with me for a while," Patty said wearily. "I need to go manage a damage control operation. And I don't just mean on the system. All my people are in a state of shock and they don't understand why I'm not. And I'll never tell them that even though I didn't believe it, I had to imagine that one of them was a skunk." She started out the door, then turned around, brandishing her coffee mug. "I'll take a refill first. This is a damn sight better than what we serve downstairs in the lounge," she said archly.

"As well it should be," Carole Ann replied as dryly as she could manage, winning a true Patty hoot of laughter through the fatigue as she dragged herself out the door and into the hallway.

Jake crossed to her and, knowing what he would say, she preempted him by hoisting Warren's present and tossing it to him. "What do you think of this?" she asked lightly.

He opened the box carefully, almost warily, and she could tell that he knew what it held. "Where'd this come from?"

"A gift from Warren," she replied casually. "A reward, actually, for being such a quick study."

"Is it loaded?"

"Of course not," she snapped at him.

"Then load it," he snapped back, tossing the box to her and hurrying out and down the hallway.

She did, and then changed her clothes, aware that if she didn't hurry, she'd be keeping Jocelyn waiting. Too late she realized, as she was standing between her desk and the closet door in her bra and panties, that she hadn't locked the door behind Jake. "Tough noogies," she muttered, thinking that everybody employed by GGI at this moment on this day had too much to think about to react to her standing around in her underwear. Still, she quickly slid into a pair of tights and a long-sleeved silk T-shirt, over which she donned a turtleneck and winter running tights, and over that, her black ski garb. It no longer was bitterly cold, but neither had spring arrived, and it was certain to be colder where they were heading, out toward the mountains and into West Virginia. If she got too warm, she always could begin peeling off layers.

She stuck her tiny cell phone into the inside pocket of her jacket on the left side, and her wallet on the other side. "And where am I supposed to put a damn gun?" She gave the weapon a baleful, distasteful look before sticking it in the side pocket, grabbed her keys, and ran out of the office and down the hall. She rode down on the elevator with several people she recognized but whose names she didn't know, and she wondered whether that meant GGI was growing too fast. How could she not know the names of people who worked for her? Then again, they didn't work for *her*, exactly . . .

She exited the elevator and jogged the short distance to the security door. She inserted her card and was allowed out of the building. Jocelyn was standing beside the idling truck.

"Sorry to keep you waiting," Carole Ann said.

"I just got here," Jocelyn replied. "Would you like to drive, or do you want me to?"

"Are you a good driver?" C.A. asked with real seriousness and expected a serious answer. She abhorred riding with timid or careless or reckless drivers.

"I'm a very good driver," Jocelyn replied with total ease and a complete absence of bravado. And they both climbed into the truck and Jocelyn set about proving the accuracy of her claim. Not only was she good, she knew the city. She had them downtown, across the Potomac, and on Route 66 by eight-thirty. Carole Ann was impressed and said so.

"Is there anything you're not good at?"

"Acting!" the young woman said with real feeling. "I'm a lousy actor." And there was such sadness in the tone that Carole Ann had to will herself not to laugh; because it was such an improbability that an ex-D.C. cop wanted to be an actor with such obvious passion that laughter was her first reaction.

"OK, Jocelyn, I'll bite. You want to be an actor?"

"Past tense. I don't have what it takes, since desire obviously isn't enough. I was a theater major at Catholic U. Excelled at 'getting into' a role. Nobody ever knew it was me on stage, including my parents. But nobody ever remembered me in a role, either. I went to New York and I went to L.A. and I never got a single job. Not one. So, I came back home and was preparing to enter grad school, thinking I'd get a master's and teach theater, when I saw a recruiting ad in the paper. Why not be a cop? And as it happened, I did very well at the academy."

Jocelyn's recitation was interrupted by the ringing of the phone. Carole Ann answered, to hear Jake asking her what county they'd be in. She told him, adding the reminder that Ruthie Eva herself lived just across the Virginia line into West Virginia. Jake was still cussing when he disconnected her. She knew he was preparing to notify the authorities in the various jurisdictions should any GGI employees encounter or uncover evidence of a crime. And though the authorities in Virginia and Maryland would not be pleased to hear from a privately licensed investigator from D.C., it wouldn't be an unusual occurrence, and Jake's status as an ex-D.C. cop would carry some weight. Not so in West Virginia.

"So why did you leave the department?"

Jocelyn stole a sideways glance at her. "Have you been reading about the D.C. Police Department in the newspaper?"

She had, and with equal parts dismay and alarm. She'd had occasion to meet quite a few D.C. police officers during her years as a criminal defense attorney; and while no small number of them were jerks and assholes, she'd never considered any of them bad cops. But it did appear that things had changed within what once had been a pretty good department. Jake and Tommy were so disgusted they refused to discuss the matter. Carole Ann followed suit, and they rode in silence for several miles.

"That song that Jake sang this morning?" Jocelyn was asking the question before she asked the question. "The thing about lighting the brimstone? What was that from?"

Carole Ann groaned. Jake and Marshall and Patty were about ten years older than Carole Ann and Paolo; and they, in turn, had ten or so years on Jocelyn and Bob. And in certain areas of life, music being one of them, ten years was an eternity. "That was vintage Stevie Wonder. Song called, 'Skeletons' from the *Characters* album. Came out in about 1984 or so."

"Gee. I was about—"

"I don't need to know that, Jocelyn."

She shot Carole Ann a sideways grin, then asked her if she knew all the lyrics from the song. She did, and sang them for the appreciative younger woman, marveling at the genius of a musical talent not much heard from in recent years.

"I love that line: 'Somebody done fired up the brimstone.' Shakespearean and biblical and Black! What a holy combination!"

Carole Ann laughed at Jocelyn's youthful exuberance, and found she shared it. She also found that she was grateful for having something else to think about, because as soon as the levity left, reality returned. The thought she'd been trying to keep at bay involved the destruction of an entire family: if the worst of bad scenarios were true, all the Islingtons conceivably could be dead. Annabelle, it appeared, already was; Richard had not been seen in two days; and Ruthie Eva had not been reachable so far this day. She muttered some curses to herself, then, aware of how Jake-like she was becoming, stopped herself.

"We're getting close," Jocelyn said, reading her tension correctly.

"Good," she responded, though she didn't know why. What would they do once they arrived? Ruthie Eva still hadn't answered her home telephone, nor had she responded to messages left at the Garden of Eden. Perhaps, she thought, driving so far out of town was a mistake. Yet, what would she do if she were back in D.C.? She knew one thing—she picked up the phone and punched a number. "Hi, Carla. From my call sheet, reach Bill Williams for me, please . . . thanks." She watched the countryside speed past while she held the phone, awaiting the connection, willing herself not to invent reasons to worry. "Mr. Williams, this is Carole Ann Gibson. I'm sorry to disturb you so early." She listened to him; sounding hearty and full of good humor, he sloughed off the need for her apology and wondered what "an old man like myself" could do for her. It was as if there'd never been a moment of tension between them; as if she'd never said a rude or hostile word to him. Bill Williams either was a forgiving man, or he was, as she'd originally thought, full of shit.

She shared with him GGI's concern at not being able to reach Ruthie Eva and the plan to send the police to check her home, unless he knew of some other place she could be. She heard the intake of breath and the lessening of his bonhomie as he sought to assure her that there was no need for that; and when she pressed him, he reluctantly acknowledged that Ruthie Eva had a fishing shack on the Potomac, up in the mountains, about thirty-five miles from her house, where she sometimes went when she was upset.

"She was upset?" Carole Ann asked, surprised. She'd been on the phone with Ruth until after midnight and the woman hadn't mentioned being upset or leaving. In fact, she was contemplating driving into D.C. and parking in front of Annabelle's building. Carole Ann closed her eyes and cursed herself as she listened to the jovial voice relay the details of an argument Ruthie Eva had had with Annabelle the previous day.

"How awful for her," she responded, forcing what she hoped sounded like a mixture of concern and sadness into her voice, for she knew that Ruth had not spoken to her daughter the previous day. "Would you happen to have the phone number at this cabin, Mr. Williams? I'd like to commiserate in person." And when his cheery tones informed her that there was no telephone in Ruthie Eva's fishing shack, anger and dismay turned to foreboding. She thanked him with a contrived cheeriness of her own, punched off the phone and waited while all the pieces clicked into place. Then she picked up the phone again. "Jake. In my safe, in the 'I' file, there's a Garden of Eden card with Ruth Simmons's cell phone number on the back. Get it quick."

Within five minutes, she heard Ruth's voice answer the phone. "Ruthie!" she exclaimed. "Are you at your cabin and are you alone?" And in the relief that followed, she demanded and got specific directions on how to get there and Ruthie's promise not to leave until she arrived.

11

AS SOON AS THEY CROSSED THE LINE INTO WEST VIR-
ginia and began the ascent into the mountains, Carole Ann's sense of
foreboding increased. Perhaps if Jake hadn't yelled and cussed so
when she told him where they were headed and why, she wouldn't be
so rattled; but it wasn't just the yelling and cussing, it was the fear she
heard in his voice. And he'd really meant it when he ordered her to
turn around and come home and to hell with Ruthie Eva Simmons.
And she'd really wanted to obey him this one time. And this was the
one time she really couldn't.

There still was significant snow cover on the ground and it was at
least fifteen degrees colder than it had been in D.C. Carole Ann
looked at the map again, checking it against Ruthie's directions. She
felt the truck slow and looked up to see a new-looking gas station-
cum-convenience store. She nodded her approval and Jocelyn turned
into the parking lot, driving to that corner farthest from the road to
park.

"What's our plan?" she asked in her quiet voice.

"I don't really have a plan," Carole Ann answered. They already
had decided that since it was likely that Bill Williams had directed

Ruthie to the remote location, it was just as likely that someone was being sent to . . . to do she didn't know what and didn't want to contemplate the possibilities. "Since we don't know the terrain, we can't sneak in, and I don't want to risk calling her again in case somebody has showed up."

"But if we go driving up to the door and she's in some kind of trouble, we could get her killed," Jocelyn said with a reasoned calmness that irritated Carole Ann.

"Then what do you suggest?"

"That I walk in," Jocelyn replied in the same tone. "You drop me off when we're within a couple of miles, then hold back and give me, say, half an hour. I'll foot it in, try to get a sense of the situation, and I'll call you. If you don't hear from me, you'll know to call in the Marines."

It was a good plan. The only difficulty facing Carole Ann was fear. It had come upon her suddenly and without warning. She squeezed her hands into tight fists and took several deep breaths. "I should give you my cell phone number," she finally managed, "in case, for some reason, I'm not in the truck."

"And why wouldn't you be in the truck?" For the first time, the calm left Jocelyn's voice.

"Shit happens," Carole Ann replied dryly, herself once again. "I don't know why I wouldn't be in the truck, Jocelyn, but it could happen and it would be advisable for you to have my cell phone number and for me to have yours, *n'cest-ce pas?*"

"*Mais ouis, madame,*" she responded, and each of them programmed the other's number into her own phone.

"Only . . ." Carole Ann began, and stopped.

"Only what?" Jocelyn asked after waiting for a completed sentence that didn't come.

Carole Ann was recalling the ringing of a cell phone in the woods—the swamps of Louisiana, really—on a dank, muggy night. "I just hope the woods aren't so sparse and naked that you stand out like pepper in the salt shaker," she said.

"I'll hug a tree if I feel the need to blend in," Jocelyn said with a laugh.

They alternately visited the bathroom inside the store, and Carole Ann was in the driver's seat when they resumed their journey. Both were quiet on the final leg of the trip, partly because each was absorbed by her own thoughts of the mission ahead of them, and partly because once they left the service station, they were on rutted, rural roads that were little more than lanes, following markers instead of street signs. But Ruth's directions were precise: barns were where she said they'd be, painted the colors she said they'd be painted; the rusted hulk of a tractor on its side was where she said it would be; and the uprooted ancient maple was where she said it would be. And, finally, the virtually invisible path that would lead to the fishing shack was where Ruthie Eva said it would be.

"Drive down about a quarter mile and let me out," Jocelyn said, studying the landscape.

"Will you be warm enough?" Carole Ann asked. "And dry?"

She nodded and as the truck slowed, her hand gripped the door handle. "Give me thirty minutes to reach the house, then drive in unless you hear differently," and as the truck slowed to a halt, she opened the door, jumped out, slammed the door, and darted into the woods. Within seconds, Carole Ann no longer could distinguish Jocelyn from the forest.

She looked at the clock, then eased the truck forward into a slight verge and backed up, then executed a U-turn. She planned to drive back toward the service station and, after ten minutes, turn around and follow the rusted tractor and uprooted tree back to Ruthie Eva's hideaway.

All morning, all the way from Washington, she had been checking to make certain they hadn't been followed. That task became easier once they left the heavily traveled interstates and turned onto the state roads. In a couple of months, they would be choked with campers and pickups pulling boats; but now, this time of year, only the locals occupied and utilized these tiny back roads, and the locals, for the most part, drove well-used, American-made automobiles and trucks. Which is why, even at a distance of perhaps a quarter of a mile, the approaching vehicle bleeped loudly—and ominously—on her radar screen. "Dammit to hell!" she yelled to herself, and forced the gas pedal to the floor. She was doing eighty when she passed the white Range Rover.

She knew she could not return to the gas station, and a quick glance at the clock told her that even if she wanted to, it was much too early to rendezvous with Jocelyn; she could put them both in danger. She checked the rearview mirror: no sign of the white Range Rover. She sped past the gas station and, making a quick decision, slowed enough to make a hasty left turn into what she hoped was a road and not merely a path to somebody else's fishing shack. It was wider than that, she thought, though it was heavily rutted, and the ruts were ice-filled, so the truck slid and shimmied. She realized that she was climbing, and wondered if four-wheel drive would help. Then she saw another road, again to the left, and decided to take it since that would take her in the general direction of Ruthie Eva's. Then, she wondered, did she want to go in that direction? Did she want to risk leading MacDonald—and she was certain that it was MacDonald driving the white Range Rover—to Ruthie Eva?

She looked again into the rearview mirror. She was alone in the woods. She shifted the truck into four-wheel drive and, miraculously, remembered the emergency call button. She studied the truck's console. There it was, next to the telephone. She pressed it and before she had completely withdrawn her hand, an answering buzzer sounded, followed by a voice: "This is Central, who is this, please?"

"Carole Ann Gibson."

"Are you in danger, C.A.?"

She hesitated only slightly before replying, "Yes. I'm being pursued by a white Ranger Rover that I believe to be driven by John David MacDonald."

"I have you located on the map, C.A. You're way off-road . . . there's a vehicle approaching your location . . ."

She looked into the rearview mirror but saw nothing. She threw the truck into gear and it jumped forward, moving slowly but steadily up the ragged road. Then, abruptly, the road ended. There was nothing ahead of her but forest, and nothing behind her but J. D. MacDonald.

"I'm bailing out, Central. I just ran out of road."

"Where is Jocelyn?"

"With Ruthie Eva . . ." She glanced hurriedly at the clock. "I'm supposed to meet her in exactly ten minutes. Central, turn this thing off so nobody can find out that you know where I am. I'm leaving the truck, continuing on foot to Jocelyn's location. I've got my cell phone. Get me some backup as soon as you can."

She turned off the truck's engine, removed the keys from the ignition, and, as she slammed the door, pressed the button that both locked the vehicle and set the alarm. Then she began running. Carefully, because she didn't want to risk an injury, but as quickly as she dared. She hadn't run in two weeks and while she found it invigorating, it also was taxing. The frigid air seared her lungs, and the higher altitude was taking its toll. She stopped and melded herself against the trunk of a massive oak. She needed to catch her breath and to use the tree as camouflage, to study her surroundings. She had run directly toward where she thought Ruthie Eva's cabin should be. She looked back and no longer could see the truck. She was aware that she was angled downhill instead of up, and she thought that was a good sign.

Her breathing was under control and her heart had ceased its beating so that she could listen to the forest. Hearing nothing but the whisper of the wind, she released her hold on the tree and plunged forward, running again, but slower, as the ground cover became denser. Then she was angling uphill again. She stopped to check her direction, but there was no point of origin. She no longer was certain where she'd left the truck, nor that she was, in fact, running toward Ruthie Eva's. She looked at her watch. She'd been out of the truck for fifteen minutes. That made her five minutes late for her scheduled arrival. Jocelyn, she thought, would allow a maximum of fifteen minutes—

What she heard could have been caused by an animal; it was a larger sound than the wind would have made, or a bird. She was out in the open. She turned, peering into the brush all around her. She began running again, her heart beating now in fear and not in exertion. She was aware that she now was running away from something rather than toward something, and she therefore was running faster and with less caution. She stopped suddenly, grabbing a sapling with both hands to keep herself from falling. Whatever was running in step with her, off to her right, didn't stop when she stopped and the sound carried, louder than anything she could have imagined. Then it, too, stopped, and silence prevailed. Someone was following her. She looked frantically around and, seeing nothing, no one, prepared to propel herself forward.

"Stay where you are, Miss Gibson, and do not move."

John MacDonald stepped out of the brush forty feet above her. His stance, and the weapon he trained on her, served to convey the inadvisability of attempting to run. She turned to fully face him.

"I knew that you were a city jogger, but you traverse the woods with the skill of a rabbit or a deer."

She looked at him steadily, seeing the man who had silently and elegantly wheeled the service cart into Richard Islington's library, poured coffee, and departed with barely a glance at his employer, to say nothing of a word in greeting. A pity, given the elegance of his language. No American this. He stood tall and still—and silent and elegant—improbably clad in a fawn suede jacket, a black wool turtleneck visible beneath it, black wool slacks, and calf-high, all-weather boots, into which the bottoms of his trousers were tucked. He stood poised and ready to shoot her if necessary. Had he already murdered his employer? He almost certainly murdered his own brother and his brother's business partner. And perhaps his employer's daughter . . . She shuddered. She didn't believe that it would pose significant difficulty for him to add her to the list.

"Why are you here, Miss Gibson?"

She still didn't speak and it was apparent that her silence was annoying him. To what extent? she wondered. So much as to make him careless enough to reveal information to her? Or merely angry enough to shoot her? She was thinking of something to say, some words that would agitate him, challenge him, when her phone rang. She'd have laughed had not his reaction been so dangerously startling.

"What is that!" he screamed, whirling around and pointing his gun into the bush. "Who's there?" He whirled around again, another three-sixty, waving the gun and firing off a round.

The phone trilled again and she yelled at him, "It's my phone, MacDonald! For God's sake, it's my cell phone!" He was unhinged and she now knew that it would be a fatal mistake to bait or goad him. "It's in my pocket," she said more calmly.

"Do you have any idea who it might be?" His face was contorted as he struggled for control.

"My office. I haven't checked in this hour," she replied as the phone trilled again.

"Then answer it, please," he said, with a degree of restored calm. "And be very careful in what you say and how you say it, Miss Gibson," he said, sounding dangerously normal.

She unzipped her jacket then raised her left hand as she gently eased her right hand inside to retrieve the phone. It trilled again as she punched a button and held it to her ear. "Hello?" She heard Jocelyn's panicked voice wondering where the hell she was. "I know, and I'm sorry. I guess I lost track of time . . . no, everything's fine. I'll call in the next hour." She held the phone toward MacDonald, both hands raised. "My office . . ."

"You already told me that and now I know you're to call them in an hour. If you're properly cooperative, you should be able to make that call on time."

She lowered her left hand slightly and opened her jacket, holding the edge between her thumb and forefinger. She lowered her right hand, with the phone in it, and returned it to the pocket. Her movements had been slow and exaggerated so that he would not mistake her meaning. She kept her hands slightly up and toward him.

"What are you doing out here, Mr. MacDonald?"

He looked at her as if she had gone mad. "What am *I* doing out here?" He shook his head in disbelief, then he laughed. "You do amaze me. And since you're so amazingly forthright, I think you deserve an answer: I'm doing the same thing I imagine you're doing. I'm looking for Annabelle. And for Ruth. Where are they?"

She struggled to maintain her aura of control and to conceal her surprise at hearing him speak of Annabelle. "I don't know where Annabelle is, Mr. MacDonald, and since I'm a little lost myself at the moment—"

"You're a liar!" He spat the accusation at her with such venom that she recoiled, and was thankful that he was as far away from her as he was. He had changed in an instant. Rage purpled his face and veins protruded in his forehead and his eyes bulged. But there was something else fueling the rage and, difficult as it was to reconcile with his behavior, Carole Ann thought it was fear.

He thought Annabelle was alive, and he'd made no mention of Jocelyn. Did that mean that he *hadn't* been following them? And if he hadn't, what was he doing here? "I'm not lying, MacDonald. I lost my bearings when I was running through the woods and I really don't know where Annabelle is."

"Kneel down, Miss Gibson."

"I beg your pardon?" She was taken completely off guard and totally startled by his direction.

"I said kneel down, and lock your hands over your head. I've researched you extensively and I don't intend to get close enough for you to display your martial arts prowess." He chuckled to himself. "Richard thought the articles made you sound too noble, citing as they did your disdain for weapons and touting your emphasis on the *arts* aspect of martial arts, and therefore he found them not entirely believable. I, however, believe every word. Now. Do as I ask and kneel down!" he said, his voice so thick with tension that the gun quivered in his hand. She obeyed.

He began to inch closer to her, keeping the gun trained on her but having to be careful of his footing. She was downhill from him, and the underbrush was a thick tangle. He stumbled and wobbled once, and quickly righted himself. The gun remained steady in his hand. He might be a novice as an intimidator, but he clearly was an expert with a gun. Even if she could manage to surprise him with a display of her own weapon, she was no expert.

"If you don't know where Annabelle is, why are you out here? How would you know to come here? And why did you evade me when you saw me on the road? Your behavior is suspicious, to say the least."

"*My* behavior is suspicious? Have you lost your mind?" she snapped at him, finally too irritated to remain frightened. "You kidnapped my partner's wife and murdered our client and destroyed his business, all the while pretending to be a servant, and you call *my* behavior suspicious? What kind of drugs are you on, MacDonald?"

He stared at her for a full minute. Then he smiled and nodded his head to her, signaling a touché of sorts. "Obviously your good press is well earned, Miss Gibson; you're every bit as tough as your notices report, though you do err in several significant respects. I did not kidnap Mr. Graham's wife, nor did I murder Mr. Childress."

"But you did kill your brother, didn't you, Mr. MacDonald?"

"Actually, no, I didn't do that, either, though I have planned in my mind, for years and years, ways to rid myself of him. He's really an awful human being." There was genuine sadness in his voice and Carole Ann was beginning to feel more and more like Alice down the bunny hole. He'd spoken of Sanderson in the present tense.

"You're going to have a difficult time convincing a jury of that, especially since nobody's seen him since Harry Childress was murdered and since he was doing his dirty deeds in your name. You have motive, you have method," with a nod to the weapon in his hand, "and you no doubt had opportunity. And unless you kill me, too, I certainly intend to contribute to your conviction." She hoped she sounded convincing because she no longer was convinced that John MacDonald had killed his brother or anyone else. Fear was wreaking havoc with the man's emotions.

"Does anyone else think I'm guilty of having committed these crimes?"

"Quite a few people, as a matter of fact. And besides, I saw your hand, MacDonald," she said, aware of a slight edge of hysteria creeping into her voice. "I know you were responsible for Grace Graham's kidnapping. I know you were there that night."

"You saw my . . . I've no idea what you're talking about." He spoke with such guileless surprise that she believed him. And yet, she'd seen the ring. Twice.

"The woman's ring you're probably wearing at this very moment, Mr. MacDonald, on the baby finger of your left hand. You were wearing it the night I exchanged the OnShore and Seaboard documents for Mrs. Graham and I saw it. That's how I knew to connect you to all of this: I saw the ring again when you served us coffee at Mr. Islington's the other day. . . ." She gasped. On his *left* hand. The kidnapper had worn the ring on his right hand.

He closed his eyes and his body sagged, as if some of the air had been siphoned from him. "Sandy, you fool," he whispered. Then he smiled sadly and there was not the slightest trace remaining of the raging, murderous pseudo-mercenary of a moment ago. "Let me tell you the story of this ring," he said softly, raising his left hand, removing the glove, and looking at the sparkling circle on his baby finger. "My brother gave this ring to Annabelle Islington when he promised to marry her. She didn't know he was a womanizing scum. She didn't know men like him at all. For all his faults, Richard Islington was a good father. Not a warm one or an openly affectionate one, but a good one. He exposed Annabelle to as much good as he could buy, and kept as much evil and ugly away from her as he could afford to shelter her from."

"Then how did she meet your brother?"

He sighed, as if he himself were the helpless, hapless father of the rebellious daughter. "They all leave the nest, Miss Gibson. She graduated from college and moved out on her own. Her father disagreed about the wisdom of that—she moved to Falls Church to placate him because he believed living in the city was dangerous, and she deliberately pursued activities and behaviors and people she knew he would oppose."

"Like your brother."

He nodded. "They met at a movie, of all places. I learned of their association purely by accident. Even after she moved out on her own, I periodically visited her, just to be certain that she was all right. And one day, Sandy was there."

"You're very close to her, aren't you, Mr. MacDonald?"

"I've known her most of her life. I began working for Richard when she was seven. I drove her to school and to ballet classes and horseback-riding and piano lessons. I was Mr. Islington's assistant, but it gradually fell to me to care for Annabelle as she grew older, and I didn't mind. She's really a very nice girl," he said almost proudly.

"Then why are you trying to kill her?" Carole Ann shot at him, wounding as she'd intended.

His head snapped back as if he'd been slapped. "I'm not trying to kill her, for God's sake! Are you mad? I'm trying to find her . . . to find out what Sandy may have told her. My brother created more trouble for me than I know of, Miss Gibson."

"You didn't know he'd used your name to buy his way into partnership with Harry Childress?"

"No!" he exploded, the anger back in full force, but without the hysterical rage. "The bastard! Annabelle told me. Apparently she surprised him with a visit at the warehouse and called him Sandy or . . . Jimmy is what she called him. And Harry Childress was standing there and asked who Jimmy was . . . is that what put you and Graham onto him? He was so scared and so angry! I, of course, enjoyed every moment of his misery, especially when I discovered my inadvertent part."

"He used the Social Security number of a John David MacDonald from Georgia who's deceased. That's what caught our attention."

He blanched. The blood drained from his face and he blinked rapidly. "That was my father," he said quietly. "He escaped to Canada to avoid the army and Vietnam back in the 1960s. He met my mother, produced me, and, with the United States Military Police on his trail, he escaped again. He was killed in a car crash when I was seven."

"So, what about the ring?"

He shrugged and looked again at his hand. "Annabelle learned that Sandy was much worse than a liar. He had numerous women, which he freely admitted to her. He also admitted that his desire to marry her was sparked, at first by her father's wealth, and then, later, when he found out about Ruthie's trust fund. She gave the ring back to him and he was going to give it to one of his other girls, some secretary at the warehouse. It had no more meaning than that to him. So I took it from him. I don't know what I planned to do with it, but I couldn't allow him to give it to some secretary or, worse, to that one who was following him all around everywhere."

Carole Ann thought immediately of the Jane Doe in the warehouse. "A young woman followed him about?"

He nodded. "She even had the temerity to show up at my home! Of course, it wasn't her fault. Sandy told her to come."

"Where is your brother, Mr. MacDonald? Since you didn't kill him."

"I don't know and I don't care. Ask that fat old bastard he works for."

Fat old bastard. The final piece dropped into place. Bill Williams, Carole Ann thought. All along it was Bill Williams pulling the strings.

When the alarm sounded, MacDonald jumped, stumbled, and almost fell. Carole Ann knew instantly that the silence-shattering whoop was the Explorer's alarm, that someone must have tried to enter it. She rolled over on the ground, crab-crawling into the underbrush, digging into her pocket for her gun. It felt familiar and comfortable in her hand. She rolled over and fired toward MacDonald; she did not try to aim. She quickly fired off two more rounds. Then, above the noise of the truck's alarm, she heard men's voices yelling. Then she heard MacDonald cry out in anguish before she heard him crashing through the brush. She scrambled to her feet and began her own scurry.

"Jocelyn, if you hear me, I'm fine," she said into her chest. "I repeat, I am not wounded and I'm moving and I hope I'm moving in your direction." She picked up her pace, running wildly and with abandon, tree branches slashing at her face. Suddenly she stopped and listened. She thought she'd heard her name called. The truck's alarm was still screeching in the distance, but that was the only sound she heard.

She began moving again, not running but picking her way through underbrush that had grown considerably denser. The gun she still held in her right hand was impeding her progress; she needed two hands to move the branches. . . . "Shit! You scared the shit out of me!" She pushed aside a branch with her left hand and came face-to-face with Jocelyn Anderson.

"Damn smart move leaving that phone on," she said in her usual calm tone.

"I thought so," Carole Ann replied, striving for an equal degree of calm.

"Where's MacDonald going?"

"If we're lucky, directly into the arms of the West Virginia State Police. Or the county sheriff's deputies. Or whoever Central called. Is Ruthie Eva all right?"

Jocelyn nodded. "Scared out of her mind, but she's fine. She says Bill Williams sent her here to meet her daughter but then she panicked, wondering why, if Williams knew where Annabelle was, he didn't just tell her."

"Good for her! How much further, Jocelyn?"

"We're there. Or here. Or whatever," she said with an exasperated grin.

Carole Ann's hackles were on their way up and her eyes opened wide. What Bill Williams had called a "shack" was, in reality, a woven wonder growing out of the underbrush. It was small, no more than one room, and it appeared to be made of the underbrush itself—it was thatched and woven—Carole Ann didn't know what to call it; she'd never seen anything like it. She stepped closer to it and touched it, in some way to convince herself that it was real. She looked inside but darkness stared back at her: a small, tidy, clean darkness. "She is a remarkable woman," she said, speaking essentially to herself and only barely aware that her words were audible.

"I'm a very simple woman, Mrs. Crandall, who has had more good luck than I know what to do with." Ruthie Eva, somehow, was behind her, dressed from head to toe in ski clothes and with a heavy wool blanket wrapped around her shoulders.

"We need to get out of here," Jocelyn said with urgency. "C.A., we'll take Miss Simmons's vehicle. I don't think we should take the time to look for the truck, and I don't think we want to talk to the authorities just yet."

Carole Ann agreed and they ran around to the side of the little cottage to where Ruthie Eva's forest-green four-wheel-drive sport utility was parked. In the spring and summer, it would be virtually invisible parked here.

"Do you mind if I drive, Miss Simmons?" Jocelyn asked, even as she was approaching the driver's side door. "We may need to move in a hurry and I wouldn't want you to be accused of doing anything illegal."

Ruthie Eva took a deep breath and handed over the keys. She climbed into the backseat, leaving the front to Carole Ann. They were under way in seconds, bumping along the lane that would lead them out to the auxilary road that would return them, eventually, to the interstate. "If you want, I can show you a back way," she said tentatively.

"Show me!" Jocelyn cried enthusiastically and gratefully. "I would do just about anything to avoid running into the West Virginia gendarmes." And, following directions, she slowed to a crawl and turned onto a road only a native would have known existed and there, before them, was the river.

"What majesty!" Carole Ann exclaimed. "No wonder you chose this spot. But why on earth do you call that a shack?"

Ruthie Eva chuckled and drawled, "Well, it ain't a house and it ain't a cabin. It's just one little room, no electricity, no running water. Just a cot and a table and a couple of chairs. I cook on the pit in the back."

"What did Williams tell you?" Carole Ann asked.

"To come up here and meet Annabelle. That she was in some kind of trouble and that he was sending her up here to be safe. It wasn't until I got here that what he said didn't make sense."

"I called you, Ruth, early this morning, and you didn't answer."

"My phone was out of order when I woke up. . . . Oh, my God! Do you think somebody . . . Bill called me on my portable because he said my line was out of order. . . . Oh, my God. If I didn't have this little phone . . ."

"*What would* have *happened?*" Carole Ann asked the question only of herself. "*Who would* have *harmed you?* And why?" She found that she believed John MacDonald's claim not to have harmed anyone. But if he wasn't in collusion with Jimmy Sanderson, then who was? "The second car," she muttered.

"The gray hatchback?" asked Jocelyn.

She nodded. "MacDonald had been following me, but he wasn't trying to kidnap me; he was hoping that I'd lead him to Annabelle. The guy with the gun *was* trying to scare me off. He's part of whoever kidnapped Grace and killed Harry Childress and torched the warehouse."

"Abduct you? Hurt you? John? John wouldn't hurt you or anyone else. And what does any of this have to do with Annabelle? Or with Richard, for that matter?" Ruthie Eva's confusion was equal parts anger and fear, a mirror image of Carole Ann's own feelings.

"I'm not absolutely certain," she began, but Ruthie Eva interrupted.

"You don't know where Annabelle is, do you?"

Carole Ann hesitated for a moment before responding. "No, I don't."

"Did you shoot John?" she asked hesitantly and fearfully.

And Carole Ann actually managed a laugh. "If I did, it would be a miracle of biblical proportions! I was on the ground, rolling away from him. I fired in his general direction, but above him. I just wanted him to know that I was armed and I prayed that he would just leave me alone. Then I heard yelling and I heard MacDonald running away, so I ran in the opposite direction."

"Speaking of which, what do I do here?" Jocelyn asked, and Carole Ann, who had turned around to look at Ruthie Eva, faced the front to see a fork in the road.

"Go right," she said, and before anyone could ask a question they passed a huge, blue MARYLAND WELCOMES YOU sign.

"We're in *Maryland?*" asked Jocelyn.

"Yep," replied Ruthie Eva. "And in about fifteen or twenty miles, you'll see the signs for the interstate."

"Way to go—"

"I know where this is!" Carole Ann exclaimed. "I know where we are! This is where they had Grace!"

12

"WHO'S GRACE?" ASKED RUTHIE EVA.

"Are you sure?" asked Jocelyn, something like fear heavy in her voice. Then she composed herself and added, "Call 'em and let 'em know we're OK and heading home."

Carole Ann reached into her pocket for her phone and found it was still on and the "low battery" light was blinking. She shut it off and extended a hand to Jocelyn, who, without a word, reached into her own pocket, retrieved her phone, and dropped it into C.A.'s palm. She punched it on and punched in the familiar GGI number. "Central, this is C.A. Gibson. We're coming in, ETA four hours." She listened, the expression on her face changing to something unreadable. She relayed their exact location, and then listened for a few moments more. "Jake," she said after an interval. "Well, I'll be damned," she said after having listened for several long minutes. Cradling the phone between her ear and shoulder, she reached for the notepad and pen on the dash and wrote briefly. "We're fine, really," she said finally, "and we'll see you soon."

She switched off the phone, sat back, and closed her eyes, signaling that she needed not to be disturbed. She thought she had gathered all the pieces and fit them into their proper places in the puzzle. She was wrong. MacDonald was as innocent as he'd claimed—he wasn't a mass murderer or a terrorist—he'd told the truth about that. And James Sanderson had an accomplice. A partner who still was very much alive and active. A partner whom Jake had identified and who, at this very moment, was closer to them than they could ever have imagined.

"Slight change of plan," she said to Jocelyn, as quietly as possible. She knew that Ruthie Eva would be aware that she'd spoken, but she thought that if she spoke obviously and only to Jocelyn, that their passenger would be uninterested. At least for a while. Carole Ann passed on the directions she'd just received from Jake, wishing she could share the information but not daring to. Jocelyn followed the directions perfectly, not needing to have them repeated or refined. "Good thing you're a lousy actor," Carole Ann muttered, and Jocelyn threw her a sideways grin.

"Where are you going?" Ruthie Eva asked suddenly and almost shrilly. "This is the way to Bill's. Why are you going this way? What are you doing? Why are we here?"

"Your daughter is here," Carole Ann responded, as they turned off Interstate 68 and onto an access road, heading north. In an oddly familiar way, the area reminded her of the Four Corners of the far West, the point at which Colorado, Utah, Arizona, and New Mexico all touched one another. The topography and terrain were vastly different here, but they'd crossed easily from Virginia into West Virginia, then into Maryland, and were now skirting the Pennsylvania border. The area was heavily forested and considered mountainous, though it was, in her mind, considerably tamer than the Chuska or the San Juan Mountains, where the lowlands were seven thousand feet. But it was beautiful here, and wild and dangerous enough for the uninitiated or the unaware.

She thought of the night she'd shimmied back and forth on the icy roads up here, alone, terrified, and responsible for the safe passage of her partner's wife. The thought, the memory of that night produced the sensation of cold and she shivered. "Here we are," she said, as they crested a gentle incline, and two GGI trucks and half a dozen Maryland State Patrol vehicles came into view, all of them hugging the almost nonexistent shoulder of an impossibly narrow stretch of road. All day Carole Ann had marveled at the fact that they were, at most, four hours from Washington, D.C., and yet their surroundings were rural. And, as she now knew, these rural woods and forests harbored the secret fantasies of many of Washington's wealthy.

Jocelyn made a U-turn and pulled up behind one of the GGI Explorers, Ruthie Eva's Sportage sitting all the way off the paved road, given its diminutive size. Carole Ann turned to face her. She'd wrapped her arms around herself and, huddled as she was in the blanket, she was the frightened child she was frightened for.

"It appears, Ruthie, that Bill Williams has some involvement in—"

"I don't believe that," she said flatly. "I won't. I can't."

"I know." She had trouble believing it herself.

Ruth was shaking her head back and forth. "That just doesn't make sense. If he wanted to hurt me or my daughter, why not just steal the money? He could have hurt either one of us years ago."

"This isn't about you and Annabelle. You just happened to get in the way. This is about Bill and Jimmy Sanderson, who just happened to be John MacDonald's brother, who just happened to be involved with your daughter, who just happened to be the daughter of Sanderson's brother's employer. This is about bad luck and bad timing." And greed, she thought disgustedly. It's always about greed.

Ever since they'd pulled onto the shoulder and parked, the activity at the area had increased to the point that it now appeared as if something were under seige. An ambulance, a crime scene van, and three more state trooper vehicles had joined those already on the scene and, as Carole Ann watched, a West Virginia State Police cruiser eased up and joined the queue. She had a momentary sinking feeling, which she quickly banished. Aside from the illegal discharge of an unregistered weapon, she had committed no crime; and since she wasn't claiming to be the victim of one, she had nothing to fear from West Virginia authorities. She hoped.

All of the activity seemed directed up a paved and graded driveway, flanked on either side by columned lampposts; this was not the kind of trail that had led to Grace, that had led to Ruthie's shack, that had provided a convenient albeit temporary escape for Carole Ann earlier that day. She assumed that somewhere up that road, Bill Williams had a house or a cabin, and that he was there or that Annabelle Islington was there. And, she realized, this is where he had to have been when she talked to him earlier. He was up here and to prevent the police from being sent to look for Ruthie Eva and raising an alarm, he told her about the fishing shack. And Jake somehow had smelled the rat.

She turned around to look at Ruthie Eva, still hunched into her blanket and all but cowering in a corner of the already small vehicle. "He sent you up here because he wanted you out of the way. Whatever he and Sanderson are up to has come unglued. I don't believe he really intended for harm to come to you or Annabelle, but he may not have been able to prevent it. You and your daughter, and your . . . Richard . . . represent money, Ruthie. Both of you would pay dearly for her safe return."

She squeezed her eyes shut tightly. "Has something happened to Annabelle? Has someone hurt her?"

"Tell me about John MacDonald, Ruthie," Carole Ann asked, wanting to avoid answering a question that she didn't know the answer to, and needing answers to other questions, like MacDonald's presence near Ruthie's shack.

"What do you want to know?" she asked in a voice devoid of emotion, in a tone so flat that the question in it almost didn't exist.

"Whatever you can tell me."

"I love him," she said simply. "I have for years. He stayed with Richard because of Annabelle. He was my eyes and my ears and my heart all those years. He gave my daughter what I couldn't, wasn't allowed to give her. We're going to be married as soon as my divorce from Richard is finalized. And I'm almost ten years older than he is, in case you were wondering. What else do you want to know?"

What else, indeed? Carole Ann thought to herself, as questions that were answered led to the formulation of additional questions; for if John MacDonald's actions were the result of his love for Ruthie Eva Simmons and her daughter, along with his need to extricate himself from his brother's duplicitous behavior, then all of the weight and responsibility for the ugliness and the madness of the past couple of months rested on another man's shoulders.

"What is Bill Williams's full name?" Carole Ann asked, and she could tell that her seemingly unrelated questions were irritating Ruthie Eva and confusing Jocelyn.

"William Archibald Williams the third," she replied a bit testily. "Why?"

"Because," Carole Ann responded slowly, "that's the missing link. It's Archibald Williams who is the attorney for Seaboard Packaging and Manufacturing, not *Wilson*. He's where all of this begins. He's the one common thread holding all these different pieces together. That's why he lied to me on the phone this morning. He didn't know I knew that Annabelle couldn't have spoken to her mother."

Jocelyn made a startled sound and a quick move and Carole Ann looked first at her, then where she was looking. There was movement all around them—all the cops were on the run, most of them with weapons drawn.

Jocelyn and Carole Ann threw open their doors and jumped out of the little truck simultaneously. Ruthie Ann followed suit, a look of horror on her face. Jocelyn was running down the shoulder, skirting in and out between police vehicles, her head whipping from side to side, looking, Carole Ann knew, for Jake or somebody else from GGI; and if she didn't connect soon, she'd be ordered back out of the way.

"Ruthie, please stay here," Carole Ann said, turning to take the other woman gently by the arm. "You could be hurt."

"If my daughter really is up there, this is the first time in her life that I can be there for her. Don't try to stop me. Please don't try to stop me."

Carole Ann released her arm and watched her run forward as the forgotten blanket first trailed from her shoulders, then dropped unnoticed to the ground. She stood where she was, trying to get a sense of what might be happening. She didn't know how far up the road Williams's place was; and since she had no idea what had prompted all the hurried activity—she hadn't heard a gunshot—she was content to wait. She needed the time to think, to sort out all the various details and twists and turns that had led her and Jake—all of them—down so many blind alleys and toward so many false conclusions. She picked up Ruthie's blanket, shook it, and wrapped it around herself. She leaned against the little green truck, thankful for the warmth.

Part of her consciousness remained tuned into the activity immediately surrounding her. She was conscious of listening for gunshots, of sounds of pain or struggle. Neither Jocelyn nor Ruthie had returned, so she imagined that Jake's presence was, so far, at least tolerated if not welcomed. Otherwise, they'd all have been sent packing by now.

She shivered and realized that she was chilly and, at the same moment, her stomach rumbled and she realized that she also was hungry. She looked at her watch. No wonder! It was after one o'clock and she'd had exactly a cup and a half of coffee all day. She shivered again and wrapped the blanket tighter and was deciding whether to go in search of Jake when movement off to her right captured her attention. She turned to look but saw nothing but the dense woods, and nothing moving within, yet she was certain that she had seen something and that it had not been a bird or the wind rustling the vegetation.

"C.A.!" She turned to see who was calling, and then quickly returned her focus to the woods. She heard and saw the movement at the same time: someone was running through the woods. She started to run, dropping the blanket and turning to look back at Jocelyn, who had called her and who already had begun to run toward her. Carole Ann ran on the graveled shoulder, not wanting to enter the forest for fear of losing her footing. Whoever she was pursuing was wearing red, and she was outrunning him—or her—at the moment; they were running almost parallel to each other, the red streak bobbing and weaving as the runner tried to dodge the slapping and scratching branches and brambles. Carole Ann knew her face would bear the marks of the similar assault she had suffered barely more than an hour earlier.

Suddenly, the red blur stilled. There was no movement and no sound. She stopped, grateful for the opportunity to catch her breath, and was wondering whether she should plunge into the woods when she heard pounding feet approaching. She turned to see Jocelyn upon her, but before she could speak, she was pushed forward, into the woods, and knocked to the ground. And at that moment, she heard the branches rustle above her and then a muffled popping sound.

"That son of a bitch!" Jocelyn exclaimed.

"What." Carole Ann was too dazed to ask a real question.

"He shot at you, the son of a bitch!"

Before Carole Ann could respond, they heard the loud crashing through the brush and both women propelled themselves up and forward, diving into the forest as if into a pool. "Look for red," she said in a low voice, and Jocelyn nodded. They ran side by side for a dozen yards, then, by unspoken agreement, they widened the distance between themselves, remaining parallel to each other but creating a vise. Carole Ann kept near the edge of the forest, with easy access to the road if that became necessary, while Jocelyn angled deeper into the woods. The prey could only continue forward, with one pursuer above and slightly behind, the other below and slightly ahead.

As had happened earlier, the underbrush thickened, slowing their movement and obliterating the periodic flashes of red. Unless,

C.A. thought, the runner had removed whatever was flashing red through the forest. "Damn," she muttered to herself as she considered that possibility. She looked to her left, hoping to be able to see Jocelyn. Failing at that, she halted and listened for sounds of movement. There were none. There was no sound. A sinking, helpless feeling overtook her as she wondered what to do. Then, remembering what happened the last time she stopped to think, she dropped to her knees and rolled behind a bush, and as her breathing slowed, she wondered how long she'd been running alone. When she stopped, she hadn't heard a sound. No one else was running; hadn't been running for a while, she thought.

She slid a hand into her jacket pocket and withdrew her gun. Whoever they were chasing already had shot at her once—shot at her using a gun with a silencer. She recalled the whoosh of the bullet through the trees where a split second earlier she'd been standing, and the delayed *pop* of the gun's firing. Then she had a sickening thought: Had Jocelyn been shot? Is that why she no longer was running, why Carole Ann couldn't hear her, couldn't see her? She rolled over toward the road. This was the way out—the only way out. He had been trying to reach and cross the road when she'd spied him initially, she was certain of that. And she didn't think it was possible that he already could have crossed without her seeing him . . .

And there he was, in a solid black, turtleneck sweater, twenty yards ahead of her, on the shoulder, looking back at her. She stood and began running toward him, running as fast as she could. She had more experience as a distance runner than as a sprinter, but she observed by the stride of the man running ahead of her that he hadn't much experience as any kind of runner. He lumbered more than ran and he'd been at it for a while now, too long, and Carole Ann guessed that fatigue would catch up with him and overcome him pretty quickly. Even though she hadn't done it for a couple of weeks, she was accustomed to running five miles a day. She was not yet winded. And she could sustain a sprint for another few yards if necessary.

Fortunately, it was not. The man's legs obviously were tired, which made them sluggish, which caused his feet to drag. And he fell, flat out, on his face, spread-eagle in the roadway. And his gun flew out of his hand when he fell. Carole Ann summoned an added spurt of energy and reached him before he could regain his feet or reclaim his weapon. It was the man who had blockaded the street and shot at her as she was leaving Beth Childress's house.

She leveled her gun at him, holding it with both hands, hoping that he thought she looked proficient enough to shoot him. She recalled how impressed she'd been with John MacDonald's display earlier and how, if Ruthie Eva was to be believed, he'd no more have shot her than she would shoot the man on the ground in front of her. She didn't need to tell him not to move. He mumbled something and dropped his face into the hard surface of the road. She could hear his labored breathing.

Then, as she was wondering what to do next, she heard Jocelyn's approach. Not because she could hear rustling in the woods from across the road, but because she could hear Jocelyn calling the man a son of a bitch. Over and over. "You shot me, you son of a bitch," she said. Then, "You son of a bitch. I ought to turn you into roadkill." Followed by, "You so much as move, you son of a bitch, and I'll blow your ass to Kingdom Come."

When she was near enough, Carole Ann risked turning her eyes from the man on the ground to Jocelyn, who had indeed been shot. Blood poured from a hole in the left sleeve of her jacket just below the shoulder. "Are you all right?"

"I'm fine," she snapped. "This was a new jacket, too, you son of a bitch."

"Why don't you sit down?" Carole Ann said. "He's not going anywhere."

"Damn straight he's not! Spread your legs as wide as you can and lock your hands behind your head, you ugly son of a bitch," she snarled, and she winced in pain as he obeyed. Then, with Carole Ann's assistance, she obeyed the directive to sit down.

"Do you have your phone, Jocelyn?"

She nodded slowly and pointed toward her left shoulder. They both winced as Carole Ann unzipped the jacket and reached for the phone in the inside pocket. She was scrupulously careful not to touch any part of the other woman's body. She'd been shot and she knew how excruciating the pain could be. She quickly punched in the numbers to Jake's cellular phone. He answered immediately. She told him what had happened and where they were and, knowing that it would be a matter of only a few seconds before they were surrounded by police, she strode over to the man on the ground, who still was breathing heavily, and squatted down before him, gaining as much eye contact as was possible and advisable under the circumstances.

"Life without the possibility of parole. That's your future, unless at some point you inadvertently crossed the line into Virginia, which has the death penalty. And they use it. Do you understand what I'm telling you?" She watched his eyes as the words took effect. "What did Harry Childress find out?"

"That Sandy was packaging coke and smack in the plant and shipping it out in the trucks."

"That's why Seaboard wanted OnShore? They got caught for laundering money, but their real operation was packaging and shipping?"

He nodded as best he could, with his face plastered to the asphalt roadway.

"Did you do the murders?"

"Nooo!" It was a whining, pleading denial that was fully believable. "Sandy did those. I set the fire late that night, like he said, but that's all I did. I swear . . ."

"Who's the other guy? And who's the girl?"

"Sandy's newest babe. Followed him around. And the guy was Archie's partner, Ed something, who was threatening to pull out and leave Sandy holding the bag. That was 'cause of you guys, GGI, you were messing up everything. But Sandy was the only one you could

219

connect to anything. Look, you gotta believe me that I didn't kill any-body! That was Sandy all by his lonesome. He's still got the gun!"

"Where's Sandy now?" She sliced into his protestations and hoped that he didn't notice the underlying anxiety in her voice, and the surprise that carried it. She made him repeat his answer as the screaming of sirens and the roaring of powerful engines obliterated his words.

"C.A.," Jocelyn called out to her in a low, urgent voice, and Carole Ann rushed over and knelt beside her. "Didn't you say that was an illegal weapon?"

She blanched and nodded.

"Then you'd better put it in your pocket. We've got enough ex-plaining to do without that."

She straightened up to see themselves surrounded by Maryland State Patrol vehicles, bars flashing red and blue. Her eyes sought out Jake, and she ran to meet him, her right hand snugly in her pocket. She repeated what she'd just learned and watched the odd mixture of surprise and admiration spread across his face. "He is one crafty bas-tard, isn't he?" he said with a rueful shake of his head. "He's out-smarted us from day one. Stay close to Jocelyn while I go earn us some brownie points with the captain." And he hurried off to confer with a Maryland state trooper who easily was six and a half feet tall. She stifled a giggle at the sight, the gigantic trooper bending almost in half to hear Jake, both of them looking, alternately, grim, ani-mated, surprised, and mad.

She turned to find Jocelyn arguing with two paramedics who were trying to load her onto a stretcher. "I can walk, you guys!" she tried to insist, and seemed not to realize that her voice held ab-solutely no strength or power.

"Jocelyn, it would be better if you rode—"

"And I'm not spending the night at some hospital in Cumber-land, Maryland, and that's the end of that," she announced in a vir-tual whisper, almost completely out of steam.

Carole Ann leaned in close to her. "I personally will call Sergeant

Carpenter, and I will send someone to pick her up and bring her to the Cumberland Hospital."

"You promise?"

"What's the number?" And, using Jocelyn's phone, she punched in the number as it was recited to her and then watched as Jocelyn closed her eyes and allowed the paramedics to lift her onto the stretcher. They snapped it into its upright and rolling position and hustled toward the rear of the medic unit.

She completed her conversation with Betty Carpenter and looked around for Jake. She noticed that one of the state troopers was searching the pockets of the perp, now on his feet, hands cuffed behind him. The trooper triumphantly withdrew a ring of keys and she knew what that signified. "I'd almost like to meet Sanderson," she said as she sidled up to Jake, who was standing alone, hands stuffed into his pockets, observing all the action from as great a psychological distance as a physical one.

"I'd like to wring the bastard's neck," he said in a tone of voice that she'd never heard before.

She took a step away from him so that she could study him, could see what was different.

"The amount of misery that man has caused, and for absolutely no good reason. He's killed people, he's kidnapped people, he's stolen and lied and . . . and . . ." He stopped himself, unwilling or unable to say more.

Carole Ann needed information but Jake needed time to gather himself, so they stood silently observing the scene before them, at once familiar and bizarre. They were not strangers to crime or crime scenes, but something was irrevocably different for them now, and they both knew it. Her hand, holding the gun in her pocket, transmitted proof of that new reality. Her ability and willingness to elicit information from a not-yet-accused man, without concern or regard for his legal rights, was further proof, as if it were needed. And the new things she felt from Jake: the sadness, the vulnerability, the weakness—he never again would be the homicide detective whose mission was to apprehend the perp. Period. He now was a man who could marvel at the capacity that human beings have to harm each other. And to be frightened by it.

"Is Annabelle—"

He nodded. "She's with her mother."

"Good," she said quietly. "Good."

"But Islington is still missing."

The sense of shock that information produced was cut by the starting up of the siren on the medic unit as it roared off with Jocelyn Anderson, en route to the hospital in Cumberland, and Carole Ann was reminded to inform Jake of the arrangements she'd made on Jocelyn's behalf. Then she returned her thoughts to Richard Islington's whereabouts. She was past applying logic or rationality to any aspect of what Jake called "this mess," yet she couldn't make sense of a still missing Richard Islington. "I need to talk to Ruthie Eva," she said.

Jake shrugged. "Let's go, then," he said, and turned toward the truck. His shoulders remained hunched up around his ears and his hands were stuck in his pockets. He was walking rapidly, but his posture conveyed a sluggishness. Then he stopped and his face changed and he turned back toward the handcuffed man being led to a patrol car. "I'm going to see them arrest Sanderson in the same place where he held Grace. I need to see that, C.A."

She nodded, caught the keys that he tossed to her, and watched him trot toward the Maryland troopers. She stood watching and waiting, feeling what it was that was fueling him at that moment as much as making certain that the authorities would permit his presence. He climbed into the backseat of one of the patrol cars and she climbed into the Explorer and turned the key, and backed up along the shoulder until she was clear to make a U-turn and head in the opposite direction. She floored the gas pedal and within seconds was in sight of the staging area.

She and Petrocelli saw each other as soon as she wheeled into the crowd of vehicles at roadside, and he jogged toward her. "How far back in the woods is Williams's place?" she asked before he could say anything.

"Quarter mile at most," he replied.

"Describe it," she demanded, and he did, describing a cross between a chalet and a ski lodge—most definitely not a shack. She told him about Ruthie Eva's "shack" and wondered if such a structure could have existed on the Williams property and gone unnoticed.

"Let's go find out," he said, intrigued, and knowing exactly what she was thinking without her having to verbalize it. "By the way, where's Jake?" And he whistled when she told him, then he said they should hurry and find Williams before he was taken away and ask him if he had another property.

Remembering the perfect camouflage that the fishing shack was, and remembering what a disingenuous liar Bill Williams was, she looked around for Ruthie Eva; asking her would be a much simpler proposition. There were several distinct groups of people huddled about, the majority of them comprised of law enforcement personnel from three different organizations: the Maryland troopers wore blue and black; the West Virginia State Police wore solid black; and the sheriff's deputies were clad in khaki. She was able to distinguish one GGI representative in two of the huddles; and in a third, there were two women surrounded by uniforms. Ruthie Eva and obviously Annabelle, who resembled her mother closely enough that at a distance, had the two of them not been standing together, Carole Ann easily could have mistaken daughter for mother.

She approached that group slowly, Paolo following, hoping that Ruthie Eva would notice her. And she took the opportunity to study Annabelle Islington. She was slightly taller than her mother, and thinner, and like probably every young woman of her age, she wore jeans and Timberland boots and a down jacket and beneath it Carole Ann could see the top of a thick, natural-colored cable knit sweater. And her body language screamed out her ambivalence toward her mother: Annabelle stood so close to Ruthie that their shoulders touched, and Ruth's arm was around the girl's waist. But Annabelle's arms were crossed tightly across her chest. She was listening to one of the police officers and she turned to look at Ruthie, as if to solicit her mother's advice or opinion. And Ruthie leaned in and touched her daughter's head with her own. Annabelle moved away, breaking contact first.

Ruthie turned her head slightly and noticed Carole Ann, who beckoned, and she slowly detached herself from the group, leaving her daughter with obvious reluctance, and striding down the incline toward them. As soon as she was close enough, Carole Ann posed her first question: "Have you talked to John? Is he all right?" And Ruthie Eva knew, as had Patty Baker on that morning that seemed like years ago, that her only possible responses were truth or lie.

She stole a quick glance at Paolo, then nodded.

"Does he know where Richard is?"

This time she shook her head.

"Does Bill have a fishing shack?"

Her eyes widened in surprise. "Sure. He had his first and that's why I built mine."

"Tell me exactly where it is, Ruthie Eva," she said with increasing urgency, remembering that Richard Islington hadn't been seen in more than twenty-four hours.

"Two and a half miles due east of his cabin."

"How does Williams get there?" she asked, still urgently but with some skepticism thrown in; she couldn't imagine Bill Williams making a two-and-a-half-mile trek through dense forest carrying fishing gear.

She described yet another cut-through trail leading from the road deep into the woods toward the river and Bill Williams's fishing shack.

"Who's in charge here, Paolo, and how's he feeling about GGI?" Carole Ann queried, looking around at the clusters of law enforcement personnel.

The left corner of Paolo's mouth lifted in an obviously forced grin and he shook his head. "There's considerable discussion about who's in charge, since we've ventured in and out of at least three jurisdictions this morning. And their feelings about GGI are mixed, to be kind about it." He stopped and looked around. "You see the stocky guy smoking the pipe?"

Carole Ann looked where he pointed and nodded. His name, Paolo said, was Topping, and he was the highest-ranking Maryland State Police official present, and he and Jake had some kind of past that had allowed them to be almost friendly with each other, while the other cops had wanted to start taking big bites out of Jake's hide. Before he could say more, she was striding toward the group huddle that included Topping—and GGI's Bob—Paolo and Ruthie trailing.

"Excuse me, sir," she said, and introduced herself to him. A range of emotions traversed his weathered face before he removed the pipe from between his teeth and returned her greeting.

"Well, Miss Gibson. I might live to regret asking, but what can I do for you?"

She told him about the fishing shack and it took him less time than it had taken Paolo to process the possibilities. He ran toward one of the other groups of cops and she saw him speak animatedly for a few seconds, and the group dispersed as quickly as if a stink bomb had been released in their midst. Four of them took off running back up the path toward Williams's cabin and they would, Carole Ann knew, charge into the woods heading due east. Four more, two Maryland troopers and two West Virginia troopers, ran down the road toward a big GMC Jimmy with tires the size of Ruthie Eva's little truck. It sounded like the roar of a jet when it was started, and it was a fearsome sight as it rumbled off down the road, gaining speed quicker than should have been possible for something so massive. It would traverse the underbrush like a BMW on the autobahn.

Carole Ann was aware that Ruthie Eva was clutching at her arm. "You think Richard is in Bill's fishing shack?"

"I hope he is, Ruthie. Because if he's not, I don't know where else to look." Then, as an afterthought, "Have you asked Annabelle if she's seen her father in the last few days?"

"No, I didn't have any reason to ask, but she did tell me that she hadn't talked to him—or to John—since she found out what a louse Sanderson was. She blamed them." Ruthie Eva emitted a wry laugh. "Kids always blame grown-ups when their world falls apart. And they never understand that if we had the kind of power they think we have, we'd never let anything bad happen to them. Never." The sadness in her voice was painful to hear.

"How will it be between the two of you?"

"Oh, God, I don't know," the woman wailed. "She still thinks I didn't want her and she still doesn't believe that I didn't know back then how to fight Richard. And now she thinks that John, instead of being her friend, is a spy. Oh, God, it's just a mess!"

Carole Ann could not begin to imagine the depth of the woman's pain. The entire time she spoke, she stared directly at Annabelle, her eyes boring a hole in the girl's soul, pleading for understanding and forgiveness.

"The one straw we're grabbing at," Ruthie said, wiping away a tear from her cheek, "is that she's confused about being kidnapped by Bill Williams. She thought he was her friend. And she knows that John risked his life looking for her. She knows I hired people to find her." She wiped some more tears, using both hands this time. Then her head jerked up and her jaw tightened. A handcuffed Bill Williams was being led down the path, encircled by state troopers. He walked with surprising agility, and he looked directly ahead of him, seemingly oblivious to the gathering in what could be considered his front yard. If he noticed Annabelle, he gave no sign. The same for Ruthie Eva. But he stopped when he saw Carole Ann and something happened in his eyes and was transmitted throughout his body. He stiffened, then a shudder coursed through his body, but his recovery was quick and masterful.

"Miss Gibson," he called out in his booming voice. "May I have a word?" It really was more of a demand than a request but she needed to know what he wanted more than she needed to display her ownership of the upper hand, so she walked toward him.

"Mr. Williams," she said.

"I do believe I underestimated you, little lady," he boomed in his country bumpkin voice, the one he'd used when she first met him. "You're even better than your notices," he said, a definite edginess creeping into the tone now.

"How long do you think it'll take for Sanderson to give you up?" she asked him in a light, conversational tone.

His eyes narrowed and grew cold. "I'd like to hire you to represent me," he said, in a flat, even voice. "Money is no object."

Not that she needed further proof, but the ability of "this mess" to continue to surprise and confound was startling. She hadn't known what to expect from the old lawyer, but certainly it wasn't this. "I don't think so," she managed to reply calmly.

His mouth curled. "Don't you still believe in those basic legal concepts, Miss Gibson: an accused is innocent until proven guilty, and every accused has the right to the best possible defense?"

She nodded. "Indeed I do, Mr. Williams. I just no longer believe that I'm obligated to provide that defense or to wait for the jury to pronounce guilt." And she watched as he was propelled forward, down the slope and toward the waiting vehicle.

"I've known that man for a dozen years." She turned to find that Captain Topping had returned. "How do good people go so bad?" It wasn't the kind of question that allowed for or required an answer, so they both stood and watched the old lawyer as he bent himself and struggled to get his bulk into the back of the trooper vehicle. He turned toward Carole Ann. "Can you give me the short version of this mess?" he asked.

"That's what we call it at GGI: 'this mess.'" She sighed and started talking and when she was finished, he sighed, his deeper and longer than hers had been. But then she'd been sighing about it for the better part of the past three months.

"Drugs," he spat out. "All this ugliness and destruction for drugs."

"For money, really," Carole Ann responded, for that was the truth of the matter: millions of dollars annually, brought in by truck, packaged, and shipped out again, an exquisite production perfected and orchestrated by Bill—or Archie—Williams, and carried out by Jimmy Sanderson, under the identity of his older brother.

"But what did they want with the Islington girl? Or her father?" And then he realized that Ruthie was still there and he apologized. She brushed it off; she, too, wanted to hear the answer.

"Insurance," Carole Ann postulated, because she didn't know for certain. "The master plan was unraveling, coming apart at the seams, and they needed some way to maintain control. But—and I'm guessing now—when John MacDonald refused to help his brother, Sanderson retaliated by abducting Annabelle. He knew that would buy him MacDonald's cooperation as well as Islington's. But GGI kept getting in the way, even though we didn't know it; we didn't know what the hell was going on. But we were getting angrier every day."

"Don't get mad, get even," Ruthie said quietly and Carole Ann laughed gently.

"That's Jake's motto. Mine, too, now."

Topping shook his head in wonder, his gaze holding steady on Carole Ann. "I quite frankly don't know whether to yell at you or invite you to dinner," he said, his face revealing true confusion.

"I respond better to being fed," she said dryly, adding, "especially since I've not eaten yet today."

The big, grizzled state trooper reached into one of the half-dozen zippered pockets on his jacket front and withdrew two packages. "Protein bars. Carob and peanut. Take your pick," he said, graciously extending them toward her.

"I'll take them both," she said with equal grace and a wide smile, snatching them from his hand. "And since I expect you'll want to keep me out here probably until sometime well past sundown, answering the same questions over and over, I'll be looking forward to dinner."

His face wanted to laugh but too many of his youthful subordinates were standing too nearby, observing and hearing in open-mouthed amazement. So he grunted, turned on his heel, and stalked away. She ripped open the peanut butter protein bar and took a bite. "Not bad," she said, chewing gratefully, wondering whether she should offer the other bar to Ruthie or Paolo, and deciding that she was hungrier than she was well bred.

13

"YOU ALL CAN WHINE AND COMPLAIN ALL YOU WANT."
Donald Smith, the GGI business manager, wagged his head first at
Jake and then at Carole Ann. "You can rant and rave about 'this mess'
from now until the cows come home. But from a bottom-line point of
view, it was a case made in heaven! Both Islingtons paid us for finding
their daughter, and Mr. Islington paid us a bonus for foiling an extor-
tion plot that could have cost him millions. Mrs. Childress paid us for
finding out who killed her husband, and she also paid the balance owed
on the OnShore contract. And I didn't have to mail a single invoice—
they just sent the checks. And every single one of them cleared." He sat
back and folded his hands in his lap as if he were in church, his satisfied demeanor daring any of them to challenge his pronouncements.

No one did.

Carla Thompkins, who ran things, let them know that Jocelyn
Anderson would return to work that day and, seeing that no one had
anything to add, she adjourned the Monday-morning staff meeting,
noting that it was the shortest on record.

Carole Ann stood and picked up her empty coffee mug. She
looked wistfully into it.

"I'll bet Paolo has made a fresh pot," Patty Baker said, coming up behind her and brandishing her own empty cup. "Let's go see," she said, leading the way to Carole Ann's office.

"You coming?" Carole Ann asked over her shoulder to Jake, who was talking quietly with Carla. He raised one finger and she left the conference room, following Patty down the hallway.

Three weeks had passed since the resolution of "the mess." For Carole Ann, it alternated between feeling like a lifetime ago and just yesterday. The surreal qualities of the events that had transpired would not release her thoughts. Only frequent appearances in courts in three jurisdictions for the arraignments of Bill Williams and Jimmy Sanderson and their cohorts on charges ranging from murder to kidnapping to arson to drug dealing kept her mind from running out of control.

She replayed the events in her mind the way she replayed favorite records when she was a teenager: the same song, over and over, until her mother or brother shrieked at her to stop. Only this time, it was herself doing the shrieking at herself to stop. As difficult as it had been—and continued to be—to accept, all the events, though perversely related, really were happenstance, as she'd told Ruthie Eva. It was an object lesson for all those pragmatists, herself included, who denied the possibility of coincidences.

"You still look dazed and confused," Patty said with a laugh, extending the coffeepot.

"In truth, Patty, that's how I feel. But from this moment on, I'm going to try to take a lesson from Mr. Smith and focus my attention on the bottom line."

"I recommend it!" she said enthusiastically. "I hope your bonus was as healthy as mine," and she turned away quickly to replace the coffeepot on the warmer, and to compose herself. "My people really appreciated you all's generosity, C.A. You and Jake didn't have to—"

"Your people kept us going, Patty," she interjected, cutting her off. "If the army of old moved on its stomach, the modern one moves on information. Whatever doubts I'd harbored about this being the information age have been put to rest. Information is what kept us from being buried under huge piles of crap." A healthy chunk of the payments deposited into the GGI bank account that made Donald Smith so happy had been spread around among Patty and the subterraneans.

"What about piles of crap?" Jake strolled in on the tail end of the conversation and looked around. "Where's Petrocelli?"

"Haven't seen him," Carole Ann replied.

"But the coffee's fresh, so he's in the vicinity," Patty added, on her way out, with a wave to them.

"Don't tell me we have another missing person."

He nodded. "Two. We need to hire somebody to work with him. Unless, of course, you're interested."

She shot him a look, the one that would freeze spit, and took her coffee to her desk and dropped into her chair. "Not even in jest, Jake," she said wearily. "In fact, I may never again leave the office."

"You wish. Don't forget your date with Sandra Cooper."

She grinned. "That's court, Jake, and I get to be the lawyer. That falls into the 'please don't throw me into the briar patch' category. I'm looking forward to that encounter." The young assistant attorney general somehow had convinced her boss that the state should file charges against Gibson, Graham for obstruction of justice and a few other things. So, instead of being a witness, as she had in the various arraignments, she, once again, would be counsel for the defense. "I'm going to chew her up and spit her out in little tiny pieces. I think that's what I need to make me feel better and finally put this madness behind me."

"You did good work, C.A.—"

She held up a hand to stop him. "I don't want to hear it. I don't want to hear another word about any of it. As it is I can't stop thinking about it. I don't need to discuss it, too."

"Well, I do," he retorted cheerily, sinking down into the sofa and stretching his legs out on the coffee table, "and I've waited long enough. You've taken the time you need for reflection and sorting out, or whatever it is you do. Now. Tell me about that Williams character. What turns an old man—and old *lawyer*—into a drug-dealing murderer?"

She pressed her temples with her fingers, then ran her hands through her hair. "The same thing that turns a good cop bad, Jake, or makes a lawyer double-bill a client. I think part of it is for the thrill of it, and I think the other part somehow is related to performance. The good cop who never will make the daring rescue that will win a commendation. The skilled lawyer who never will argue precedent-setting law before the Supreme Court. Bill Williams was a good lawyer, but not a great one. He never was going to be the guest of the week on *Court TV* or be interviewed by Marcia Clark and Johnnie Cochran."

"Hell, C.A., how many lawyers get that chance? How many cops rescue babies from burning buildings? How many Jonas Salks or Charles Drews are there? How many are there ever going to be?"

"You know that and I know that. Most of us know that, so we just go about doing and being the best that we can. But what happens to those people, Jake, who want more? Who want to be king of the hill? What are they supposed to do with that desire when the realization strikes that it's never going to happen?"

"Well, most of 'em don't become murderers or deal drugs," he said darkly and without a trace of sympathy.

"No, but quite a few become substance abusers or self-destruct in a variety of other ways. Bill Williams's path was extreme. Yet he did some good, Jake. He genuinely cared for Ruthie Eva and Annabelle."

"The hell he did! He kidnapped that girl, C.A. He had somebody do it, which is the same damn thing. Tied her up and blindfolded her and scared the shit out of her mother, out of both her parents, for that matter. That's caring for somebody? Then he had the bald nerve to think you'd represent his ass? Bastard!"

She didn't try to argue. Jake didn't feel sympathy for criminals. Period. "There is one thing I want to know from you," she said. "Describe the look on Sanderson's face when you and half the cops in western Maryland and West Virginia showed up to corral him."

The look on Jake's face shifted dramatically as he recalled the moment, hardening into the visage of the homicide detective who has seen too much ugliness. "What do you call those people who are so full of themselves they're not able to think about other people? Shrinks have a name for it."

"Narcissistic?"

"That's it! He first looked totally unconcerned, like he couldn't be bothered. Then he was pissed off and kept wanting to know where Cameron was. That was the one you and Jocelyn bagged. Then, if you can believe it, he started to whine about how something was always going wrong for him, how his plans were always being screwed up by some idiot or other. That's why he had to kill Childress and the guy who was Archie's go-fer, and his own girlfriend, for cryin' out loud, whose name he couldn't remember! The bastard! He blamed *them* for screwing up his plans. Then he blamed us for 'interfering.' Can you believe that? And the whole time he was acting and sounding so superior. So I got in his face.

" 'Do you know who I am?'

" 'No, should I?'

" 'Yeah, I think you should know a man if you're going to steal his wife from the safety of his home. You remember her name, don't you?'

"That got to him and he backed up like he expected me to hit him."

"You mean you didn't?"

He laughed. "Did you get a good look at Tiny Tim?"

She laughed again, fully this time, not at all surprised that the gigantic trooper was assigned a diminutive moniker. "I take it he was keeping an eye on you?"

He nodded. "That was our agreement: I could go along if I promised to behave. And behave meant I couldn't smack the guy." He shrugged. "And you know how I believe in keeping my word." And they both giggled at that. Then, still smirking, Jake recounted Sanderson's efforts to find his brother all that night and the next day.

"Tiny Tim told me that when Sanderson finally got him on the phone, MacDonald hung up on him."

"Could we have been more wrong about him?" she asked, sounding as guilty as she felt.

Jake snorted. "His own damn fault! He had no business following you and Paolo all over town."

"Oh, could you try to show a little compassion for once in your life! The man was being squeezed from all sides, Jake. His brother was scamming him, the kid he loves like a daughter hates her mother, who just happens to be the woman he loves. He loses a big development deal out in California, which would have bought him independence from Islington—"

"And he's living happily ever after. So what, he had a few bad moments. He's probably already forgotten about them. I'll bet Miss Simmons has seen to that."

Carole Ann laughed and conceded the point. She knew that Ruthie was living, at least part of the time, in MacDonald's Georgetown Park home, within walking distance to Annabelle's DuPont Circle condo, and that the young woman had been very receptive to the relationship between her mother and her friend. "I plan to pay Ruth a visit out in Eden in a week or so; I'm in need of some major pampering. I thought I'd invite Grace to go along."

"Grace who?"

"Your *wife*, Gracewho."

He snorted. "My wife would never spend that kind of money to lay around in some mud."

Carole Ann returned the snort and followed it with a laugh and a suggestion that her partner get better acquainted with his wife's proclivities. He stood up to leave, the pretense that he was ignoring her in full force. "By the way," he said, and reached into the inside pocket of his jacket and withdrew several folded documents, which he gave to her.

"What's this?" she asked, a frown disrupting her humor.

"Your permits to carry a concealed weapon. Issued by D.C.,

Maryland, and Virginia." He read the expression on her face and in her body and he took them from her hand and placed them on the desk. "You don't have to do anything with them. They just exist, C.A., that's all. If there's ever a question, if there's ever a need, they exist, OK?"

She nodded. It was anything but OK but that was a conversation that she most certainly didn't intend to have.

"Oh, I forgot to mention, your friend, Gracewho, wants you to come to dinner on Saturday and she said you have to bring that wine you brought the last time that she liked so much."

"I'll let you know," she said quietly.

"Why can't you let me know now?"

"Because I don't know now, Jake. I don't know what I'll be doing on Saturday."

"You'll be doing what you're always doing: watching movies and eating popcorn."

"And maybe that's what we'll want to do and maybe not but I'll let you know!" She was irritated and in a mood to let him know it. She was so busy gearing up to be annoyed with him that she missed his shifting of gears.

"What 'we'?" he asked innocently and almost gently.

"Warren's coming into town Friday morning."

"What for?" Jake growled, eyes narrowed.

She fixed him in a stare that he held with his own angry gaze until she relaxed her face into a sly grin. "Why do you think, Jake?" she asked sweetly, and laughed when he blushed.

"Well," he sputtered. "In that case, ah, I, ah. . . ." Then he cleared his throat until she thought he'd choke himself, then he glared at her. "Does your Mama know?" he asked in a stage whisper and, just before the giggle began, he ran out and left her standing in the middle of her office, mouth open, speechless.